Vivienne

RICHARD HOYT

A TOM DOHERTY ASSOCIATES BOOK
NEW YORK

This is a work of fiction. All the characters and events portrayed in this book are either products of the author's imagination or are used fictitiously.

VIVIENNE

Copyright © 2000 by Richard Hoyt

All rights reserved, including the right to reproduce this book, or portions thereof, in any form.

A Tor Book
Published by Tom Doherty Associates, LLC
175 Fifth Avenue
New York, NY 10010

www.tor.com

Tor® is a registered trademark of Tom Doherty Associates, LLC.

ISBN: 0-812-57862-7
Library of Congress Catalog Card Number: 00-031814

First edition: December 2000
First mass market edition: November 2001

Printed in the United States of America

0 9 8 7 6 5 4 3 2 1

For my daughter Teresa Nellie Hoyt

. . . quaeque ipse miserrima vidi
et quorum pars magna fui.

(. . . I saw these terrible things
and took great part in them.)

Virgil, *The Aeneid*

Vivienne

1

ORDINARILY THERE WOULD have been an unmanageable mob of anti-war protesters gathered outside the Pacific Club with their banners and placards, but to avoid embarrassing their famous guest, Gen. William C. Westmoreland, the sponsors had held off notifying the press until the last minute, including Jim Quint's paper, the *Honolulu Star-Bulletin*. This was to be a cozy lunch so Westmoreland could explain the Tet offensive without having to shout over kids screaming into bullhorns or being trapped in a melee of war protesters.

This was 1968, however, and word of Westmoreland's appearance had inevitably leaked so that a passionate band of a couple of dozen radicals—restrained by police officers—had gathered at the entrance to the club at the last minute bearing a huge white banner saying: *STOP WASTING LIVES! OUT NOW!*

Quint, giving thumbs-up antiestablishment handshakes to the familiar figures on his beat, worked his way through the enthusiasts as they gave him encouragement. A young man wearing yellow sunglasses and a red sweatband looped his arm around Quint's shoulder and gave him a squeeze. "Give it to 'em, Jim. Do it!"

Surrounded by radicals, looking past the phalanx of Honolulu police officers, Quint saw Vivienne for the first time.

A stocky, bearded radical wearing a ragged blue T-shirt clenched his fist and murmured in a deep, earnest voice, "Don't let us down, Jim. Tell it like it is."

She was sitting in a white Mercedes Benz sedan parked in the shade of a banyan tree at the edge of the parking lot, reading something in her lap.

A plump girl with Joan Baez hair, no bra, and a see-through blouse shouted, "Right on, Jim!"

As Quint passed through the line of police officers and drew near the Mercedes, Vivienne looked up at him with outsized brown eyes. There was something about her that made him think she wasn't from Hawaii, more likely from somewhere in Southeast Asia, maybe even Vietnam. She was, in a word, elegant.

Their eyes caught and held for a heartbeat that nearly gave him goosebumps. A siren, she was. Quint paused by the open car window and mopped some sweat from his brow. He wondered who that young woman was, sitting there in her expensive Mercedes. He said, "The man inside is going to tell us all about it." By the man, Quint meant Westmoreland. By it, he could have meant Tet, Hue, or the war in general. All the same really. The war was twisting the country.

She grinned. "What do you think?"

She had an accent with a hint of French that Quint recognized as Vietnamese. He briefly held his lower lip in his teeth. "About you or about the war?" What a lovely, desirable young woman. She was extraordinary. Quint's stomach turned.

She laughed mischievously. She was wearing a white blouse with the top two buttons unfastened. She had not left the top of her blouse open to be provocative. That was clearly not her way. It was hot and humid. She was being sensible. "What you think of the war, not me, silly. That's where you're going isn't it? To hear General Westmoreland give the official explanation of Tet." She folded the newspaper and began fanning herself.

Quint said, "I think we're swimming in a big tub of crud." He wanted to get an angle on her blouse, to see what was down there, but he didn't want to come off as boorish. He thought she likely knew his mind was more on her blouse than the war in Vietnam.

"I take it you're a reporter," she said.

Quint wore a handlebar mustache and a mane of tangled brown hair that fell to his shoulders. "Yes, I am as a matter of fact. How'd you know?"

"Hard to believe they'd book a rock band for General West-moreland, and you've got a notepad sticking out of your hip pocket."

So Quint had. "Good deduction. I'm Jim Quint of the *Star-Bulletin*. I'm substituting for the regular military reporter." He smoothed his mustache with the top of his forefinger. "And you are?"

"Vivienne Lambert. Well, Jim Quint! So this is what you look like. I read your stories in the paper every day. So does my husband. They make him grind his teeth. He thrusts your stories at me, looking like he could kill. Very pleased to meet you." She extended her slender hand through the window.

As Quint shook her hand, he inadvertently groaned. Well, groan didn't quite cover the territory. An envious, wistful, longing moan was more like it. Although he quickly suppressed the sound, he was immediately embarrassed. He was aware that his face was flushed. Mr. Cool, he was. Class all the way.

Vivienne laughed. She had been flattered. She watched him with renewed interest. "I especially liked your series of vignettes on hippies in Waikiki. You didn't judge. You just described and quoted, letting your readers decide for themselves what they thought. English is my third language, so correct me if I'm wrong, but you wrote those stories in the second person, present tense, didn't you? I'd never seen anything like it in a newspaper. It worked."

She really had been reading him. And with attention too. It was Quint's turn to be flattered. He said, "It's something they're calling the 'new' journalism, which really isn't new at all. It's the use of literary devices in journalism. I used the present tense to make the vignettes sound more immediate. I wrote them in the second person to put the readers in my shoes without the intrusive references to myself."

"You weren't the story, they were, so you kept yourself out of it."

She had it nailed. Smart woman. Quint said, "Aren't you hot out here?"

"I . . ." She hesitated, then held out her blouse and blew on her chest. This was a simple, unembarrassed gesture. She said, "It was a whole lot hotter than this where I grew up. My husband is an army colonel. I'm waiting to take him home when he's finished."

Of course. Quint knew that. No way under heaven that this female was not taken. An army colonel. The alpha male scores.

She glanced at her watch. "His plane from Saigon was probably late. He should be along any second now."

Quint had already revealed himself. To hell with pretending to hide his emotions. "A very, very lucky man, your colonel," he said. Looking wistful, he sighed deeply and gave her a rueful smile.

"Thank you," she said, watching him.

"What would you do?" Quint asked.

"Do about what?"

"About the war? You're Vietnamese. I'm curious. Assume you're the American president."

Vivienne laughed at that idea. "Let's see." She thought for a moment. "I would hold a national lottery for visits to Vietnam. Pick a few thousand names from lists of registered voters. Let them talk to people in the streets of Saigon and live with a family in the provinces. After they returned, I'd wait for one month so they'd have time to talk to their family and friends and be interviewed by journalists like yourself, then I'd hold a binding national referendum?"

Quint grinned. "I see, the old word of mouth. What do you think they would conclude from their trip?"

She shrugged, looking mischievous.

"You're not going to say?"

"Like you said, I'm a Vietnamese national. My husband is an American army colonel. Do you think it's smart for me to be completely honest to a newspaper reporter?" She was suddenly alarmed. "I hope you don't put my lottery idea in the newspaper. My husband would kill me."

Quint laughed. "No problem. You're a little pistol, aren't you?"

"I'm maybe a little too impulsive. I'm an artist, not so good with words. I try to paint the truth."

"I'd like to see your paintings." Quint thought Vivienne was some kind of artwork herself.

She sighed. "Hard to imagine how that would come about."

"Yes, I guess that is hard to imagine." Quint glanced at his watch. "It's been fun. See you later, Vivienne," he said. He gave her an admiring salute and continued on his way.

Behind him she said, "*Au revoir*, Jim." There was a sad, wistful quality to her voice, as though she were saying good-bye to hope.

Quint glanced back. Still fanning herself, she was watching him intently with her outsized Asian eyes. She gave him a knowing little smile. Boy sees girl. Boy likes girl. Girl sees boy. Girl likes boy. Girl is married.

Quint sighed. Such frustration.

Vivienne laughed.

2

AWARE THAT HIS editor Charles R. "Chick" McGyver was watching him, Jim Quint circled the long table looking for the card with his name on it. Why was McGyver watching him like that? Quint had a slight glow from the freebie Scotch that he had consumed at the pre-lunch socializing, and it was hard to keep his mind off the officer's young Vietnamese wife waiting under the banyan tree. Was he obviously drunk?

He pretended not to notice McGyver's interest in him and glanced about the room at the captains and colonels and admirals and generals, all dressed in formal uniforms, their chests covered with medals and ribbons. The decorations were a military affectation that Quint found slightly sophomoric. The civilians from the Johnson administration all wore suits that made them look like Wall Street brokers. The journalists and wire service reporters from the mainland all wore suits and ties. Oahu was a tropical island. Why did they insist on wearing those silly costumes in that heat?

It was this urge to display that Quint found amusing, a sentiment perhaps touched by the spirit of the times. These men were, collectively, the Establishment, the dreaded, allegedly monolithic nemesis of the boomers who had taken to the streets in defiance of the war. Quint thought it was a kick that the kids had enlisted Ike into their cause, finding any excuse to quote his warning of the military-industrial complex; sweet Ike, who Norman Mailer claimed was the only old woman elected president of the United States, had fingered the enemy in his farewell address.

Quint wore a blue aloha shirt plastered with outsized yellow flowers, dark blue bell-bottomed trousers with vertical pin-stripes, and sandals. Wearing shoes was stupid in Hawaii. Bad enough that he was the only person at the table without a proper haircut. He had never gone for crew-cuts and considered going to a barber every ten days an affectation that wasted money better spent on Primo beer. He had grown up shoveling manure on a Montana cattle ranch and regarded neckties as a hangman's noose. There was a rack in the newspaper office with proper jackets in various sizes and an assortment of ties that were intended for such occasions, but he never used it. Now he understood the reason for McGyver's look, or thought he did. He had blown off the jacket and tie, and this had embarrassed McGyver.

If there was anybody present in the Pacific Club that day who looked like he belonged on the Group W Bench it was Jim Quint. In his best-selling song of the previous year, Arlo Guthrie had wondered if he was "moral enough to join the army, burn women, kids, houses and villages—after being a litterbug." Quint harbored doubts about the Vietnam War and had sideburns and an upper lip that looked like it belonged on Wild Bill Hickok. Was he moral enough to be in General Westmoreland's restaurant that day?

QUINT FOUND HIS assigned spot and sat before a plate of marinated avocado halves sprinkled with slices of white onion and bits of crisp bacon. A reporter for the *Los Angeles Times* was seated on his left and a man with a whole bunch of muscles, a Green Beret colonel with bloused boots, on his right. The seating was no accident. Each reporter had been assigned an officer or administration official whose job it was to prime him or her with the latest pitch. The Pentagon had sent down the word. Get these reporters one-on-one, and for God's sake talk to them. Give them the military's side of the story.

From the Pentagon's point of view, 1968 had not had an auspicious start. On January 23, Captain Lloyd Bucher, commander of the *U.S.S. Pueblo*, an intelligence ship monitoring communications in North Korea, had allowed his vessel, together with its classified codes and equipment and its crew of eighty, to be captured by the North Korean navy. No other American navy commander in the history of the republic, not one, had allowed his vessel to be captured on the high seas.

Captain Bucher was either a tragic victim of circumstance or a monumental screw-up and maximum coward, depending on one's point of view. Few people were neutral with regard to the fate of poor Bucher. Famous sailors from John Paul Jones to Bull Halsey were said to be turning in their graves at such abject cowardice. There was widespread sympathy for the imprisoned sailors of the *Pueblo*, but Bucher and the navy were excoriated for their incompetence. How had the navy allowed that to happen?

The next awful load of bad news arrived on January 31. North Vietnamese and Vietcong forces launched a coordinated attack in the central and southern provinces of South Vietnam. In a twenty-four-hour period, eighty-four thousand of General Vo Nguyen Giap's combat troops struck all the capitals and major cities, including Saigon, and the ancient capital of Hue, just south of the 17th parallel that divided Vietnam. In Saigon, the Vietcong succeeded in blowing a hole in the wall of the U.S. embassy, which would have fallen had it not been for the heroic efforts of the marines defending it. Hue was not so lucky. The Vietcong captured Hue.

The assaults by Giap's forces were launched within hours of a previously announced truce between the combatants that was to take place during the holiday period known as Tet, the Vietnamese lunar New Year. Civilian casualties were said to be "high," although no numbers were reported. There being no statistical measurement of the tears and heartbreak, the territory of pain was ceded to the antiwar radicals who escalated their rhetoric with each reported disaster. The startling, sobering ambush became known simply as Tet.

From the Pentagon's point of view, any good news was occasion to take on the critics of the war. With American units surrounding Hue and closing fast, General Westmoreland's intimate little chat with the media in the Pacific Club was timed to coincide with the expected retaking of the city. After his rounds of conferring with Johnson administration officials and Pentagon brass, Westmoreland had adjourned to the elitist watering hole for an intimate chat with reporters.

Fred Fielding hadn't had a choice of whom to cover the talk. His military reporter was on vacation, and Quint was the only warm body available.

The *Times* being more powerful and influential than the *Star-Bulletin*, its reporter had drawn an admiral who was presumably in charge of aircraft carriers operating in the Tonkin Gulf and along the Vietnamese coast. Quint didn't feel slighted. He felt he had a greater chance of learning something useful from a soldier who had likely served in the field with the grunts.

Quint's assigned officer, a Green Beret and rugged stud with zero body fat, had "Lambert" on his name tag. Quint thought people with muscles like sculptured marble were likely addicted to the endorphin highs of exercising until their bodies screamed. Lambert had to be Vivienne's husband, the lucky son of a bitch— the macho yin to her delicate yang. A grimacing bead of sweat with his hair cut shorter than a cocklebur, he had a self-assured way about him that suggested he rarely had doubts about anything.

Four straight years of war gone wrong, matched, month by month, by increasing rage back home had largely stripped the country of ambiguity. Everybody, it seemed, had a personal identifying tag that put him or her into a bin of absolutes—hawks, doves, hippies, yippies, draft-card burners, Panthers.

Quint immediately fit Lambert into his mental catalog of stereotypes. Lambert was a military officer therefore his tag read *Unrelenting Hawk*. That meant his world would likely be as clean, clear, and unambiguous as his ice-blue eyes. He would be confident of who was who and what was what. He would have clearly identified friends and enemies. If a red target popped up, he would shoot at it. If it were blue, he would hold fire.

Quint knew Lambert had no choice but to be friendly to what

he likely regarded as a pipsqueak. This was a media event, and Lambert was likely under specific orders to suck up to his assigned reporter. He no doubt cursed his luck for having drawn a longhaired, know-nothing asshole. But if Quint quoted him in a bullshit little our-boys-are-doing-their-damnedest feature that was picked up and moved by the Associated Press, he would have fulfilled his mission.

"Jim Quint."

"Del Lambert." They shook manfully. "Are *you* the guy from the *Star-Bulletin*?" He seemed mildly surprised.

Lambert had likely expected Tom Benson, the *Star-Bulletin's* regular military reporter. Quint said, "Tom Benson took his family for a drive across the mainland, avoiding all interstate highways. He sent us a postcard showing the highest point in Indiana."

Lambert smiled, studying Quint intensely. "You're the reporter who writes about draft-card burners. I've read your stuff."

Quint tried the salad. "You and Aku." He was referring to a popular Honolulu disc jockey, Hal Lewis, who called himself J. Akuhead Pupule, that is, J. Crazy Tunahead. Aku, or plain Tuna, did not approve of Quint, whom he accused, almost daily, of glorifying traitors and snot-nosed cowards who didn't have the spine to risk their lives for their country. American chickens, they were. Lately, as the Vietcong infiltrators had shot up Saigon in their daring Tet offensive, Aku's denunciations of Quint had gotten especially bitter. He routinely referred to Quint as the *Star-Bulletin's* house hippie.

Lambert laughed. "Aku doesn't like you, that's a fact. He's supposed to be the highest paid disc jockey in the United States. Gotta lot of people out there listening to him. The other day he called you a traitor. Did you know that? Dared you to sue him. Why didn't you?"

Quint shrugged. "Not good business for us to encourage libel and slander suits. Besides, he's entitled to his opinions." In fact, Quint was highly entertained by Aku's calls to famous people, Mao, say, or Queen Elizabeth. While operators, bureaucrats, and yes men listened, stupefied, he'd say, blandly, "This is J. Akuhead Pupule calling from Honolulu, Hawaii. I'd like to speak with Marshal Tito, please." Who, they'd say? Calling from where? You want to speak to whom?

"I like his phone calls," Lambert said.

Quint agreed. "Those're good, I'll give him that. What is it you do?" He knew Lambert wasn't there by accident. He had to do something big time important to have rated a seat at the table with Westmoreland and all the brass and reporters. This was a speech intended to influence public opinion.

"What do I do?" Colonel Lambert smiled grimly. "I've been part of General Westmoreland's G-2."

"Intelligence. Doing what?"

"Trying to run down the CBS film of the Lon Be massacre three years ago, if it still exists. That and flying back and forth from Vietnam to Honolulu to brief congressmen and Pentagon brass. But now I've been rotated, reassigned to Ft. Shafter to make it easier."

"Giving up on the Lon Be film?" At Lon Be on the Mekong Delta three years earlier, the Vietcong had slaughtered eighty-three people including CBS reporter Vince Carelli and his Australian photographer, Terry Henson, who had apparently been filming the invaders when he went down.

"No, we're still trying. CBS wants it most dearly, and we're more than willing to oblige if we can."

"With Johnson running for reelection this year, I bet you are. You people been giving congressmen the straight poop about Vietnam?"

"We do the best we can. And we did know about Tet in advance."

"But you still lost?"

"We did *not* lose," he said evenly.

"No? But you perhaps underestimated the strength of the Vietcong. Would you concede that?"

Lambert stiffened slightly. "They were stronger than we had expected, yes."

"Still briefing hot-shots?"

Lambert nodded. "Means shuttling back and forth between Honolulu and Saigon, Honolulu and Washington. Our problem is as much political as it is military. You might have deduced that from reading your own paper, smart guy like you. The first couple of trips to Honolulu were fun for the wheelers and dealers. Their wives got a freebie trip to Hawaii. They all thought winning the war was no big deal. Everything was hunky dory. But now they're saying it's getting harder for them to spring the time to come here, so I have to fly to Washington. More air time for me."

"You've become a kind of politician then. A lobbyist for the army."

He cocked his head, studying Quint "I'm a professional soldier, Jim. A bird colonel. A graduate of the Citadel. Regular army. I do what it takes to win the battle."

Even if it meant kissing the butts of politicians and reporters like him, Quint thought. "But I take it you'd rather be in Saigon where the action is, instead of here in the land of aloha."

"I say again. I'm a soldier. I follow orders."

"What do you think about Lloyd Bucher?"

"He's navy. I can't speak for the navy."

Quint said, "I know, just curious is all. A victim or coward, do you think?"

Lambert eyed Quint mildly. "I don't want this to be printed in the *Star-Bulletin*, but I think Lloyd Bucher is chickenshit in the extreme and a disgrace to his uniform. If they ever get him out of Korea, they should throw his ass in the brig."

"I see. Tell me about Hue."

"We'll have Hue back today or tomorrow. We're talking hours away here."

"And victory?"

He shrugged. "Months away probably. If we're allowed to do what we have to do. Otherwise it could be a long haul. Nobody beats us in battle. Nobody. But I suspect you . . ." He left the sentence unfinished. He looked about.

Was Lambert more intelligent and complex than Quint had

expected? Possibly. But then Quint had found that most stereotypes assumed human qualities when he had met one personally.

Lambert said, "What do you say I scare us up another round? We're supposed to keep you guys happy. Do us both good. We've got lamb chops coming up. You like lamb chops?"

3

JIM QUINT'S CONVERSATION with Colonel Lambert was interrupted by waiters who took their salad plates; other waiters appeared with plates of lamb chops and tiny boiled potatoes, and still others filled their glasses with red wine. Quint in fact loved lamb chops. The only ones he had seen in the supermarkets were from New Zealand, dark red with crusts of yellow fat and frozen hard as rocks. But these, he supposed, had been flown in fresh for the occasion. They were delicious. Who had paid for them? The Pacific Club? Or had they come by military transport, comfort food for Gen. Westmoreland, faced with the awful chore of explaining Tet to the American people?

The *Los Angeles Times* guy sitting next to Quint had probably written a check to pay for his meal. The *Times* presumably had the wherewithal for such gestures of independence. All the news without fear or favor and all that. But Quint was writing for the *Honolulu Star-Bulletin*. His publisher, Chinn Ho, either had better use for his money or assumed that none of his reporters could be bought off for lamb chops.

Either way, for Quint there was, at least for the moment, such a thing as a free lunch. He was an unembarrassed eater. He dug in. The lamb chops were delicious. Tender. Cooked just right, slightly pink inside. The red wine was good too. All Quint had to do was hold up his glass and a guy in a white jacket appeared as if by magic to top it off. Couldn't beat that.

Munching on a piece of lamb, he asked Lambert, "Tell me, what happens now, after Tet?"

"That's what we're here for, isn't it, to hear General West-moreland explain the military situation?"

Quint laughed. He thought, *good fucking luck*. "Let me guess. Westy's fourth and long on his own goal line. He'll give us a Lombardi. Go, fight, win. Never surrender. Do what we have to do. Let Hawg Hanner bust a few butts. Send Jimmy Taylor up the gut followed by Max McGee or Boyd Dowler on a fly pattern. Let Paul Hornung run for daylight. Et cetera. That's his job. What do you think will happen? Where is this all taking us?"

"Tet was a setback, that's a fact. But we'll win the war if we're allowed to. The United States Army has never been defeated. Never. If we can't beat these slopes, we're hurting." Lambert stopped, looking stricken. Something was bothering him big time. "Do me a favor will you, and don't quote me using that word in a story. Your readers just won't understand."

"Which word is that?" Quint knew damn well which word.

"Slopes."

"Oh, that. No problem." Lambert was married to the Viet-namese beauty waiting for him outside in the heat. What was wrong with him? Jesus!

Del Lambert studied Quint. "And you," he said, "What do you think?"

What did Quint think? That's what Vivienne had asked. "About what? The Mamas and the Papas? The Grateful Dead? Honkeys and pigs?"

"The war."

"What I think is irrelevant," Quint said. He found it hard to take his eyes off the ribbons on Lambert's chest. What did they mean anyway? Did anybody know really? If Lambert faked a few, just tossed in a color here and there, a random green or red or yellow, would anybody ever spot them?

Lambert frowned. "But you do have an opinion. I read your articles in the paper. I know you have an opinion."

"Oh, sure. I have an opinion."

"Well?"

"I'm not sure I like the war a whole bunch."

Lambert said, "That's what I like. A man with a robust opinion. Not afraid to speak up. Where did you go to school?"

"The University of Montana."

"Do they teach history at the University of Montana?"

"Why yes, they do," Quint said.

"Did they teach you what happened on September 29, 1939?"

"Neville Chamberlain went to Munich where he turned over the Sudetenland to Adolf Hitler. He returned to London carrying an umbrella and good news. He thought he had bought peace."

"Appeasement. They call it appeasement. It led to World War Two. I don't know about the umbrella."

"I understand your argument," Quint said. "You might be right." Quint didn't really believe that. He thought he was right and Lambert was flat wrong.

"But maybe not right also, is that what you think?"

Quint shrugged. He got the feeling that he was sitting beside a human hand grenade with the pin halfway out.

4

THE WAITERS BEGAN clearing their plates and replacing them with peaches and cream and cups of coffee. Seeing the dessert, Quint brightened. "Look at that, peaches. Okay! Probably flown here straight from Georgia. An all-American dessert."

Lambert and Quint dug into their peaches and cream.

Lambert said, "When I said I was familiar with your stories, that's an understatement. I bet I've read every article about free-thinking hippies and chickenshit draft dodgers that you've ever written. Beats hell out of me why anybody would give a damn about what they think one way or another."

Quint grinned. "Well, I like a fan! But that's not surprising. You're an intelligence officer. I suppose collecting newspaper clips is part of your job. What are you doing, starting files on everybody I interview, starting with A for Abercrombie, Neil?"

"Abercrombie! Jesus! There's somebody who will go far. By devoting so much energy to the views of draft dodgers and ass-holes who are encouraging soldiers to frag their officers, you're furthering their cause. Have you ever thought of that?"

Lambert hadn't answered Quint's question about starting files on the people he interviewed. Quint shrugged. "Neil has never advocated fragging soldiers. No way. But what if they're right about the war? It's always possible they're right. In any event, I don't suppose they're to shut up anytime soon."

"Not with you clinging to their every word, I agree."

"That's the point of their theater."

"Theater? What theater? And what point?"

"The theater of constant turmoil. The point is to keep me

writing about them. People with money hire press agents. This is democracy, remember. American pluralism and all that. If all you have is energy, a lot of bodies, and conviction, you do what you have to do. A draft card burning is a dramatic little show to gain attention. Theater."

"More like a public circus."

Quint grinned. "It has elements of a circus, I'll give you that. In the end, they might be judged wrong. But for now, they're deliberately breaking the law to call attention to what they think is a screwed-up war. Maybe it is. Maybe it isn't. It'll be years if not decades before we know."

Lambert gave him a look.

"This lunch is theater too, if you think about it. Only more like opera—highbrow, invitation only, very formal, with neckties, ribbons, shined shoes, and lamb chops, and starring the famous *castrato*, General William C. Westmoreland, singing *a cappella*. A clean, pure soprano if you go for that kind of thing."

Lambert clenched his jaw.

Quint thought it was great sport to torment Ball Bearing Buns by ridiculing Westmoreland. He might as well have been stretching Lambert on the rack. They ate in silence. Quint thought about Lambert's wife. Good-bye, she had said to him in French. Quint remembered the touch of sadness in her voice. He especially remembered her little smile.

THE DAY AFTER Tet, President Johnson, whose advisors were presumably on top of the war that was costing the taxpayers $25 billion a year, had solemnly informed his countrymen that the Vietcong attack had been no surprise at all. According to Johnson, what actually happened was that the previous week intelligence officers had told General Westmoreland to expect what Vietcong soldiers were being told was a "decisive campaign" that would produce a "final victory." But Westmoreland's hands were tied. He couldn't make anything public without tipping his hand. And besides, the Vietcong had failed to produce anything like a final victory. In fact, they had suffered huge losses. For those reasons, this was really a win for the defenders.

The administration's critics said, well, tell that disingenuous story to the marines who lost their lives defending the embassy compound. And if the intelligence had been so damn good and nobody had been fooled, why had the South Vietnamese and their American sponsors allowed the Vietcong to capture Hue? That was victory? All the Pentagon and White House "yes, buts" couldn't erase the obvious fact that somebody had screwed up, big time. How had all that been allowed to happen?

Both the kids in the streets and their skeptical elders concluded that the much touted "light at the end of the tunnel," the national metaphor for the promised victory in Vietnam, was growing ever dimmer. With each reported debacle, the antiwar clamor increased.

JIM QUINT WAS the one who broke the silence. He felt he'd served his time in the military. What was Colonel Lambert going to do? Knock his teeth out right there in front of God, Chick McGyver, and General Westmoreland? He said, "I've been reading those stories about Khesanh."

"And?"

"We've got five thousand soldiers surrounded by twenty thousand North Vietnamese troops. Our people are getting shelled day and night. We have to make dangerous flights in and out to keep them supplied with food and ammunition. I took a look at Khesanh on the map. I don't pretend to be General Grant or George Patton or anybody, but for the life of me, I can't figure any tactical or strategic reason for us to pay that kind of price for a place in the middle of nowhere. I don't understand. Why don't we just pluck those poor bastards out of there and give 'em a hot meal and a change of clothing?"

Lambert gave Quint a patient look. First, Quint had suggested draft-card burners might be right. Then he'd called Westmoreland a *castrato* in an opera. A soprano. Now this, questioning the army's resistance at Khesanh at great cost to the defenders. Lambert said, evenly, "You know about Dienbienphu?"

Dienbienphu was the 1956 Dunkirk for the French army then fighting what was called the Indochina War. Quint said, "Sure, I know about Dienbienphu. At least a little. As I understand it, we're intent on proving we can do what the French couldn't."

"They were colonialists."

"And ours is the morally uplifting mission of stopping the spread of communism in Southeast Asia. I've heard the pitch. I get the drift." With a wife like Vivienne, Lambert called them slopes! Quint found it impossible to get that out of his mind.

Lambert finished off his peaches and cream and followed it with a sip of coffee. He started to say something, then stopped. He thought a moment, studying Quint. Then he grinned broadly, as though something had just occurred to him. It was like he had had a pot flash, although he had probably never smoked weed in his life. "Say, I was wondering . . ." Lambert let it drop, but something was on his mind.

"What?" Quint said.

"Nothing." He took another sip of coffee. Then, he said, "Okay, why not? I'm curious about something, Jim. Are you married or have a girlfriend?"

First the look, then the leap from Dienbienphu to Quint's love life. Quint wondered what that was all about? "I lived with a girl for a little over three years, but we split a couple of months ago. She said a person is either part of the solution or part of the problem. I'm forever thinking about both sides, and I do my best to be fair to everybody in my stories. In her opinion, that made me an establishment cop-out."

"Part of the problem."

"Exactly. I was either for her or against her. Me being in the middle annoyed the hell out of her. Questions, questions, questions. She couldn't handle ambiguity. She wanted answers and commitment. Fire and passion and all that."

Lambert found that amusing. He smiled. "Ahh, too bad."

"She's probably a Weatherman by now. They know who the

bad guys are and what to do about them. Boom!" Quint used his hands to make a mushroom cloud. He could tell by the look on Lambert's face that he was about to ask him her name. "Just kidding," Quint said quickly. "A joke. Really. Everybody thinks I'm part of the problem. Aku. You. My ex-girlfriend. Probably half or more of my readers."

The host stood to introduce General Westmoreland, and it was time for Quint to get to work. He cleared a space for his notepad and got his pencil ready. At the top, absently doodling, he printed "Vi . . ." Jesus, Lambert was watching him! He'd nearly screwed up. Quint turned the word into "Vietnam," then added below, in script, "Gen. W. C. Westmoreland, Pac Clb."

5

GENERAL WESTMORELAND GAVE what Jim Quint had predicted, a rah, rah, speech. No, the Vietcong had not taken the American army by surprise at Tet. Yes, the command had underestimated the strength of the attack. Yes, the Vietcong had very nearly overrun the American embassy. But no, they had not won and would not win. In fact, Tet showed the very opposite of strength. It was an act of desperation. The Charlies had gathered all their resources to strike one treacherous blow. They didn't really think they could win a military victory. It was propaganda they were after, hoping to convince the American people that the war was a doomed, losing effort.

Westmoreland paused, presumably giving the reporters time to note for their readers that the VC had suffered a big defeat at Tet. The Americans had emerged victorious.

Westmoreland said the art of war was knowing how to counterattack. Check out Napoleon's ill-fated Russian campaign. Look at the Battle of the Bulge. What's the first thing Bart Starr does after Willie Woods intercepts a pass? He throws long. In fact, the American army would regroup; aided by the determined, freedom-loving South Vietnam army, they would push Uncle Ho back where he belonged. The South Vietnamese army and their American advisors would soon reoccupy Hue. The rest was inevitable.

Quint murmured to Lambert, "See. Vince Lombardi and Bart Starr. What did I tell you?"

Lambert looked at Quint mildly. "Easy to predict. This close to the Super Bowl."

"By the way, exactly how was it you people missed the buildup of Tet? That happened right under your noses. No offense, but I'd have thought that would be hard to miss." Quint knew this was a verbal equivalent to kneeing Lambert in the balls, but after all they were engaged in a form of combat. Attack and defend was what the news was all about. It was his job as a journalist to attack. Westmoreland was here to defend the Tet screw up.

"You're not listening to what the man is saying. We didn't miss Tet."

"You just forgot to place a call to Hue, right?"

Lambert said, "The answer to your objections is coming right up. Get your pencil ready."

"Coming right up? You helped write his speech?"

Lambert said nothing. Quint understood why he had been so touchy at Quint's having predicted a reference to the Green Bay Packers. His failure to reply said yes, he had helped write Westmoreland's speech. In the Pentagon's dictionary, victory and defeat were loose concepts, to be redefined according to circumstance. But there had to be blame assigned somewhere. The public would insist on it. Someone had to be held responsible.

Westmoreland leaned over the table, his long, lined, handsome face earnest in the extreme. He said, "In recent months we have noticed that critical information we send up our chain of command inevitably finds its way back to General Giap's staff. We're obliged to ask ourselves, How is this happening? The only logical answer is chilling. We believe we have a *prima facie* case that the North Vietnamese are obtaining information about American intentions from the highest levels of the Pentagon and the administration. Our intelligence tells us, accurately, we think, that Hanoi is being helped by sympathetic Americans, not by the KGB. This assistance to the enemy is both strategic and tactical, in the theater and at home."

Quint perked up at that and scribbled a quick note. There was a story here after all, although he couldn't decide if it was a comedy or tragedy. He knew these uptight soldiers weren't about to shoulder any blame themselves. It was the radicals who had done it. Of course! *They* were responsible for Tet. Traitors within.

Quint was aware that Lambert was watching him. Lambert had had a hand in writing Westmoreland's speech, and he was understandably curious about how it was playing. He would have preferred Tom Benson, who played freebie rounds on military golf courses, but he was stuck with a longhair who asked disconcerting questions.

Westmoreland said, "This underscores national security implications of the government's concern about the domestic antiwar movement in the United States. The antiwar radicals are not exercising legitimate First Amendment rights when they actively aid and abet the enemy. They are not benign. This is more than a clear and present danger. It is nothing short of treason."

Lambert said, "There you go, Jim. See, there was some news here after all. You can put that at the top of your story."

"Aiding and abetting the enemy? Traitors? That'll make people choke on their coffee. I'll put it at the top, you can bet the farm on it," Quint said. Quint felt that if Westmoreland could have gotten away with it, he would have blamed the press. This was as close as he dared come.

Quint was curious about something else. "Say, I've been wondering. You're not one of *the* Lamberts by any chance?" The wealthy, powerful Lambert family was one of a half dozen dynasties of the former Sandwich Islands, descendants of Protestant missionaries who, along with the military, owned most of the land in the state.

Lambert grinned. "Yes, I'm one of those Lamberts. The only one not in the shipping business or growing pineapples. When I was coming in today, I asked my wife if she was getting bored waiting. You know what she told me?"

"Don't have any idea," Quint said.

"Yes, you do. She told me she'd talked to Jim Quint from the *Honolulu Star-Bulletin*."

"That was your wife?"

"You know it was."

Quint tried to suppress his embarrassment. "A real beauty. Good for you. She was sitting in a Mercedes reading a book when I passed the open window."

"No need to explain, but I have to admit, I'm curious, why didn't you tell me you met her?"

Quint licked his lips.

Lambert grinned. "She's enough to give a brass Buddha a hard-on, that's a fact. Did she tell you she reads your articles too? For reasons that escape me, she thinks you're a good writer."

"There's no accounting for taste," Quint said.

"Possibly too good a writer considering your subject matter. You two talk about the war, did you?"

"She wanted to know what I thought, and I told her."

"I see. And did you ask her what she thinks about the war? She's Vietnamese. I'd think a guy like you'd be naturally curious."

Quint said, "I asked, but she passed on answering."

"Dumb, Vivienne is not."

"I didn't think she was."

Lambert smiled lazily, his pale blue eyes boring in on Quint. "I got the impression she likes you. You flirted with my wife did you, Jim? Come on now, 'fess up."

"I just said hello."

Lambert looked scornful. "I bet. Say, I'd like to have a husband's privilege of introducing you to her myself if you don't mind."

Quint blinked. A husband's privilege?

Lambert said, "There's something about her I bet she didn't tell you. Only take a minute. Hard to believe you'd have any objection to that."

That sounded mysterious to Quint. "Sure," he said. He was grateful for any opportunity to meet Lambert's wife again. Had she been out there in the heat waiting for Lambert all this time?

QUINT WAS AWARE that Chick McGyver was watching him as he headed outside with Col. Del Lambert. McGyver was clearly annoyed by something more than his appearance. Was he somehow sore because Lambert was friendly to him? If that were true, Quint found it an odd reaction. Weren't reporters supposed to get along with everybody from street people to heads of state? McGyver should feel pleased that he had established rapport with the intelligence officer who had likely helped write Westmoreland's speech, and a Lambert at that. For all McGyver knew, Quint had scored a news source that would prove valuable to the *Star-Bulletin* in the future. Maybe McGyver was envious? Officer editors were supposed to be the ones chatting casually with Lamberts, not sandal-wearing hippie reporters, journalistic foot soldiers.

For all of his misgivings about Quint's beat, Lambert was amiable enough as they strolled outside together. "Vivienne is trilingual. She speaks fluent French in addition to English and Vietnamese. She was named after a French nun in Saigon. She's a Catholic. Also she's an accomplished artist."

"Oh? What kind of art?"

"She does both acrylics and watercolors. She's good with faces. She does people and portraits. Street scenes. Peasants in fields. That kind of thing."

"Interesting," Quint said and meant it.

Lambert continued, "Most Asian art is highly stylized. The portrait, with its emphasis on the character of an individual human face, is a product of the western imagination. From Leonardo's *Mona Lisa* to portraits of Henry VIII, Lord Nelson, and George Washington, we know what people from the past looked like. There is no such tradition in Asia. There are highly stylized birds and mountains that we associate with the decor in Chinese restaurants. The Japanese have elaborate, formal rules for everything from flower arranging to serving tea. Buddhism, which spread from East- and Southeast Asia from India, holds that individuals rise from the great river of humanity and sink back in, blending into the waters. It is the larger race or civilization that counts, not individuals within it. The use of Mao's face as a political icon, copying the Soviet's use of Lenin's image, is a recent phenomenon in Asia."

Lambert was no bonehead military officer. Quint was impressed. "Who taught her to paint?"

"A Jesuit priest," Lambert said. "She believes surface is reflection. And by reflection, I don't mean just light. Her art is why I was attracted to her. In addition to the obvious of course. She's beautiful. She lives an examined life."

They stepped out into the heat of the parking lot. Quint whipped on his shades and the floppy, wide-brimmed hat that he used to protect his beak from the tropical sun.

"Vivienne," he said. "An elegant name."

"She's an elegant young woman, but of course you know that already. Racially, she's basically a Malay, as are all the women in Southeast Asia. I say Malay. They're a duke's mixture actually."

"Oh?"

Lambert led the way, heading for the Mercedes under the banyan tree. "Vietnamese, Thai, Cambodian, Laotian, Indonesian, and Filipino. Different religions and cultures, but racially they're a mix. You're looking at a little Chinese, a touch of Khmer, some Burmese. Whatever. They vary, but generally they have rounder eyes and slightly darker skin than the Chinese, Koreans, and Japanese. Took me months to get permission to marry Vivienne—me being an intelligence officer and all. What a drill!"

"I can imagine," Quint said, wondering why Lambert was so intent on introducing him to his wife.

When Quint saw Vivienne again, he wondered even more. Beautiful hardly described her. She was maybe eighteen or twenty years younger than her husband and apparently smart as hell. Quint supposed it was foolish to expect a Lambert would commit himself to any old beauty.

With her extraordinary, large brown eyes Vivienne watched her husband and the longhaired reporter draw near. She seemed surprised, and pleased, to see the two of them together.

Lambert said, "It didn't take so long did it?"

"No problem," she said. "I was reading and the time flew by. I got a little breeze too." Vivienne obviously hadn't told her husband about Quint's groan. She gave him a mischievous hint of a smile, a teasing, private thank-you for their earlier moment.

If Lambert noticed anything untoward he didn't show it. "Turned out I sat beside Jim Quint here, the reporter you met earlier. We had a good talk."

"You get a good story, Jim?"

Quint said, "It was a story, I guess; parts of it are hard to believe but you never know. I suspect our readers're probably more interested in the Celtics and Lakers."

Watching Quint, Lambert said, "I told you that I've spent the last three years trying to recover the CBS film of the Lon Be massacre. Well, Vivienne is from Lon Be. The Vietcong murdered her entire family that day. Her mother and father. Her grandparents. Her three brothers and two sisters, plus two nieces and a nephew. They tortured her father while the others watched, then wasted them all with AK-47s. I say again, her entire family. Every one of them."

Quint took a deep breath and let it out through puffed cheeks. He thought, *thanks a whole bunch, asshole.* He said, "I'm truly sorry that something like that happened, Mrs. Lambert."

She said, proudly. "My grandfather was the mayor of Lon Be."

Lambert said, "Tell me, how would you feel if that happened to you, Jim? What if some bastard just stepped in your family's house one day and wasted everybody, then torched the place as a form of exclamation point? How would you feel?" Having scored his dubious point, Lambert cocked his head in triumph.

"It would make me goddam furious. I wouldn't sleep until I put the bastards in the grave."

"They'll pay one day," Vivienne said mildly.

Lambert said, "You asked me why we refuse to pull our troops out of Khesanh. That's precisely why."

No way was Quint going to argue the war with the Grimacing Bead of Sweat standing there in the parking lot. He said, "Your husband tells me you're an artist, Mrs. Lambert. Good with faces, he says."

Vivienne blushed faintly. "I learned in school."

"Not many portrait artists in Vietnam, I wouldn't think. I'd like to see your work sometime."

Lambert, curiously intent, seemed almost to be studying him.

"Say, Jim, would you like to have lunch with me at the Willows? A soldier and a journalist. We could talk. Maybe swap stories."

No good reporter in Honolulu turned down an invitation to have lunch with a member of the Lambert family. Wondering why the colonel was interested in him, Quint found himself saying, "Lunch at the Willows. Sure, why not."

"How about tomorrow?" Lambert said.

Lambert was serious. Quint hesitated. "It'll have to be later in the afternoon. Our last deadline is at two o'clock. That's for the green streak final. Street sales and all that."

"Three o'clock then. How about three o'clock? We can take our time and have a leisurely talk."

"Three o'clock, sure." Quint found it borderline impossible to keep from sneaking another look at Vivienne, who momentarily caught his eyes then looked quickly away. He'd never in his life had such a flirtatious, searing moment with a beauty like her. And with Colonel Ball Bearing Buns standing right there. Jesus!

"Tomorrow at the Willows it is." Lambert extended his hand and shook.

Quint shook Vivienne's slender hand. "It was pleasant meeting you, Mrs. Lambert."

She looked him straight on. "Yes, it was. Maybe we'll meet again sometime."

The protectors had disappeared. Quint walked numbly to his car. *Maybe we'll meet again sometime.* He slipped behind the wheel and started the engine. The Mercedes was leaving the lot.

He gave a quick peek back. She was watching him through the window. A beautiful Vietnamese. The wife of an army colonel. A Lambert.

He gave her a wave.

Vivienne glanced at her husband then back at him. Then she was gone.

6

THE *STAR-BULLETIN* CITY room, painted a pale, industrial green—said to be the hue of puke after Primo and pistachios—was a clutter of desks mashed between square concrete supports. The dark room lay between the clattering linotypes and the long city room. The linotypes, each with a pot of hot metal, sent one line of type at a time cascading down a chute to go *plop, plop, plop* into a tray. Their muted *click-clack* had been the background sound in newspapers, rather as a lowing, industrial wind, metallic and mechanical, for the better part of a century.

The network television news was flown to Hawaii on commercial airline flights from the mainland. Local channels reported the national and international news without visuals. CBS's Walter Cronkite, ABC's Howard K. Smith, and NBC's Chet Huntley and David Brinkley got their turn at 11 P.M. This meant Honolulu was the last city in the United States that had anything resembling competition between morning and afternoon newspapers. While television had sent most afternoon dailies under on the mainland, the *Star-Bulletin* was still publishing the green streak final for tourists in Waikiki.

Copy was edited and headlines written at the rim, a semicircular desk on the makai side of the city room. Mauka and Pearl City of the rim were the *ch-churg-churg-churging* Associated Press machines that extruded, inch by inch, news of the latest disaster, travesty, or scandal from the mainland. The stories were lined up, coming at the city room twenty-four hours a day.

After a sleepless night of remembering Vivienne Lambert's large brown eyes looking into his as they shook hands, Jim Quint drew a ration of Yamani's coffee and survived the morning drill of waking people up to get quotes, then settled in to work on a story about Project Mohole. Mohole was touted as an effort by geologists to bore through the crust of the earth. Scientists, needing public support for their research, ordinarily loved to have reporters write about their work. The drilling was being done by Brown and Root, the Texas company that was an enthusiastic financial backer of President Johnson. Forced to rewrite vague press releases on what seemed like a major story, he wondered why Brown and Root had chosen to drill in the middle of the Pacific Ocean. He tried to wangle a trip to Mohole, but Brown and Root sent him a form letter rejecting his request without explanation.

"Jim, I'd like a word with you, please."

Quint looked up. It was Chick McGyver, standing in the door of his office. "Sure," Quint said. Trouble. Had to be. He felt a flutter in his stomach. He got up and went inside.

McGyver retreated behind his desk and gestured for Quint to sit.

Quint sat. He didn't dislike McGyver. At least McGyver wasn't a total fraud like the *Advertiser's* editor Peter Burberry, who rewrote dust jacket blurbs into "reviews" to assure a steady flow of freebie review copies. He used the books to decorate his office. Quint once spotted a novel by Anthony Powell called *Books Do Furnish a Room* and burst out laughing. There was serious doubt that Burberry actually read books—he was known to be a passionate fan of *Gunsmoke* on the tube—but he liked to affect the air of a thoughtful gentleman and intellectual. McGyver was more straightforward. It was simply his job to see that his editors and writers didn't offend his circle of friends or anybody else who counted. As such, Quint considered him only a marginal fraud.

McGyver cleared his throat. "Jim, I'm concerned about your appearance at the Pacific Club yesterday. That was General William C. Westmoreland speaking, and the commander of the Pacific fleet was there. And you showed up wearing an aloha shirt. You were the only person at the table without a tie."

Quint wanted to say admirals and generals let farts and put their pants on one leg at a time, same as him. But he restrained himself, doing his best to look properly contrite. McGyver couldn't sack him for the offense of wearing an aloha shirt, the Newspaper Guild would see to that. On the other hand, it was in his best interest to get along with his editor.

"You were sitting next to a member of the Lambert family."

"The youngest son, Del," Quint said. "The only one not in shipping, ranching, or pineapples."

McGyver didn't like Quint referring to a Lambert by his first name. He colored. "Colonel Lambert."

"Colonel Lambert, yes. Interesting guy. We had a good talk. He introduced me to his wife afterward, and he invited me to lunch at the Willows today."

McGyver looked amazed. "He did? Colonel Del Lambert? He's in charge of military intelligence in Vietnam."

"I don't think he's in charge, but he's apparently a biggie of some kind," Quint said. He wanted to add that Lambert and his colleagues couldn't have been all that great, or they would somehow have gotten word to Hue about the Vietcong buildup for Tet. "He's the officer in charge of trying to retrieve the CBS film of the Lon Be massacre. Who knows, maybe I'll come back with a story? I'm doing military while Tom is on his vacation."

McGyver seemed genuinely puzzled about something.

Quint wondered if he was annoyed that Quint was going to have lunch with one of the Lamberts. That was like a butler having lunch with a baron. Perhaps it offended his sense of propriety that Quint had entered the much-coveted territory of suck. McGyver was editor of the paper. *He* was the one who should be invited to have lunch with Del Lambert, not a longhaired nobody like Quint.

Or was there something he wasn't telling Quint?

McGyver was either mystified or pissed, one or the other. He shuffled some papers on his desk. He had the presence of an earnest chipmunk. He avoided eye contact with Quint. Whatever it was that specifically bothered him or had stimulated his curiosity, he had obviously decided not to tell Quint.

He decided to return to the original subject. "For most assignments, an aloha shirt is just fine, Jim. This is Hawaii, not Boston or Chicago, and the state earns a lot of revenue marketing them. But the next time you go to cover a speech by General Westmoreland at the Pacific Club, I want you to wear a jacket and tie. Simple respect. That's why we keep them on the rack, for occasions like this."

"I'll try to remember, next time," Quint said. "You want me to say hello to Del for you?" Quint was aware that flipping McGyver a verbal finger meant he would forever be a reporter, but he didn't want to be an editor anyway. He wanted to be out there in the mud and blood and spit. He left McGyver's office wondering what it was the editor was holding back about Col. Del Lambert.

THE WILLOWS WAS a popular bar and eatery not far from Honolulu Civic Stadium where the Islanders played baseball in the AAA Northwest League. The Willows had an airy, tropical motif and featured tables around an interconnected network of pools filled with large, colorful goldfish—some were in fact black, some orange, some yellow, some white, and others were speckled, or a combination of those colors.

It turned out that Del Lambert was a regular there. A solicitous waiter immediately steered Lambert and Quint to Lambert's favorite table that was in a choice location by the fish pond. They settled in and ordered martinis on the rocks. They admired the goldfish and talked about the Islanders' acquisition of the aging knuckleballer Hoyt Wilhelm, after which Lambert adroitly steered the conversation around to the radicals on Quint's beat. George Sarant, who was president of Students for a Democratic Society; Neil Abercrombie, a fire-breathing orator who was a graduate student at the University of Hawaii; a radical named John Witek.

"Do they trust you?" he asked casually.

Quint shrugged. "I can't do business without their trust. I won't talk about them to an intelligence officer, if that's what you're thinking. Are you collecting dossiers on them?"

Lambert smiled. "What do you think about the Oliver Lee business?"

Oliver Lee was the current *cause celebre* at the University of Hawaii. Lee, an assistant professor of political science, was also advisor to the Students for a Democratic Society. A small band of SDS zealots had used a departmental ditto machine to produce leaflets urging soldiers in Vietnam to frag their officers. They passed these out in Waikiki, inadvertently thrusting one into the hands of the wrong person, the patriotic Fred Fielding, who went bananas. As it happened, the university administration had mailed a letter to Lee informing him that he was to get tenure. In the furor that followed, the university withdrew the letter. Question: Was the act of sending the letter the same as giving Lee tenure?

"I have to cover that story," Quint said. "Both sides," he added.

Lambert raised an eyebrow. "There's only one acceptable side to that story, pal. Those adolescent little fuckers urged enlisted men to murder their officers. How are we supposed to prosecute a war with shit like that going on back home?"

"Oliver Lee didn't advocate fragging. The SDS kids did. He didn't see the leaflet. How was he supposed to know what was in it?"

"He was their advisor. He was responsible. He should have known. They used a machine bought by the taxpayers." Lambert leaned forward, studying Quint.

Quint sighed. Lambert, along with Gov. John A. Burns, was an obvious believer in the doctrine of *in loco parentis*, in which professors were supposed to function as surrogate parents for their students. This was a screwed notion as far as Quint was concerned. "Okay, you want my opinion, you've got it. Oliver Lee says he doesn't believe in the fragging business. I believe him. He says he's a professor, not their father. They say if they're old enough to be drafted, they're old enough to be treated as adults. I agree with him. Lee also says he can't tell them what to think. They're entitled to their opinion, however wrongheaded. I agree with that. I think he got screwed, but I can't let my personal feelings color my stories."

"Do you think enlisted men should frag their officers?"

"Hell no, what do you think I am?"

It just struck Quint that nowhere in their conversation at the Pacific Club and now here at the Willows had Lambert asked him whether or not he had served in the military. Quint was old enough to have been eligible for the draft. Quint had either served or somehow avoided it. Given the subject of the American participation in the war in Vietnam and Quint's coverage of the anti-war radicals, Quint thought it was a logical question. Harmless enough. In fact, Quint had been drafted and served in Germany as an analyst of high altitude reconnaissance photographs. Quint said, "Why haven't you asked me if I've served in the military?"

Lambert said, "You were drafted. You were trained as a photo analyst at the Bird. I went to school there too, as you probably suspect. We have that much in common."

"You checked my service record?"

Lambert seemed unconcerned. "Sure. Why not? Easy to do. I was curious. It's one thing for a draft dodger to glorify draft-card burners. More honorable if you've done your time. I'll give you that one. What do you think of the Peace and Freedom Party?"

Quint grinned. "This is a union state. People here vote for Democrats. They might agree that the war is wrong, but they'll do what their unions tell them and vote for Democrats."

"Gene McCarthy go far, do you think?"

"Not likely," Quint said.

"You like Bobby?"

"I think he'd get farther than Gene, but Johnson will figure out a way to cut either one of 'em off at the pass. I'm suspicious of anybody who once served on Joe McCarthy's staff." By temperament, the charismatic Del Lambert was opposite Quint in many if not most ways, yet Quint respected him. He was a soldier, yes, but a soldier out of conviction, Quint thought, not because he was afraid he couldn't make it on the outside. He did not appear to be parroting anybody's line. He might even have lived an examined life. He was sensible enough not to be accusatory in his disagreements with Jim, which Quint appreciated. He was genuinely curious about why Quint thought as he did, which Quint found flattering.

Quint didn't doubt his own beliefs, but he knew that it was easy to say something dumb in the presence of someone who was more experienced than he was. Quint was wary of coming off as glib or arrogant. Lambert made him feel too young to have been given the responsibility he had with the *Star-Bulletin*. Sometimes he found it hard to believe that he, at twenty-six and still a kid really, was interpreting the cultural revolution for Hawaii's readers. Where did he get off? Perhaps that was what Lambert was thinking.

Lambert hesitated a moment. "By the way, I was right. Vivienne likes you. It's obvious."

"She does?" In what way? And why had Lambert pointed it out? Quint's stomach fluttered.

Lambert said, "Talked about you all the way home. She wanted to know what the two of us talked about at the Pacific Club. It was not just small talk either. She was genuinely curious. No accounting for taste, I guess. I told her you look like Wild Bill Hickok or Wyatt Earp. She had no idea who they were. Of course you like her too, I could tell."

Quint blinked. Had Lambert noticed his private little moment with Vivienne? Was Quint about to get a chewing out by a jealous husband?

Lambert grinned. "You can close your mouth, Jim. It's okay. Every male who lays eyes on her falls in love with her, I know that. Why should you be any different?" He paused, assessing Quint's reaction. "Ah, see, I was right. You too. I thought so. No reason to be embarrassed."

Quint thought he must have looked like a dog caught eating a turd.

Lambert seemed unconcerned. Like he said, he was used to

men admiring his wife. "You'd be astonished at the hòrseshit I went through to marry her. Hard to let a woman like that slip through your fingers."

"She's good looking, that's a fact," Quint said. "What happened to her family was a terrible thing."

"The Charlies are unrelieved cocksuckers, something people here in the states don't fully appreciate. They just unloaded on that village, wasted everybody who couldn't make it to the jungle fast enough." Lambert checked his watch. "Well, I better be getting back. I've got to go to the airport to help meet some members of the House Armed Services Committee. It'll only take a few minutes, but I have to be there. Tomorrow we'll brief them about the light."

"The light?"

Lambert grinned ruefully. "The one at the end of the tunnel. They've got constituents nagging them."

"The light getting a little brighter, do you think?"

"After we get Hue back which should be a matter of hours now, it'll be a whole lot brighter, guaranteed. Say, how would you like to come to our house for supper tonight? Vivienne can make you some Vietnamese food. I bet you don't have anything to do except lope your goat or get loaded with the gang at the Columbia Inn. I know Vivienne would like it. What do you say?"

Vivienne would like it? Quint thought about Chick McGyver, wondering what it was that McGyver hadn't told him. "Sure. Why not?"

Lambert paused, thinking about something then. "There's something else I suppose I should tell you. You'll find out about it anyway, if not from Vivienne then somebody else."

"Find out about what?"

"That I might be a little crazy." He grinned.

"Crazy?"

"Maybe not entirely round the bend—just part of the way." He looked amused.

"I see." Quint thought there was something spooky about Lambert's eyes.

Watching Quint, he said, "Don't you want to know what's wrong with me?"

"I get the feeling you're going to tell me anyway."

He grinned. "I can't sleep. I'm gripped by rage." He watched Jim carefully. "I've spent six years in Nam. That has to affect a person."

"I suppose it would."

Lambert said, mildly, "Every time I come back to Honolulu it gets worse. I just cannot abide this radical, war protesting, pacifist horseshit. It drives me fucking nuts. You read anything about that shrink R. D. Laing?"

Quint nodded. "The guy who says the psychopaths are sane. Everybody else is crazy."

"You know, every time I pick up your newspaper, I get the feeling that I'm landing in a combat zone that's just as confused as the one I just left. It's like I can't turn a page without seeing another one of your bullshit pieces quoting more blather by yet one more pimple-faced longhair or posturing college professor. Then something occurred to me. The war in Vietnam has triggered a civil war back here, but this is something nobody wants to admit. By that reckoning, you're a kind of war correspondent."

Quint looked puzzled. "I am?"

Lambert bored right through Quint with those ice-blue eyes of his. "Covering ignorant chickenshits and scumbag traitors. I know the fire on one side of the pond. You write about the flames on the other. I find that interesting. Well, are you going to accept my invitation or not? The question before the house is simple enough: Have you got a spine or are you what makes the grass grow green?"

"Which is?"

"Chickenshit. Nature's very best fertilizer. Vivienne likes you. Her husband the colonel invites you to dinner."

"Sure. Why not? I'll be there."

Lambert laughed. "Thought so. I tell you what, Jimbo. We're gonna have an unusual evening. One you won't forget. Guaranteed."

7

JIM QUINT WAS in a pensive mood as he drove his Datsun sedan up Tantalus Drive, passing the National Memorial Cemetery of the Pacific, locally known as Punchbowl, on his right. Here were the most expensive residences on the island. On one side of Mt. Tantalus, the grand homes tucked back into the rain forest overlooked the University of Hawaii and the East-West Center in Manoa Valley; on the opposite side, the houses faced Pearl Harbor. A select few residences, the grandest of grand houses tucked into the tropical undergrowth on the makai side of the loop, got a more panoramic view of everything from Diamond Head to the vessels anchored at Pearl.

As Quint drove he thought about the Greek mythological figure Tantalus, the root of the English verb *tantalize*. It was an interesting choice of a name for the mountain overlooking the queen city of the Pacific. Tantalize was the act of exciting somebody by exposing something desirable and keeping it just out of reach. Honolulu's wealthiest and most powerful lived on Mt. Tantalus, up there in the swirling mists of desire, just out of reach.

Following Col. Del Lambert's directions, Quint turned off Tantalus Drive onto a narrow, private lane that led downhill to an abrupt end, and there was Lambert's house, although *villa*, in the European sense, was perhaps more descriptive. It was far too grand and elegant to be called a mere house. The sprawling residence, tucked into tropical undergrowth and overlooking the city lights, was stained a rustic brown to blend into the mountain and had a shake roof. Large windows and sliding glass doors faced the makai, or seaward, side of the house. The glass doors opened onto a series of decks built on stilts. The windows and decks took advantage of the amazing view that extended from Diamond Head to Pearl Harbor, although the latter view was blocked somewhat by a second, smaller ridge.

There was nothing surprising about the size or location of the house. This was, after all, the residence of a Lambert. As money went in Hawaii, this was old money. The good fortune of the Lambert family was part of its inheritance from the Rev. Josiah Lambert, who in the early nineteenth century landed in the Sandwich Islands with the mission of introducing the Lord to the brown-skinned heathens who lived there. In return for delivering them from Lucifer and securing their spot in the Christian afterlife, the thoughtful reverend bought large chunks of their land for his family at giveaway prices; this was a biblical transaction: As ye shall give, so shall ye reap.

The present-day Lamberts did not talk about their good fortune nor show it off, the boorish practice of new money. The Lamberts knew the painful truth of a terrible cultural catch: Contrary to the enthusiastic urging of advertising copywriters, class was not for sale. Those who believed they could buy class demonstrated that they didn't have any. Let the misguided bourgeois scramble for every buck; the serene Lamberts, untouched by having to perform untidy labor, observed the amusing hurly-burly from the privacy of their clubs and secluded estates.

Lambert had said little of his wife's background. An artist by imagination, Vivienne had attended a Catholic school where she had learned to paint, which suggested she was from an upperclass family, but Quint couldn't imagine that any amount of wealth could have prepared her for this. She must have felt like an Asian Cinderella. He parked his Datsun and walked uphill on a flagstone path through an immaculate garden of manicured evergreens and rang the doorbell.

Lambert answered the call with a smile on his face and a drink in his hand. When Quint met him at the Pacific Club, he'd been in uniform, his chest plastered with fruit salad and an intelligence service patch on his shoulder. Now he was dressed in Bermuda shorts showing hairy, muscular legs and a Hooker's green aloha shirt with yellow ochre flowers. He was so lean he looked bulletproof. But for all his power and muscle and his decisive blue eyes, he seemed amiable enough.

He said, "Well, Jim, I see you found the place all right. Come on in."

Quint stepped inside a foyer, looking for Vivienne, who was not to be seen. Were there maids and butlers, he wondered?

Lambert said, "We gave the help off tonight so we could relax. Vivienne is in the kitchen. She wanted to do the cooking herself. I hope you like Vietnamese food. It can be quite good. The influence of the French. Their colonials had to endure the heat and the bugs, but they weren't about to put up with bad food."

"Oh, well sure, whatever," Quint said.

"Drink?"

"Whatever you're having."

"Scotch," Lambert said.

"That sounds fine."

Lambert led Quint into a spacious den, the walls of which momentarily stunned him. They were covered with photographs of visitors to the Lambert residence, almost all of them featuring Vivienne and a guest.

Vivienne—a delicate, doe-eyed Vietnamese beauty in her midtwenties and flat beautiful—was an amazing presence in the photographs. At around five-foot six inches, she was tall for a woman from Southeast Asia. Quint felt there was something about natural beauty of whatever race that just jumped right out. It was indefinable. It just was. Whatever it was, Vivienne had it and then some.

And the guests with her in the photographs were not ordinary folks. They were top generals and admirals including General William C. Westmoreland, the commander of the Pacific Fleet, Rep. L. Mendel Rivers, Sen. Scoop Jackson, and other members of the House and Senate armed services committees. In one of the photographs, beautiful Vivienne was posed with a boozy looking

Rivers. In another she served Sen. Jackson *puu-puus* on a tray. In a third, she was standing beside the South Vietnamese president Nguyen Cao Ky.

Quint had attended press conferences by scores of brand-name visitors to Hawaii and interviewed several of them. When visiting power players from the Pentagon and the White House visited Hawaii to discuss the latest bad news from Vietnam, they adjourned to Lambert's sprawling house to talk things over in privacy. Here they had security, a good view, and a hostess who was the stuff of wet dreams.

If the news about the receding light at the end of the tunnel didn't cheer them up, the presence of Vivienne almost certainly would.

Lambert gave Quint a generous glass of Scotch on the rocks. He said, "Vivienne and I do a lot of entertaining, as you can see. It's private up here. People can relax."

Quint took a sip of Scotch, which was smooth and mellow. He hadn't paid any attention to the bottle, but the whisky was delicious. It *tasted* expensive. "And you don't have to pay a lot of attention to the budget—being a Lambert and all."

Lambert smiled. "There's that too."

At which point Vivienne entered with a platter of egg rolls. She set them on a coffee table, glancing up at Quint with her brown eyes. She said, "Welcome to our house, Jim. You'll find these crispier than the Chinese variety. They're made with translucent rolls of what we call rice paper."

Quint tried one. She was right. It was crispier. And better. "They're delicious," he said.

"I've steamed some mahi mahi and made a fennel sauce for it. Fun to cook for myself once in a while."

Quint gestured to the photographs on the wall. "I see you and Scoop Jackson and President Ky hit it off."

Vivienne accepted a glass of white wine from her husband. "They are nice men and sincere. They're doing their best in spite of all their problems."

Mired down in a screwed war while the country comes unraveled, Quint thought. He said, "They do have their problems, that's a fact. You know, Colonel, no matter how much you repeat the claim, it's tough for most Americans to believe that Tet was somehow a victory for the Americans and South Vietnamese. It's got your critics pumped. If you don't mind my saying so, your need is for a propaganda coup that cuts the other way. A big thump that creams the Charlies. Get some sympathy rolling your way."

Lambert studied him. "You read my mind, Jim. That's precisely what we need, and exactly what I'm going to deliver."

"You?"

"Why not me? Who knows, maybe starting tonight. Here, have another hit of whiskey. Put us in the mood." Lambert, the accomodating host, freshened their drinks.

8

*T*HE HUGE DINING room had an equally large window that overlooked the twinkling and blinking of the Honolulu city lights. In addition to steamed fish with fennel and the mandatory white rice, Vivienne had prepared a crispy chicken noodle salad, a soup of pork and shrimp with rice noodles, and strong, sweet coffee with a layer of cream on top. Quint thought it was delicious. During the supper, Quint could feel her watching him with interest. Quint wondered about Lambert's mysterious claim that he was going to deliver a propaganda coup to help the American cause in Vietnam. What kind of coup?

Who knows, maybe starting tonight.

Did Quint's unexpected dinner invitation have anything to do with Lambert's ambition to retrieve the Lon Be film? He couldn't imagine what.

Quint knew that the dictionary described "charming" as the quality of pleasing or delighting. In his experience, somebody who is charming ordinarily has the capacity to be interested in something besides themselves. By either definition, Vivienne was charming. She never ventured information about her past. Quint had to seek it out. He learned that her father, the only son of a prosperous Vietnamese businessman, had been a history professor in a college established by the French in Saigon. One of his books, a history of colonialism in Indochina, had been published by Gallimard in Paris, one of the top publishing houses in France.

Most attractive of all, in Quint's opinion, was Vivienne's apparent lack of interest in things material. He quickly lost interest in people who felt they were defined by what they consumed. That was not Vivienne. She had married a rich man, yes, but if she had married Lambert for his money, she showed no sign of it.

After supper, at Lambert's urging, Vivienne showed Quint her studio, which featured brilliant overhead lights for work at night and a skylight for daytime painting. If she wanted she could open a sliding glass door and paint on a spacious deck. She had rendered remarkable city scenes, from Saigon cafe life to the wretched poverty of Third World streets. And Lambert had understood her talent. On the surface, light and color. Beneath that, delight, joy, pain, and despair. Her world was in her studio. Her pride was in creation. As she felt, so she painted. She had recently tried her hand at some Hawaii scenes—a young man carrying a surfboard, a huge Hawaiian or Samoan carrying a garbage can, tourists in aloha shirts with leis around their necks. But her Hawaii scenes lacked the passion of her Vietnamese paintings. She was Vietnamese. Her heart was in Vietnam.

With Lambert at his shoulder, Quint went slowly from painting to painting, studying the faces. There was an enigmatic quality about Vivienne, reflected in her paintings, that Quint did not understand.

She watched Quint, pleased. "You like them?"

"They're very good indeed," Quint said. "I'm envious."

"Envious?"

"Of your talent." He wanted to say envious of her husband too, and felt it likely showed. Then he thought to hell with it. He said, "And of your husband."

She hesitated, looking him straight on. "Thank you." She rested her hand on his momentarily then moved on.

Vivienne's father had been an intellectual. Vivienne was the closest thing Quint had ever seen to an Asian bohemian. The idea of a bohemian—someone indifferent to conventional standards of behavior—was ordinarily as foreign to the Asian imagination as an artist who painted faces. These were clan-based societies. Individuals did not assert intellectual independence, *they belonged*. Quint found it curious that an artist like Vivienne could fall in love with a soldier and marry him, even an American officer who would spirit her from the dangerous war zone. Except for her sister Genevieve, she had lost her entire family in Lon Be. Quint supposed she was open to any form of escape from the memories.

"Tell me what it was like growing up in Lon Be," Quint said.

Vivienne glanced at her husband.

"That's in her past," he said.

Her face clouded with emotions that Quint found ambiguous. Was she angry? Sad? What?

"No, I want Jim to know. No reason he shouldn't and no reason to lie about pleasant memories," she said. "It is sad to remember Lon Be, that's so. Before the war, it was a lovely, peaceful place. I had a wonderful childhood there before I was sent to the Catholic school in Saigon. But all the good memories have been eliminated by the war and the monstrous outrage of what happened on December 14, 1965." She glanced at Lambert then back at Quint. "Tell me again the name of your hometown in Montana. Bison, was it?"

"Bison, yes. Give me a home, where the buffalo roam."

"How would you feel if soldiers came by one day and killed everybody in Bison, including your parents and grandparents, your brothers and sisters, and your aunts, uncles and cousins? I bet that kind of thing happened in your American civil war or close to it. People in the South are still fighting that war if I'm correctly guessing the reasons for the popularity of Alabama's Governor Wallace."

"I wouldn't like it one damn bit," Quint said.

"This is not a civil war. It's an invasion by North Vietnam," Lambert said. "There's no mistaking that. The facts are clear."

Vivienne eyed him coolly. "Whatever. The Vietcong slaughtered everybody in my family. Surely you read about it here in the United States. A barbarous atrocity." She looked mildly at her husband. "Committed by uncivilized savages. Isn't that so, Del?"

Lambert's face hardened. "The Thanhs had committed the sin of being Catholic, and Vivienne's grandfather, a rice merchant who owed his prosperity to the French, was the mayor of the village."

"Del was advisor to the army of the Republic of Vietnam."

"We were teaching them counter-insurgency tactics."

"Counter-insurgency," she repeated, rather unnecessarily, Quint thought. There was an odd tension in the air. The conversation was an apparent test of wills between Vivienne and Lambert that Quint had no way of understanding.

Lambert said, "I met Vivienne in Saigon three months after the Lon Be tragedy. She was twenty-two. I was thirty-six. Perhaps the war and the massacre isn't a good subject for Vivienne."

"No, no," Vivienne said quickly. "I think Jim should know the whole story, don't you? You Americans are committed to the truth, I'm told. 'Ye shall know the truth, and the truth shall set you free.' Who was it who said that?"

Quint said, "It was Cicero, I think. Or somebody."

Lambert said, "Vivienne and I were quickly engaged, but because of my intelligence assignment, it was a struggle to get permission to marry her. Finally, in July 1966, we married and moved to Honolulu."

Quint didn't think he was getting the whole story about the Lon Be incident, but decided it was impolite to pursue it. The tension between Vivienne and her husband seemed almost lethal.

Vivienne said, "I think Del wants to get off the subject of Lon Be. Tell us more about yourself, Jim."

Quint said quickly, "My father was the foreman of a cattle spread outside Bison, Montana."

"And that is where in Montana?"

"Just north of Yellowstone National Park. I grew up fishing for trout on the Madison, Gallatin, and Yellowstone Rivers, all of which flow north at that point, ending up in the Missouri River."

Lambert said, "Jim graduated from the University of Montana."

Vivienne asked, "How is it you became a newspaper reporter?"

"I was a journalism major. I wanted to be a newspaper reporter because that was a way I could earn a living with a typewriter."

Through the small talk, Quint struggled to keep his eyes off Vivienne. Her presence was disconcerting. It was like sitting next to an Asian Catherine Deneuve and pretending she wasn't there. It was borderline impossible for him to keep his eyes off a woman so beautiful and desirable. Like Quint, Vivienne was naturally curious. The sole exception to her generous intellect was the subject of the Vietcong. She professed to dislike the Communists, which was understandable under the circumstances, but she was a passionate defender of her countrymen. Quint assumed she was a nationalist. He wanted to know more about her, but after he had learned the civilized minimum, he backed off on the questions. She was Lambert's wife, after all. Quint was a guest.

Lambert, on the other hand, had a Manichean imagination. As a soldier, he believed in hierarchies and authority. He defined the world into comfortable zones of black and white, evil and good. He was certain of things, and he wanted certainty and order in his life. Vivienne wanted to know all sides of a question, a habit she had no doubt learned from her father.

After supper, they adjourned to the den; there, surrounded by the photographs of the power players in the Johnson administration, they enjoyed some brandy and sweet, pungent Costa Rican cigars.

Vivienne was lonely, Quint felt. And haunted. Finally, Quint, glancing at his watch, started to rise. "Looks like it's time to go home," he said.

Lambert held up the palm of his right hand, motioning him to stay seated. "No rush. Where do you have to go that's so important?"

Vivienne said, "Del's right, Jim. No rush. Do stay for a while longer." She was not being polite. She was sincere. She didn't want Quint to leave.

Then, casually, Lambert said, "Tell me, Jim, would you like to see Vivienne naked? She's a beauty. She really is. I've been thinking it would be a treat for you."

Vivienne naked? A treat for him? Quint glanced at Vivienne. Vivienne blinked.

Lambert grinned broadly. "Vivienne's got a fabulous body." He might as well have been observing that redwoods are big trees. Vivienne started to speak but Lambert shushed her with a motion of his hand. "Sensational in fact. A shame to keep her entirely to myself. Share the bounty. Isn't that what you hippies say?"

Quint stood. "Listen, I think I better be . . ."

Lambert cut him off with his hand. "No. Stay, please. You're my guest. I want you to see my wife naked. I don't see what's so shocking about that. Beauty like hers should be shared and appreciated." Lambert continued, "Vivienne?"

Vivienne stared at her husband in disbelief. "What in heaven are you talking about?"

Lambert said, "I think you heard me clearly enough. I want you to take your clothes off for our guest. Show Jim what you look like. What will it hurt? We're all friends here. Who knows, maybe we'll soon be real close friends." He looked amused, then his face suddenly turned hard. "Do it. Do it now."

Vivienne said, "You want me to disrobe in front of our guest?"

"That's exactly what I want? You're a beauty. I want him to see what you look like. No harm done."

Vivienne was barely able to mask her rage. Quint was embarrassed and wanted to get the hell out of the house. What Lambert felt was unfathomable. What on earth had motivated him to order his wife to strip for Quint's benefit? Madness? What? That Lambert had planned all this in advance seemed somehow clear to Quint. That he was conducting a silent, unspoken struggle with Vivienne was equally clear.

9

VIVIENNE STARTED TO rise. Her husband wanted her to strip. The arch of her spine and the tilt of her chin said it all: She was the educated daughter of a history professor, not a Saigon hooker. She would not remove her clothes on anybody's casual order, her husband included.

Lambert barked, "Sit!" His face was hard.

She sat. "An officer and a gentleman!" She made a scornful puffing sound with her lips.

Lambert looked disgusted. "Oh, don't be so damned conservative and predictable. Listen to what I have to say! I've been watching you two tonight. Those little looks. The pregnant silences. It's obvious that you like Jim, and he certainly likes you. So why not give him a treat? Where's the harm?"

Vivienne's eyes met Quint's briefly then she looked away.

Lambert ran his tongue under his lower lip. He didn't mind a test of wills. "I'm not asking you to give him a blow job for Christ's sake. Not on the first date anyway. That's not good. A little skin. Where's the harm?"

Quint glanced nervously from Vivienne to her husband. "Like I started to say, I better be on my way. It's getting late. Really."

Lambert frowned. "You stay. Are you turning down my offer?"

Quint cleared his throat. At the Willows Lambert had said he was gripped by rage. He hadn't addressed the question of whether or not he was dangerous.

Lambert said, "You don't want to see Vivienne naked? I find

that hard to believe. You told me you had a girlfriend, so I assume you're not queer. Turning her down is an insult! Show the lady some respect, Jesus Christ!"

Quint said, mildly, "No offense, Colonel, but I believe the best way to show her respect is to be on my way."

Lambert held up his hand. "Wait, wait, wait. Just one damn minute." His face tightened. "You're the one who is always talking about the truth. Isn't that what we're talking about here? The truth. Truth matters. Cut through the pretense. Well, clothes sure as hell don't enhance the truth. They cover it up. If the truth is so damned beautiful, let's see it. That miniskirt doesn't leave a whole lot to the imagination anyway. Stand up, Vivienne."

Vivienne remained seated. "I will not."

"And I say you will!" If ever there was a man in the grip of rage, it was Del Lambert at that moment. The look in his eyes was spooky.

Vivienne looked at Quint and said, evenly, "With all his education, my husband does not understand the nature of pride. To him, other people's feelings are curious, if not unfathomable."

Lambert said, "Quit wasting everybody's fucking time and just stand up and do it, Vivienne." To Quint, he said, "Humor me, partner. Let's see where it goes. What do you say?"

"I . . . Listen, I . . ."

"You've never seen a pair of tits like those in your life, guaranteed. They're truly prime," Lambert said. "Isn't this the new morality? Out with the old ways. Old-fashioned monogamy and the rest of it. Freedom. Isn't that what we're supposed to want?"

Quint tried to avoid looking at Vivienne, but it was impossible.

"You and Vivienne both like to make everything an intellectual game. Munich was September 29, 1939. This is February, 1968. They're not easily compared, you say. Everything is relative. You believe there is no such thing as absolute right and wrong that can be chiseled in stone or encoded in the Bible. Some wars are good and some are bad, depending. Let's just strip that idea bare and see what happens in the here and now. Is it wrong for a man to share his wife's beauty with a guest? We'll call this the Vivienne War. This is the territory of the V. Hey, look it over. Check it out."

"You think I'm a Saigon bar girl?" Her chest visibly rose and fell.

Lambert looked disgusted. "The truth is you want to take your clothes off for him. We all know it. I'm your husband. This is my turf. I'm still in charge here in my own castle. We're putting an idea to the test, remember. I want you to please me by showing him what you've got. Give him a treat. If it's okay by me, where's the harm?" He grinned broadly.

"This is not good, truly," Quint said.

Vivienne studied her husband as Darwin might have observed a beetle.

Lambert said, "Oh, for heaven's sake, Vivienne. You're not being raped. Once you get started, it'll be easy. The most natural thing in the world." He looked calm enough, but his voice suddenly took on a threatening edge, "Come on now, unfasten the goddam button before I lose my temper. Do it."

At that moment, Vivienne seemed to have made up her mind about something. In an emotional transformation that was startling in its swiftness, Vivienne calmly stood and put her hand to the top button of her blouse. "I don't strip for American soldiers, but I'd be pleased to take my clothes off for you, Jim."

Lambert looked pleased. "Well, okay. She'll do it for you, Jim. I thought so. The blouse is the best beginning. Holds the treasure of Oriental tits. Not too fast, Vivienne. One button at a time. Make it artful."

Vivienne cocked her head, grinning. "I might as well make it as sexy as possible." She was mocking Lambert. "Are you sure about this, Del? I want you to be absolutely sure."

"I've started this and I mean to finish it. We're accepting the proposition that there's nothing inherently wrong for a man to share his wife's beauty. It's simply a cultural prohibition. Let's see if that's right or wrong." He looked at Quint mildly and cocked his head.

Quint did want Vivienne to take off her clothes. He did want to see her. He found himself looking into Vivienne's eyes as a lover would. They held the rebellious, understanding moment for what seemed like weeks. A surge of adrenaline twisted his stomach. If Vivienne was to strip, Lambert had to pay a price, and there would be consequences for both her and Quint. Had to be.

Vivienne unfastened the top button of her blouse. "This is for you, Jim." To Lambert, she said, "You can stop me at any time. Later, it may be too late to, what is the word you military officers use, to disengage?"

Lambert looked amused. "Let's have the next button," he said. "Exciting stuff, eh, Jim?" He looked as though he'd never seen his wife naked.

Quint sat dry-mouthed.

Vivienne unfastened the next button. She was not just stripping; she was discarding her marriage, although from what Quint had seen it wasn't much of a marriage.

Vivienne unfastened the third button. To Lambert she said, "Are you sure? I want you to be absolutely sure."

Lambert had gone too far to withdraw from the game. His pride was now on the line. He had started it. He would see it through. "Let's have the next button," he said.

She opened the fourth.

She removed her blouse. She flipped it to one side. "Shall I continue?"

"Let's see it all," Lambert said.

She reached around and unhooked her bra.

She dropped the bra, revealing elegant breasts capped with outsized nipples that were brown spikes.

Lambert clapped his hands enthusiastically. "See there! What did I tell you? Wonderful, eh, Jimbo? They're to die for!" He groaned in appreciation.

Vivienne arched an eyebrow and gave Quint a shy smile. She was splendid in the extreme. Then she unzipped her miniskirt and dropped it. She had a slender, supple body, as graceful as a willow. She was wearing lime-green bikini underpants that were a highlight on her pale, copper-colored skin.

"Well, Jim?" she asked. She pulled on the band of the underpants.

Quint licked his lips.

Vivienne glanced at her husband. "You want them off, Del? I'm certainly game if that's what you want."

Lambert said, "Drop 'em. You said it's my call. I say why go halfway? Let's see what you've got down there. One way or another, the V is what life is all about, Truth time."

She quickly peeled the underpants over her hips revealing a modest wisp of black fleece.

Lambert was looking at his wife like he'd never seen her naked before. Quint wondered if this was as erotic for Lambert as it was for him. Did familiar territory suddenly become desirable if it was being displayed to a competitor?

Lambert said, "Go ahead, Vivienne, turn around. Show him the complete package. Isn't she something, Jim? Look at her. Splendid!"

Vivienne turned, showing Quint her profile, then again so Quint could appreciate her butt.

She faced Quint again, communicating entirely with her extraordinary eyes. Absently, she ran the fingers of her right hand down her groin, covering herself.

"She's a beauty. No doubting that," Lambert said. "Okay, you can hold her for a moment, Jim, go ahead."

"What?"

"Don't just stand there with your mouth open. Go ahead, stand up and give the lady some reassurance. Fine by me. In fact, I encourage it."

Quint blinked.

"Do it man. Don't stand there like a fucking moron. A man offers to let you embrace his naked wife? A world-class beauty. How often do you think you're going to get a chance like this? Go for it. Take advantage. Hold her. Do it."

Vivienne said, "I would like that, Jim. Please."

Quint drew Vivienne's warm, slender body against his.

In his ear, Vivienne whispered, "Thank you."

He gave her an extra squeeze by way of reply.

She whispered, "You should know I'm doomed."

Lambert said, "Don't be bashful, Jimbo. Kiss the lady for Christ's sake. Show a little class. Give her something to think about. Let her know you care."

Quint brushed his lips softly against Vivienne's, a lover's kiss. The heat of her body seared. Soft, soft, soft, she was. Delicate. She arched her torso against him. The tip of her tongue found his and they talked wordlessly.

Watching this, Lambert said, "Look at that! Okay! You two do like one another, don't you?"

Vivienne suppressed a small sound in the back of her throat.

"Break it off. Do it now," Lambert said.

They did.

The three of them fell into an odd, reflective silence.

You should know I'm doomed.

Finally, Lambert said, "I thought you'd like her." He looked pleased. "See, what did I tell you? She did want to show off. She likes it. She liked the kiss too, I could tell. Had those tongues going. A little stolen passion there. You think I didn't notice that? You whispered something in his ear, Vivienne. What was that?"

"I said 'thank you, Jim.' "

Lambert said, "No, no, no. It was something more than that. You two are a wicked pair. Naughty, naughty!"

Quint ignored him. "You're the stuff of dreams, Vivienne."

Vivienne smiled. She looked radiant. "I'm glad you're pleased."

Lambert seemed suddenly irritated. "Fun's over. Point made," Lambert said. "Put 'em back on."

Vivienne pulled on her underpants and snatched her bra from the floor. Knowing Quint was watching her, she took her time dressing. Without looking at her husband, she said, "You were right after all, Del. It was sexy. Seemed like the most natural thing in the world. It's been a while since I've been held and kissed like that. I liked it!" She seemed not to care what Lambert thought of that statement.

Lambert clenched his teeth momentarily then grinned broadly. "All truly beautiful women would like to show their stuff for a guest if they were given a chance. They like driving men crazy. If they tell you anything different, they're lying."

Lambert rose in a manner that said it was time for Quint to leave. "You know that shrink is always telling me to be honest. 'Don't repress your feelings,' he says. 'You've been under incredible pressure. A little anger is normal enough. Let it all out. Put it right there and see what it's all about.' Tell me something, Jim, you think that's really a smart idea or does it just sound good, all liberal and understanding? I mean being honest about everything. Don't you think a little useful lying and suppressing of emotion is what we all use to keep everything from flying apart?"

Quint wasn't about to stall. The husband said it was time to leave, then it was time to hit the road. Enough was enough. He said, "Thank you, Vivienne. I'll treasure the memory."

"I assure you the pleasure was mine."

Inasmuch as good manners required that a gracious hostess saw her guest to the door, Vivienne accompanied Lambert to the door to see Quint off.

At the door, Lambert said, "Boy yearns to see beautiful girl. Beautiful girl secretly wants to show what she's got. Husband agrees. They share the bounty. No harm done." He slipped his arm around Vivienne's waist. "I suppose I should tell you that Vivienne only has a two-year green card. She either stays with me or she's on the next flight back to Nam. She knows that. Right, Vivienne?" He gave her a squeeze.

Quint closed his eyes.

Lambert smiled. "Disappointed? I'm a military officer, after all. What did you expect? I've been trained never to enter unknown territory unless it's on my terms. I have the Immigration and Naturalization Service on my side. I'm a member of one of the most powerful families in the state. Vivienne is an alien. She signed a prenuptial agreement so she has no rights to my property in the event of a divorce. In short, she is totally, completely under my control. When I say she's mine, I mean it in more ways than one. Have you been reading that feminist shit you've been running in the *Star-Bulletin?* That sentiment does not apply in this household."

Quint said, "Good night, Vivienne."

Before she could answer, Lambert said, "No, no. I'm not finished." He looked at Quint, "You know, Jim, I think Vivienne likes you. I can see it. The two of you had a real moment there. High emotion. Kind of fun watching. Sexy as hell. Good for the old ego, I suppose. You know how I got the idea? We're on Mt. Tantalus. This house is on Tantalus Drive. We had to read the classics at the Citadel. I thought, 'Why not honor the Greeks with an erotic tease?' "

He paused, pleased with himself at being so clever, then said, "I suppose I was being kind of hard on you two, putting you through that and then ending it abruptly."

Quint glanced at Vivienne.

Lambert said, "Yes, she is pretty. A terrific beauty, in fact. I bet you'd like her for your own, wouldn't you? The two of you could live happily ever after."

Vivienne said, "My mother-in-law tells me that after Del learned Edgar Rice Burroughs had once worked as a reporter for the *Advertiser*, he read the entire series of Tarzan novels. Tarzan was an English nobleman separated from his parents as a baby and raised by apes. Wasn't that the story?"

"Something like that," Quint said.

She said evenly, "Do you suppose they have baboons for professors at the Citadel?"

Lambert grabbed her by the arm.

Vivienne twisted angrily from his grip. She was furious. "What do you propose to do now? Teach me a lesson in front of our guest?"

Quint started for his car.

Lambert held up his hand. "What if I ask you back and we take our little exploration in the new morality one step further? You'd like that, wouldn't you, Jim? No telling what might become of a beginning like this if the husband is generous enough and has a little imagination. I tell you what. I have to go back to Vietnam in the next couple of days to help my successor learn the ropes, but I'll be back. Why don't I give you a call when I get back, and we can set something up? You like that?"

Quint caught Vivienne's eyes.

Vivienne said, "If he calls, say yes, Jim. I would like that very much."

Lambert said, "See there. She likes you. Right now you feel compelled to make a civilized gesture. I understand that. But you'll come to your senses. You won't be able to help yourself, curiosity if nothing else. You two can lie in your separate beds and think about one another. Get those frustrated hormones pumping. Very romantic."

Watching Quint, Lambert put his hand on his wife's hip. "Course you have to earn the right, Jimbo. Ain't no free lunch at Del Lambert's place. No sir, by God."

"Earn the right?" Quint asked.

Lambert gave Vivienne a gentle push and stepped outside, closing the door behind him. He and Quint were alone. The night was warm. A gentle breeze stirred. Below them the city lights lay spread out in a vast, twinkling arc from Diamond Head to Pearl City that was partly obscured by the underbrush of the adjoining ridge. Lambert said, "Beautiful isn't it? The jewel of the Pacific. The crossroads of North America and Asia. From up here it looks tranquil and peaceful. But it's just as deceiving as the warm nights over Saigon. What's going on down there, just like every city in the United States of America, is a motherfucking civil war."

"Aw, come on."

"Oh? You think I'm wrong? You know, Jim, I've been following those assholes who wasted Vivienne's family for three years now. The Pentagon thinks that CBS film is just the emotional kind of eye-opening shocker it needs to turn people around back home. I've been thinking about nothing but Lon Be day and night. Not to put too fine a point on it, but I've become a regular

Javert. I've got an analytical imagination. Always have had. What is it I'm pursuing, I ask myself. What is this all about?"

"All this? What do you mean?"

"The war in Vietnam. The violence here in the states. I've concluded that one way or another, on a personal, political, or military level we're talking about animal passion. Human guts. Viscera. The old reptilian brainstem in action. And don't tell me I read too much Edgar Rice Burroughs as a kid."

"I don't understand what this has to do with me."

"Well, look, Jimbo, it doesn't take Dear Abby to figure out there's a little tension in our marriage. But tension comes and goes in marriages. Nothing is forever. As it happens you found her sitting in that Mercedes at precisely the right time. I regard her as a form of commodity, and you as a kind of buyer. Vivienne has something I want. Get it for me and I'll give you passion in return. She's yours. We'll both be happy as clams at high tide."

"What?"

Lambert smiled. "She likes you, there's no doubting that. I could see it in her face. I'm proposing a swap. Straight up. Nothing complicated about that. I'm a generous man. And I am an honorable man. A deal is a deal: You come through for me, I'll give you Vivienne and some start-up money on the side. You'll be wanting your own house. I've got a few bucks. No problem."

Quint said, "Does this have to do with Lon Be?"

Lambert said quickly. "Is that what she whispered in your ear? Something to do with Lon Be?"

Quint shook his head no.

"Vivienne knows what I want. If she gives it to me, I'll set her free and you get to eat rice every meal." Lambert clenched his jaw. "Look, I don't want to stand around playing games with a pipsqueak. Deliver for me or think about her and pound your pud. Give me what I want and you get the pretty lady."

"Simple as that? No problem."

Lambert frowned. "I know you don't get it, but we're talking about passion here, Jim. Remember that. Think about it when you're driving home tonight. Keep it in mind tomorrow morning when you're writing those bullshit stories of yours quoting whiners and chickenshit draft dodgers who're pissing on their country."

"I've got to go."

"I'll give you a call before I leave for Nam. Think about my offer."

"Hard not to think about an offer like that," Quint said.

Lambert grinned. "You might be aiding and abetting chickenshit whiners, but I never said you were dumb."

Quint walked back to his car. As he opened the door to get in, he glanced back at the house. Vivienne was watching him from an open upstairs window. Catching his eyes, she gave him a wistful little wave. Bye, bye, Jim.

Quint fired up the Datsun's engine. He was in love. He had gotten himself sucked into a dangerous game.

10

OFFICIALLY JIM QUINT'S beat was supposed to be higher education and science, but owing to the Vietnam war and everything that went with it, he wrote about hippies, yippies, and political radicals, and did an occasional science piece whenever he could spring the time. This combination was an unlikely beat, but this was the *Honolulu Star-Bulletin*, not *The New York Times*.

Quint's day began at 6:30 A.M. The deadline for the early afternoon edition was not until 7:30 A.M., but the rule was that no source could be phoned at home until a civilized 7 A.M. This gave reporters a half-hour to shake off hangovers and study stories the city desk had clipped from the morning *Honolulu Advertiser* and another thirty minutes to call sources and write fresh versions. The resulting bedlam required a nimble mind, quick fingers, and strong coffee.

If journalism was literature in a hurry, writing on deadline was a form of sprinting. Far from being a form of donkey work, writing fast, clean, accurate copy was a real skill—hard to do. The clock was ticking. The deadline was drawing closer. The din in the city room got louder. The shouting got more frenzied. Time, tides, and deadlines wait for no man. Tick, tick, tick. Hurry, hurry, hurry.

The next morning a skinny little Chinese man in baggy pants and rumpled aloha shirt stood over Quint's shoulder and watched him work on deadline. Although he looked like a Hotel Street bookie, Chinn Ho owned the *Honolulu Star-Bulletin*. Most newspaper owners regarded their property as a license to print money.

To be sure, Ho liked to make money, but he also regarded his paper with the enthusiasm of a wide-eyed kid with an electric train. He liked to watch it run. Like Harriet Gee, the court reporter sitting at the next desk, Quint was an expensive part, like gold glove shortstop or smart point guard. Ho was obviously amazed that Quint could simultaneously ask questions and write a story with scowling editors yelling questions at him from the far end of the room. That's not to mention the distraction of having the copy boy yank each sheet of paper from the carriage when he got to the bottom line. When he got well into a story, Quint simply had to remember how it had started.

With each take Quint sent to the city desk, Ho somehow looked at once admiring, approving, and encouraging. As he worked, Quint found it hard to keep his mind off Del and Vivienne Lambert. As Lambert had said, tension in a marriage wasn't unusual, but Lambert's offer to barter his wife as a form of commodity certainly was. He had deliberately sought to inflame Quint's imagination. Quint was now wild with desire. What male who liked females wouldn't be? Ordinarily Quint didn't mind it when Chinn Ho stood watching over his shoulder. Now, his presence was disconcerting and Quint could hardly keep his mind on the story at hand.

Quint wondered how kamaaina families like the Lamberts felt about a rich little upstart Chinese buying Honolulu's afternoon newspaper. Thurston Twigg-Smith, the gentleman publisher who owned the morning *Advertiser*, was surely more to his liking. Their shared ownership of most of the state united the Lamberts, Twigg-Smiths, and Joneses. An odious Chink had muscled into the proper, civilized club of wealthy old kamaaina families that owned everything in Hawaii. From their perspective, that was not good. They regarded the frugal Chinese as conniving and crafty and clannish. The Chinese were grubby little scavengers. Jews with squinty eyes. Everybody knew that.

There were people saying Joe Namath had the stuff to lead the Jets to a Super Bowl title. The American Football League? Sure he did. The rhetoric of change and revolution was seeping into every conceivable nook and cranny of American life.

After the 7:30 deadline was past, Quint turned his immediate attention to the nine o'clock deadline, which was for papers on the outlying areas of Oahu. He would rework his stories yet again—for the eleven o'clock deadline of the edition circulated in the metropolitan sprawl from Diamond Head to Pearl City.

When he finished his work for the nine o'clock deadline, Quint sat back for a breather.

You should know I'm doomed.

What had Vivienne meant by that? It was most likely connected to whatever price it was Lambert was placing on her. But what? Quint remembered her standing naked in front of him and the warmth of her body as he had held her briefly. He thought about her waiting patiently for her husband under the banyan tree. No fucking way he would have waited for somebody that long in the sweltering tropical heat. When he had first seen her sitting there on the front seat of the Mercedes, she appeared bored or maybe indifferent. He remembered it clearly: Vivienne's husband had told her to wait for him to finish his duties at the Westmoreland lunch. So she had waited, opening the door to catch the breeze.

"Hey Jim!"

Startled, Quint snapped out of his reverie.

Steve Sanger was standing in front of him. "Time for another cup of mud."

"Fogged out," Quint said. He stood and joined Sanger for their post–nine o'clock stroll to the back shop to buy another cup of coffee from Yamani's pot. It was their custom to mumble editorial comments on their way back, a practice that annoyed Fred Fielding.

As they passed Babs Parsegian's desk, Sanger murmured, "Another donation to destroy our fun."

"You'll live," Babs said, not looking up from the story in her typewriter.

The issue of the *Star-Bulletin's* "coffee pot rebellion" was likely what Lambert had meant by the horseshit that enraged him every time he returned from Vietnam. Those reporters who were in sports bought their deadline coffee from a pot run by a typesetter named Yamani, who used the profits to spring for a year's-end bash at a Japanese tea house—that is, a Honolulu version of a Japanese tea house. The women who served their sushi, sake, and sashimi wore kimonos and there was much good-natured goosing, squealing, and fondling of tits. Yamani gave them to believe this cultural practice was a commonplace entertainment for Japanese gentlemen.

At the end of 1967, as usual, the female reporters who bought their coffee from Yamani's pot had not been invited to the annual tea house party.

The previous year they'd said nothing. Then, bam. Rebellion. In a matter of weeks, snide comments and wry observations escalated quickly to amiable disputation. The more emboldened among them told their male colleagues that they were tired of listening to their leering, giggling references to the good time they had had at their annual bash. Next year the women would be included or they would by God know the reason why, and it had better be good.

To Quint and his male friends, this was not a promising turn of events.

The tip-off to this lurking feminist revolution was their use of the newly coined word "sexist" in reference to the tea party. None of them had ever heard that word before. Racist, they knew. "Sexist" was a recent invention, the creation of yet another class of rebelling complainers.

The coffee pot rebellion was led by Babs and Miki Hasegawa. They were buying their coffee from Yamani's pot, they said. The profits from the pot paid for the party. Ergo they should be invited—a simple matter of fairness.

The reply from the males was simple enough: Did they invite themselves to the women's stupid baby showers and Tupperware parties? No, they did not. There were other pots where the

women could buy their coffee. Why in the hell did women want
to ruin male fun? What was the point?

The women were undeterred. How, pray tell, would their presence change the fun?

The male's annual party was, uh, genital in nature. A male
kind of thing. The men didn't want to give that up.

The women said they had no intention of changing the nature
of the sport. They just wanted to participate. What was wrong
with that? Rest assured they would not get in the way. The males
could carry on as before, playing grab ass with the "hostesses"
and the rest of it. No difference. Nothing would change. Et cetera.

Carry on as before? No difference? Nothing would change?
Right.

The males all knew what had provoked this grumbling. The
only reason the women were buying from Yamani's pot was so
they could feel put-upon. The men all knew the drill. Nag, nag,
nag. The women weren't going to ease up until the men agreed
to invite them next year. When that happened, the tea party
would be forever destroyed as anything exceptional or memorable.
No more pretend geishas dragging their boobs across the reporters' faces as they served more sake and Kirin beer. No more
casually goosing the geishas as they brought more sashimi.

An organization called the Society for Cutting Up Men, the
brainchild of a young woman named Valerie Solanis, was often
in the news. The joke at the Round Table was that Babs Parsegian
and Miki Hasegawa were going to open a Honolulu local of the
dreaded SCUM. Ha, ha, ha.

THE ELEVEN O'CLOCK deadline came and went with no call from
Lambert.

Quint went to lunch in the newspaper cafeteria upstairs. He
made telephone calls to his sources early in the afternoon, telling
himself to remain calm; Lambert wouldn't have proposed any
kind of swap unless he planned to follow through. Of course
Lambert wouldn't call right away. He would make Quint wait.

Let him remember the naked Vivienne. Let the hormonal desire drive Quint crazy.

Quint didn't think he was fooling himself in concluding that yes, Lambert was right in assessing the result of his Tantalus offering. Judging from Vivienne's body language and the hunger and desire in her brown eyes, she was genuinely attracted to Quint. That had been apparent all through dinner and during the small talk when she had shown him her studio. She was independent, intelligent, and proud, all qualities Quint admired. It was almost as though Lambert weren't there. Then there was the strip itself. And the embrace. The warmth of her body. The kiss. Her body arching against his. The sound in her throat.

Quint was convinced that if he and Vivienne had the time and privacy to kindle the spark it would almost certainly lead somewhere grand.

Del Lambert had offered Vivienne as a form of commodity. He proposed to barter her. For what, Quint wondered? What price would Quint have to pay for the transfer of such intelligence, heart, and exotic beauty?

The three o'clock deadline passed. No call.

Quint reluctantly rose from his desk and left the *Star-Bulletin* city room, strolling slowly, thoughtfully, across the parking lot to drink beer with Steve Sanger and the other regulars at the Round Table in the Columbia Inn.

11

JIM QUINT RECEIVED no call from Del Lambert the next morning either. That afternoon Quint and photographer Warren Roll rode together to the campus of the University of Hawaii for another round of the Oliver M. Lee controversy that was taking up more and more of Quint's time. Every campus in the United States seemingly had a *cause celebre*, and Lee was the one in Hawaii.

The Board of Regents, which oversaw the state's public colleges and universities, met in a room in the East-West Center, an institution much coveted by the Department of Education, but currently run by the State Department. The center, located next to the University of Hawaii, was intended as a place where scholars from East and West could meet for cross-cultural studies.

The question of Dr. Oliver Lee's future being at the top of the agenda, protesting students jammed into the room and encamped outside to listen to the testimony via public address system. It wasn't so much that the students were all that worked up about what had happened to Lee. Few of them had ever been in his classes. And it wasn't that Lee had a reputation as a sensational teacher or scholar. It was rather, in Quint's opinion, that the university had clearly screwed him. This enabled the students to take the moral high ground and posture in righteousness.

Since the Waikiki fragging pamphlets had won a figurative trophy for competitive crazy, a much-prized radical encomium, the SDS leaders could hardly admit it was a dumb tactic. Guilt was too bourgeois, suggestive of *Leave it to Beaver* and *Father Knows Best* for any self-respecting radical firebrand to admit. But Quint was willing to give them the benefit of the doubt. Maybe they did feel they had a moral responsibility to get Lee's tenure back.

Quint called this the "Lee case" in his stories so he didn't have to rehash its origins in every article. After a while his readers were assumed to understand what the controversy was all about, even if they didn't really. "Conservatives" were assumed to hate Lee. "Liberals" were sympathetic. In time, the original facts of the controversy had become irrelevant, tucked into a nut at the bottom of the story. It was "we" and "they." Passions were inflamed. Nobody wanted to yield an inch.

Quint, always alert for the pithy, the succinct, or memorable excess, listened for the better part of two hours as various wannabe firebrands took turns competing to see who could call the regents the most outrageous names. The regents took all the abuse stoically, including Monsignor Charles M. Kekumano in his priestly garb, who fielded the names with an odd, lethargic blinking, like a turtle sunning itself. In his stories, Quint used the word 'siege,' presumably in a figurative sense. But watching the drama that afternoon, he realized that was wrong. The regents were literally under siege, doing their best not to look frightened at being mashed into the same room with furious students.

As was the custom, the chief sorehead spoke last, sort of a revolutionary keynote speech. This was George Sarant, president of the University of Hawaii chapter of the Students for a Democratic Society. Sarant, wearing yellow-tinted sunglasses, launched into his tirade with his arms waving. At a certain point he paused, as if suddenly seized by inspiration. Leaning forward, wagging his finger like a scolding mother, he thundered into the microphone, "You, gentlemen, are a punctured prophylactic fucking the dead body of this prostituted university!"

The room exploded with applause. Quint could hear enthusiastic hooting and shouting outside and cries of "right fucking on!" as George Sarant's alliterative Ps reverberated across campus like machine-gun fire.

ON THE WAY back to the office Warren Roll wanted to know if
they could swing by Ala Moana Center so he could do some
shopping for his wife's birthday. Jim Quint had plenty of time to
write his story, so he turned off Kapiolani Avenue into the parking lot of the shopping center.

Quint retrieved his paperback copy of Tom Wolfe's *The Electric Kool-Aid Acid Test* from the glove compartment of his Datsun
and took it with him inside. Roll took off to do his thing, leaving
Quint to read over a cup of coffee in an Orange Julius shop. He
quickly settled into Wolfe's nutty account of Ken Kesey and Neal
Cassady and the other Merry Pranksters and their psychedelic,
hallucinogenic adventures on their mythic bus.

There was this kid who got on the bus at one stop and off at
the next town, then on again. He couldn't make up his mind.
Finally, Kesey took him aside and said he'd have to make up his
mind. He had to be on the bus or off it. He couldn't have it both
ways. He had to make a commitment.

It struck Quint that he was a lot like that kid. He wanted to
get on the bus and have a look around, but didn't want to be part
of it. He was curious. He was sympathetic to the rebellion inside
the bus. But he was an outsider, emotionally incapable of joining
any cause or group. The crazies on his beat all knew that. What
they had no way of knowing was why. He wasn't sure himself. It
was arrogance, perhaps, or some form of self-imposed psychological isolation. But the fact remained that he was emotionally and
intellectually incapable of being a passionate believer in any form
of cant, dogma, or cause, not even those muddied, ambiguous
identities promoted by the Democrats and Republicans. He could
not picture himself in any parade or demonstration holding a
placard for a newspaper or television photographer. The idea of
placing a bumper sticker on his car was enough to make him laugh
out loud. What truth could be reduced to a slogan?

Well, okay, he was forced to concede, never eat yellow snow.
Never stomp on a paper bag in a cow pasture.

After a few minutes of reading, he looked up momentarily to

rest his eyes. There Vivienne was, striding through the glut of bodies in the center of the mall, beautiful Vivienne, wearing sandals and a simple black tube dress molded to the delicate curves of her elegant body.

Look my way, Vivienne, Quint thought. *I'm here. I can't get my mind off you. Look this way.*

As if by magic, Vivienne did just that. She gave him a shy smile and her large brown eyes met his straight on. But she made no move to come in his direction. She looked about uncertainly. Was she going to continue on her way? Had his waiting for her to call all been foolishness?

Quint popped up, his heart thumping like Ringo's drums, and wove his way through the crowd until he came face to face with Vivienne.

They looked into one another's eyes for a moment, saying nothing.

Then, Vivienne said, softly, "I can't stop thinking about you, Jim."

"Same here. That was some kind of evening, I have to say."

"Wasn't it ever?" She seemed embarrassed.

"One of life's wonderful surprises. You were beautiful. Every man's fantasy."

She said, "You won't think badly of me if I tell you I'm glad I did it. I wouldn't take it back for anything. I enjoyed it. Truly."

"You whispered in my ear that you are doomed. What did you mean by that?"

Vivienne hesitated. "I . . . Nothing. I shouldn't have said that."

She was a terrible liar. Quint said, "When I was about to leave and he closed the door, he told me there's something you know or have that he wants. Just what was unclear. He said if I can get that for him, he, uh . . ." Quint wondered if he should tell her everything. What human being wanted to be treated as a commodity, something to be bartered?

Vivienne finished the sentence for him. "He'll give me to you. Turn me loose. He told me the same thing. You're naturally wondering what it is he wants."

Quint grinned. "The thought had occurred to me."

Vivienne sighed.

"Not going to tell me that either?"

"Can't."

"He said he was after a propaganda coup to boost public opinion in the United States. I take it this has to do with Lon Be."

"I can't give him what he wants. No, I take that back. I won't give him what he wants, and I can't tell you anything more than that."

"Can't or won't?"

"Can't. Won't. It doesn't make any difference."

Quint felt like he was standing outside of his body watching himself. "He said he wants to invite me to your house again."

She thought about that for a moment. "What did you tell him?"

"I told him no."

She frowned, then said quickly, "But you didn't mean it. You'll change your mind?"

Quint grinned. "Of course, I'll change my mind. What do you think?"

She looked both embarrassed and pleased. "Thank you. Like I said, it was a pleasure. I wouldn't have guessed it, something like that. After I got started it seemed like the most natural thing in the world. Maybe Del was right. Nothing wrong with it whatsoever." Looking straight into Quint's eyes, she said, "I liked being held and the kiss. I can't get it out of my mind."

"What if he goes further next time? What if . . ." He let it drop.

She smiled shyly, then glanced at her watch. "I think I better be going."

It was Quint's turn to look embarrassed.

She said, "Rest assured, I hope he contacts you, Jim. I've been wanting to call you, but I can't." She bit her lower lip. "Del is having me watched. He's very possessive."

"Does he monitor your calls?"

"He . . ." She reached out and took Quint's hand, squeezing it tightly. "Don't call me. I'll call you. Be patient. I have to go. Just remember that I'll be thinking about you."

"I want you," Quint said.

"I want *you*." Vivienne turned and joined the crowd of shoppers.

Quint's stomach twisted as he watched her disappear.

You should know I'm doomed.

AFTER HIS SESSION at the Round Table that night, Jim Quint, slightly inebriated and unable to get Vivienne out of his mind, drove up Tantalus Drive until he found a place to turn off the road not far from the Lambert residence. He got out, binoculars in hand, and hiked up the road until he found the entrance of the driveway that led to the Lambert residence. Through the foliage, he could see lights.

Quint eased down the driveway and circled right around the double garage that held Del's Mercedes and Vivienne's Austin Healy TR-3. Quint remembered that the trees and undergrowth on the smaller ridge Ewa of the house partially obscured Lambert's view of Pearl Harbor. He groped his way down this ridge and soon found a spot in the thick brush where he was able to see the main deck entering Lambert's study and beyond that the smaller deck outside Vivienne's studio.

A brooding Lambert sat at the white table on the main deck with a drink, staring down at the city lights. On the deck outside her studio, Vivienne, bathed in light from a fixture mounted above the sliding glass door, sipped a large glass of what looked like iced tea as she worked on a large canvas on an aluminum easel.

Quint found an open view in the underbrush and sat on his rump, focusing his binoculars on Vivienne. He also found himself twisted by envy. Vivienne was with Lambert and not him. Hiding there in the brush watching Lambert and his wife, he imagined himself a Vietcong watching an American compound. If he had had a rifle he could easily plant a round in the side of Lambert's head. Splat! Just like that. Lambert would never know what hit him. Vivienne stared at the canvas for a full twenty minutes then picked up a stick of charcoal and began sketching on the canvas. She abruptly stopped, obviously discouraged. She put down her pencil. She stepped back, studying the canvas. She sipped her tea. She began sketching again. She stopped. She stepped back. She made another adjustment.

After an hour of this, Vivienne returned the easel and canvas to her studio and turned off the light.

Quint checked the radium dial on his watch. It was midnight. Lambert remained on the lanai staring out into the darkness. Quint slipped off his branch and hiked back to his car.

12

JIM QUINT'S WRY, sardonic friend, Steve Sanger, had helped his father dig graves in an Iowa cemetery when he was growing up, and Quint liked to razz him that this experience had somehow affected his outlook on life. When Quint arrived for work the second day after Vivienne's strip, Sanger greeted him with his usual mischievous grin. Nodding in the direction of the wire service machines, Sanger took a sip of coffee from a white Styrofoam cup and ran the palm of his hand across his balding forehead.

"They're now saying the American command in Saigon told Washington to expect Tet, but for some inexplicable reason they didn't bother to warn the Americans or South Vietnamese Army in Hue. Clean Gene says it figgers. The numbers are coming in. I knew you'd be excited so I made some notes."

Sanger looked at a notepad on his desk and read them aloud. "Let's see now. Two thousand eight hundred civilians were killed. A hundred and forty-two dead marines were killed and another eight hundred and fifty-seven were seriously wounded, which I take it means stumps, poop bags, and seeing-eye dogs, that kind of thing. The South Vietnamese lost three hundred eighty-four men with another eighteen hundred wounded. The dirty Commies lost five thousand one hundred thirteen dead plus stumps and poop bags beyond count. Served 'em right."

"Good stats," Quint said. "But a little crazy, don't you think?"

"Of course. That's what makes it fun. What we've got here is cheap victory at twice the price. Six thousand seriously damaged homes. Another forty-four hundred completely destroyed. Great stuff!" Steve looked up, still grinning. He knew Fred Fielding was eavesdropping on the conversation. Talk like this sent Fielding's blood pressure soaring to dangerous levels. The joke among the reporters was if they pushed him far enough, they could croak him and get a city editor who knew how to laugh once in a while.

Sanger said, "Don't you just love all those numbers, Jim? It's like watching a football game. Yards gained and lost. Passing yards. Running yards. Punts. Penalties. Field goals. All in all, Hue turned out to be a win for the white hats, but it was a close call. Sort of like Bart Starr sneaking it into the end zone against the Cowboys."

"Grist for the table, I take it."

Steve giggled. "That's the way I see it. Simple multiplication will tell us how many grief-stricken moms and dads and gramps and grannies are crying in their beer." Grinning, he took a quick peek at Fielding out of the corner of his eye. Fielding's view of the world was remarkably similar to Lambert's and members of the Board of Regents. They were defenders of the faith and felt themselves under siege by barbarians.

Steve pretended not to notice the wild look on Fielding's face, but he continued, unrelenting. "If we put our minds to it, we could estimate the amount of bodily fluids expelled by heart-stricken moms and dads on receiving the news—total gallons of vomit, tears, and the rest of it. Can't figure the volume extruded and expelled by grieving brothers and sisters though. That varies. Bigger for Catholics and Mormons, and casual reproducers in places like Watts and Boone County, Kentucky."

"All because some moron forgot to place a call to Hue."

"Looks like that's what happened," Sanger said. "Maybe the officers in charge were too busy dorking hookers in Saigon. Couldn't be bothered. Your pal Lambert one of those who fucked up, do you think?"

To spare Fielding further torment, Quint looped around to the wire service machines to check out the day's ration of death and disaster, mother's milk to Quint's favorite cynic, Ambrose Bierce, who once wrote a story about hogs feeding on the corpses of fallen soldiers following a Civil War battle.

The lead story of that day was about the "pacification" of Hue, a neat term, Quint thought. One story called the failure to notify Hue of the coming Tet offensive the largest intelligence screw-up since the inexplicable failure of the Roosevelt administration to pass along critical information to the fleet at Pearl Harbor. There were also stories about demonstrations at the University of California at Berkeley and at Columbia University. But these were lethargic efforts at best, tear gas had been released and the usual arrests, but no blood or bodies.

Quint had noted that the universities in northern latitudes seemed more rebellious and politically active than those farther south, and Quint wondered why that was. Was it possible that the sun soaked up energy elsewhere devoted to riot and rebellion? The students at such places as the University of Minnesota were still pinned inside their apartments and dorms by the bitter cold, but when spring broke, they'd paint their placards, unfurl their scatological banners, and enter the fray with all the energy they could muster. Quint felt this was likely a simple matter of pride. If students rioted at Berkeley, students in Minneapolis had to demonstrate that they were concerned crazies and not ignorant, callous hicks from the Midwest.

The antiauthoritarian enthusiasm had even spread to Europe, which Quint thought was interesting because nobody there was being drafted by the American army. Rebellion, it seemed, was fashionable everywhere as though an odd virus was working its way around the planet, affecting brains everywhere. In Berlin, SDS leader Berndt Rabehl had led a demonstration urging black American soldiers to mutiny at McNear barracks. In Paris, the firebrand Daniel Cohn-Bendit had led Maoist and Trotskyite chants of "Ho-Ho-Ho Chi Minh!" In Italy, the cry was "Che-Che-Che Guevera!" But these efforts hardly rated a paragraph each on the Associated Press A wire.

"Anything good?" Quint asked the wire service editor, Carl Zimmerman.

"Naw, usual horseshit," he said. "Slow day."

Thinking of Lambert, Quint said, "You going to run that story comparing Hue to Pearl Harbor?"

"Probably," he said. "Pearl Harbor happened here in Hawaii. More interesting to local readers than the rest of the Hue stuff. Natural hook."

"Sanger says you've got some good body counts from Hue. He's wondering why they don't move totals of body fluids expelled by grieving relatives."

Zimmerman laughed. "Sanger!" He ripped some more paper from the machine and threw it in a wastebasket. "And who gives a damn about students in Europe?" He rolled his eyes in disgust. "Why do they send us this crap? It's a waste of paper."

Behind Quint, Fielding said, "Jim, don't forget, you've got a draft card burning this morning at the university. Take Warren with you. Tell him I want pictures of something besides girls showing their fronts. We all know they've got 'em."

"Good luck with that," Quint said.

"He might try taking the picture of somebody burning his draft card. That's what the story is about." Fielding considered that for a moment. "And one more thing. This time I want you to verify the fact that these kids are burning their draft cards. By that I mean you are to physically inspect the cards. You only count confirmed cards. I don't want the little traitors getting their names in the paper for burning their library card."

Like confirmed kills, Quint thought. He said, "Got it."

Fielding looked sour. "I don't know why we cover this stuff in the first place. It's gotten so any kid with a beard on his face and a dime in his pocket can call himself an ad hoc committee and announce a press conference, and we'll all show up, pencils and cameras at the ready." He thought a moment then said, "On second thought, Jim, maybe the colonel has a point."

"The colonel? What point?"

Fielding, looking slightly embarrassed, cleared his throat.

"What colonel?"

"Uh, Colonel Del Lambert." Fielding pretended to be busy with the story in front of him.

"I see. Say again what point?"

Fielding sucked air between his teeth. "Colonel Lambert is an intelligence officer with the army. One of *the* Lamberts."

"I know who he is."

"He's been trying to get you sacked for a couple of years now. He's sent us maybe thirty or forty letters complaining about your coverage of the radicals. The guy is apparently obsessed. He just will not give it up. He says you're consciously aiding and abetting traitors. Now that he's been rotated back from Vietnam, he apparently hasn't got anything better to do than write letters bitching about your stories."

"Oh? Trying to get me fired? Why hasn't anybody told me about this?" Now Quint understood the reason for Chick McGyver's curiosity about his lunch with Lambert. He'd been receiving letters of complaint from Lambert and throwing them in the round file without telling Quint. This put Quint's unusual relationship with Del and Vivienne in a new light. He had blundered into a minefield without knowing it. Why would Lambert match his wife up with somebody he hated?

Fielding looked embarrassed. "I suppose we should have said something, but you've only been doing your job. We decided if Lambert wants to get his frustrations off his chest by writing pissy letters, let him. We've got a newspaper to publish. Only now he wants to know, once again, if we aren't overdoing the coverage of draft card burnings. Is it really news any longer that some pimple-faced kid is burning his draft card? Maybe he's right this time. It is getting a little boring, you have to admit."

Fielding and Lambert had a point. Quint couldn't deny it.

Fielding frowned. He didn't want to appear to be taking orders from an army colonel. Hard to admit that. He said, "Chick and Hobe and I have been thinking along the same lines, as it happens. I tell you what, Jim, if all those kids have got to offer is rhetoric

and burning draft cards, I want you and Warren to go on to your
next assignment. We've got real news to cover. We'll give 'em
the nut in the obits so they'll get to read their names in the paper.
Who gives a damn what they burn? If they were serious about
protesting the war, they'd pull a monk. Warren could really get
a picture then."

Fielding meant the Buddhist monk in Saigon who had been
sore at the war and so soaked himself in gasoline then sat cross-
legged in the middle of the street, match in hand. An AP photographer had caught him going up in flames. The picture topped
the A wire that day. Look at this readers! A burning monk! What
a shot! Shock, shock!

At three o'clock when Quint stood to go join the regulars
drinking beer at the Round Table, the phone rang.

"Hey, Jimbo, me. Colonel Lambert. Got a minute?"

"Sure, I've got a minute," Quint said.

"Thought you might. Say, I was wondering if you'd forgotten
the other night. My wife stripping for you. Your embrace. Her
whispering sweet somethings in your ear. Your little kiss."

"Hard to forget all that," Quint said.

"I bet. Plenty of loping the goat for you, eh? Thinking about
Vivienne. Squirt, squirt, squirt. Waiting for me to call, were
you?"

"I didn't know whether you would or not."

"Say, my wife whispered something in your ear. I don't believe
I caught that."

Quint said, "That's because it was intended for me."

"What was it?"

"Nothing important," Quint said.

"Sweet nothings between wannabe lovers? I don't think so. I
think you're lying. Remember my offer? A straight quid pro quo.
I get what I want. You get the pretty lady."

"I remember."

"Can't beat a deal like that. I suppose you've been wondering
what that's all about?"

"Aw hell no. Hadn't given it a thought."

"You can be a smart ass and risk me telling you to shove the fuck off or you can calm down and maybe we can work something out. I say again, my offer still stands. You have to give to get. Ain't no such thing as a free lunch in this life, pal. That's part of the lesson of Vietnam, by the way. This is a way for you to score a beautiful woman and do your country a favor at the same time—unless you think that's traitorous to the cause of the International League of Chickenshits and Leftie Morons."

"You mentioned, ah, the possibility of . . ." Quint couldn't bring himself to finish the sentence.

"Of inviting you up for another visit with my wife. I know I did. Not good to call you too soon. Fun making you wait and wonder. I live on Tantalus, remember. The more you think about sweet Vivienne, the better the odds I'll get what I'm after. And I will get what I'm after, make no mistake. By the way, did you ask her what I'm after when you talked to her at the Ala Moana Center?"

"Are you having her followed?"

"Hey, pal. I know everything my wife does. Where she goes. Who she talks to. *Everything*. Never doubt that for a second."

"By the way, I just learned from my city editor that you've been writing crappy letters complaining about my coverage of the radicals for a couple of years."

Lambert laughed. "Oh that," he said cheerfully. "Not just crappy letters, Jimbo. I've been flat-ass trying to get you sacked and sent packing to whatever hole you came out of. If I had my way, they'd take every motherfucking so-called journalist like you and string him up by the balls. Or tits as the sex requires. But reasonable gentlemen can disagree."

"Reasonable gentlemen. Right."

"You know, Jimbo, I know you think you're being fair and everything. Mr. Objective. But you know the one thing I bet has never occurred to you is by casually omitting the more lunatic assertions of their crazed speechifying, you make them sound more convincing than they really are. You pick and choose. You omit the paranoid and the impossible and the illogical. Is it really

fair to your readers to sort through their rambling nonsense looking for the one zinger of a quote that scores a point with your
more rational readers?"

"You think I do that?"

"I know damn well you do that. But set that aside for the
moment. My feeling for your coverage in the *Star-Bulletin* doesn't
have anything to do with offering you my wife. I take that back.
Yes, I guess it does. I wanted to choose a lover for Vivienne that
I knew she would like. I haven't forgotten my promise to invite
you up again. I just want you to have time to think about her
before I take the next step. You understand that, don't you,
Jimbo? I hope my trying to get you sacked doesn't mean you've
lost interest in my wife."

Quint said nothing.

"You'd be a damned fool to let a few hard feelings get in
the way of a beauty like Vivienne." Lambert laughed easily and
hung up.

THAT NIGHT JIM Quint drove back up the mountain. Imagining
himself as a Charlie, he parked his car and hiked up the hill to
the entrance to the Lambert residence and then made his way
down the flanking ridge. This time Lambert was gone, but Vivienne was on the deck behind her studio. Glass of iced tea in
hand, she studied the large canvas. Then she leaned against the
rail, looking down over the city lights.

Quint, nestled in the brush at the top of the ridge, felt an
overwhelming urge to go to the door and knock, but thought
better of it. For now, watching her was enough. Better to let
Lambert make the next move.

Vivienne returned to the canvas, her face intense as she concentrated. She painted a few strokes then stepped back. She re-
worked the same small portion of the canvas, then stopped again,
examining what she had done. She returned to the rail. She took
a sip of tea. She went back to the canvas. She studied it. She
went·back to the rail. She held her face in her hands.

Was she weeping?

Quint was stricken. He wanted to paw his way up through the underbrush and bang on the door and hold her and tell her dammit everything would be all right. But he didn't.

Vivienne took the canvas back into her studio. The lights went out.

Quint checked his watch. Midnight.

As Quint was walking up the driveway to the road, a pair of headlights rounded the corner. He stepped back into the brush. It was Lambert in his Mercedes. From the brush, Quint watched Lambert park the Mercedes then get out. He unzipped his pants and took a long, hard piss, lacing the ground. Quint heard him sing loudly,

> *"I got a gal, and she is a delight.*
> *Poke her in the butt from morning till night."*

13

As Jim Quint drove Warren Roll down King Street on their way to University Avenue to the campus in Manoa Valley, he went through the usual, tiresome drill of controlling his photographer. "Listen, Warren, you've gotta be cool while I'm talking to these kids. I know you don't like what they're saying, but I can't do my job if you piss them off and they clam up. It's not good. You know that."

Roll scowled.

"This is my beat," Quint said. "These kids need to be reassured that I'll be fair to them. They have to trust me. Believe it or not, it turns them off when somebody calls them cowards to their face. You gotta give me a break." Quint suspected that Roll's only real complaint was that the students were having fun and he wasn't. He had apparently endured maximum discipline growing up, and by God he wanted succeeding generations to suffer the same form of cultural boot camp.

"Some beat. Little chickenshits," Roll murmured. He didn't take offense at Quint's little lecture. Once reminded, he would keep his mouth shut, although it wouldn't be easy.

"Maybe they're right," Quint said mildly.

"About what?"

"About a lot of things. About the war for sure. Can't blame them for not wanting to sacrifice themselves in a totally screwed war."

Roll looked pop-eyed. "You agree with them?"

"I think there are some real tough questions the Johnson administration hasn't answered very well."

Roll looked offended. "Like what tough questions?"

Quint knew he had Roll going. He'd forced Quint to give him his little warning, so Quint figured he'd have a little fun. Quint said, "For one thing, that's a whole lot of blood and treasure to squander on what looks suspiciously like a civil war."

"Civil war? North Vietnamese Communists are invading South Vietnam. If they capture South Vietnam, you're looking at Laos, Cambodia, Thailand, Malaysia, and Indonesia with the Philippines thrown in for funsies. If that happened, where would we be? Take a look at the map. Toppling dominoes."

"And you have to wonder about the use of napalm and chemical defoliants."

"Burn their hinies. Toast their little weenies. Serves 'em right. What we ought to do is pull a Dresden on Hanoi or even pop a nuke. The war would be over before sundown."

"Also these guys train and train and train to be soldiers. The professional soldiers stayed in because they like it. They don't want to sit around on their butts. They *want* to fight. All this talk about how war is hell. If war really was hell to anybody but the poor bastards who were drafted, they'd figure a way to pull out."

"Bullshit."

"Of course if you're in college or graduate school you're too good to shed your blood in a rice paddy. Tell me, Warren, does that strike you as fair in any elementary sense? If the war is so hot-damn necessary, why do some butts get put to the fire while others drink beer in frat houses?"

Roll glared at Quint.

Quint said, "That's not to mention the assassination of Diem. Make a person wonder who was behind that. If it was the U.S. maybe we would be thinking about our priorities. You'd have thought we'd have learned something after the Kennedy business."

"You agree with them. You do. A peacenik."

Quint shrugged. He knew there was no sense trying to argue with him about the Vietnam War. Roll was a visceral patriot. In his mind, one did not question a president when boys were in the field. His mind was locked shut on the subject.

THE DRAFT CARD burning that day was scheduled in a large room with a raised dais or platform on one side that was presumably used by speakers at small conferences. The window of the campus post office was to the left of the dais. There were tables on either side of the window piled with IRS forms and ZIP-code directories, together with tethered pens for the last-second addressing of letters and packages. The students gathered in the room to witness the burning and cheer on the jeering of the establishment fuck-ups and militarists who had lost all those people at Hue. They wore the fashionable counterculture costumes: headbands, beards, and ponytails for the males; no bras, and miniskirts or cutoffs for the females.

As Quint and Roll waited for the radical leaders to arrive for the scheduled burning, a girl in the miniest of miniskirts bent over the left table to address envelopes. Her underpants were grossly inadequate to the task of enveloping her buns. Roll spotted her handsome behind immediately. Plump it was. Succulent. Roll liked it a lot. He turned to the room and put a finger to his mouth to shush the room, and without a word fell to his knees directly behind the rump of the girl who was concentrating on her task. He aimed his camera directly up at her butt, which strained against translucent fabric. He turned and grinned at the room, coming off as a naughty, wicked little boy.

The students in the room began snickering and giggling. Roll, with a happy look on his face, his lens less than a foot from the promised land, clicked away. The girl sensed something was wrong. As she started to turn, Roll popped to his feet, all innocence. Charlie Chaplin couldn't have done it any better. The room broke out in laughter. The girl looked puzzled. What was so funny? The laughter turned to guffaws.

Quint and Roll were both well-known to the students. Roll was the good-natured asshole and congenital war hawk who loved to shoot pictures of girls, and Quint was the Wild Bill Hickok reporter who smoked pot and secretly agreed with them—at least on the issue of the war in Vietnam. Quint didn't suck up to them, but he didn't put them down either.

At length, the hirsute radical leaders arrived, attended by their coterie of admiring females. It was no coincidence that the television cameras arrived almost simultaneously. The radicals liked to read about themselves in the paper, yes, but even more important to them was being on television that night. The lead firebrand that day was John Witek, the earnest young SDSer who had distributed the controversial fragging pamphlets in Waikiki that had gotten poor Oliver Lee in such hot water. Time for Jim Quint to spring into action. He popped onto the dais.

Witek was all smiles when he saw Quint. "Hey, Jim, what's up?"

Quint said, "How many cards today?"

"Four."

Quint frowned. "I'm supposed to make sure they're genuine, true-blue draft cards. No pretensies. Fielding is concerned that you're burning library cards."

Witek looked concerned. He knew there was more to it than that. "What's wrong?"

"Fielding says our readers are getting bored reading about draft card burnings. At first he told me that he wanted me to examine the cards myself to see if they were real, then amended that. He said if you've only got cards, I'm supposed to bug out and give him a nut to bury in the obits."

"A nut?"

Quint grinned. "It doesn't have anything to do with sanity. It means a short kiss-off paragraph. Put it in a nutshell. Hence, a nut. Nobody reads the nuts. They're conditioned to believe any story worth reading is on the front page of a section."

Witek didn't like the sound of that. "What are you saying?"

"You'll still have television. We both know television reporters can't ignore a match torching a draft card. That's like an alcoholic turning down another shot of whiskey."

"Kiss us off with a paragraph?" Witek looked pissed. "The motherfucker. He can do that?"

Roll arrived, reloading his Nikon.

"He can do pretty much whatever he wants. He's the city editor. It's his football. He makes up the rules. If he wants a nut, he gets a nut." Quint shrugged in commiseration. "You'll have to jazz up the show. No other way."

"What'll it take?"

Roll slung the camera back over his shoulder. "Fielding claims the readers are bored reading what you little peckers are saying, but sex never fails. Right, Jim? Of course you'd have to come up with your own idea, not us." He winked at Witek.

Witek ignored the pecker comment. He perked up. "Hey! That's not bad. Okay, how about this? Suppose we've got a couple of girls with a pair of big ones who don't mind showing them off?"

"Hey, that'd be good," Roll said. "I can shoot 'em at an angle so all our readers will see is their backs."

Quint cried, "Hey, Warren!"

Roll looked surprised. "Hey, what? We're helping the forces of good. Right, pal?"

Witek grinned. "Exactly. You guys are in the wrong business. Just give us a few minutes."

Quint looked resigned. "We're not going anywhere."

Roll was thrilled. "Topless girls! Be like giving Fielding a whiff of smelling salts. He'll have babies!"

"Wonderful," Quint said.

"You know all that talk about you being an asshole? None of it's true, Jim. You're okay, really."

Roll was an imaginative photographer. He'd come up with a real grabber of a picture. Quint's byline would be under the story of the draft card burning. The combination of photograph and story would likely drive Fielding wild. Quint said, "I take it back about you too, Warren. You're nothing short of a genius. A professional all the way."

Roll giggled. "I got a shot of that girl's butt that'll make Fielding's day, guaranteed. What an ass!"

Quint said, "What did the girls wear when you were young, Warren? Skirts halfway to their ankles. Sweaters with dickeys. See, you do too like this generation. What we're seeing here is progress. Freedom, not restriction. Honesty, not repression."

14

THE NEXT AFTERNOON Jim Quint strolled across the parking lot headed for the Columbia Inn and his Round Table companions. As Quint turned onto the sidewalk, he saw Vivienne waiting for him under an awning just down the street. She caught his attention with a quick wave of her hand, and he hustled quickly to meet her.

Vivienne, looking embarrassed, glanced about, checking the streets. "I was wondering if you might like to go for a drive this afternoon. I've brought my watercolors, and the afternoon light is good."

"We can go to the North Shore," Quint said.

"We'll be followed," she said quickly. "You have to expect that."

Quint laughed. "I'll get my car."

"I'm parked just around the corner."

"Meet you there," Quint said. He returned quickly to the parking lot, and hopped into his car. He drove around the block, pulling in behind her Austin Healy. They threw her watercolors and painting gear into the trunk of his Datsun.

They slipped onto the front seat. Without saying a word, they came together hungrily, tongues twisting. She pushed her small body hard against him. He grabbed her butt with his left hand. She slipped her underpants down and pulled his right hand between her legs. Then just as quickly she pushed his hand away and opened her thighs.

Quint unzipped and entered her, thrusting so hard she banged her head against the door window. She was exquisitely small inside and sweet and hot. They leaned back, joined, indifferent to the possibility of passersby.

"Love me," she breathed.

"Yes."

"Help me fight him. Together."

"Yes."

"As one. Swear it."

"I swear it, Vivienne."

"Whatever the dangers."

"Whatever the dangers," Quint said.

Quint saw a middle-aged Asian woman with a white plastic shopping bag pass behind them on the sidewalk. She saw what they were doing and looked quickly away. After a few feet she glanced back, amused.

Vivienne arched her back and cried out. Since the windows were down, Quint imagined they could hear her all the way from Diamond Head to Pearl Harbor.

The woman on the sidewalk gave the Hawaiian gesture that was wildly incongruent with her age, sex, and likely upbringing. Grinning broadly, she waggled her thumb and forefinger, Hawaii's famous hang-loose shaka sign, and continued on her way.

Vivienne twisted on the seat. Quint could hardly stay in her. Then he too felt the wave.

They rested, legs tangled, breathing heavily.

"Did I remember to say good afternoon, Vivienne?" Quint grinned. "If I didn't, hello there." He wiggled his hips.

"Good afternoon, Jim." She nudged him back. Smiling lazily, she wiped sweat off her forehead with the back of her arm.

THEY HAD BARELY entered the valley of pineapple fields on the far side of Pearl Harbor when Quint, again checking his rearview mirror, saw that the light green Chevrolet sedan that had been following him from Honolulu was still behind him.

Vivienne, following his eyes, said, "Still there?"

Quint nodded. "Are we in any kind of immediate danger?" he asked.

She shook her head. "If I thought we would be, I wouldn't have come."

"Who is he, a private detective or someone from Del's intelligence unit?"

"One or the other," she said.

Quint laughed. "Yogi Berra said when you come to a fork in the road, take it."

They passed Waialua and came at length to Haleiwa and crossed a small, white bridge across the Anahulu River, hardly larger than a mainland creek, which emptied into Waialua Bay. On Pauena Point at the far end of the bay, they passed a small park, Haleiwa Beach Park.

Although this was the middle of August, and the big waves were in the winter, there were surfers all along Kawailoa Beach. They circled Waimea Bay, which hardly qualified for the designation, being hardly more than a dimple in the shoreline, and passed through the village of Waimea. On the far side of Waimea, Quint pulled his Datsun into Pupukea Beach Park and parked. There was a good view of Sunset Beach where athletic young men were hanging ten on azure curls that welled up from the Pacific.

As they got out of the Datsun, Quint said, "Would you like to take a walk before you start your painting?"

"Sure, I'd like that," she said. They walked together hand in hand in silence with Vivienne carrying a small metal case of painting gear and Quint the folded aluminum easel.

Vivienne said, "Pupukea. That one's pretty easy, but I ordinarily have a terrible time with these Hawaiian names. Del is no help. He's always gone, and when he is home, he doesn't have time for that kind of thing. All he can think about is the war and people he thinks are traitors."

"People like me."

"You're high on his list."

Quint said, "You know, when I first came to Hawaii, I had a hard time with the Hawaiian place names too. The missionaries who rendered the Polynesian words into print had a limited type font, so the language wound up heavy on Ks, Ws, and vowels. My first assignment was a terrible car wreck on Kalanianaole Highway. When I came back into the city room and tried to pronounce it, everybody burst out laughing. You pronounce every vowel separately. But once you get the hang of it, they flow like rippling water. It's a beautiful language."

"Say the name of that highway again."

"Kalanianaole," Quint said. "The Hawaiians have a number of all-purpose words that are especially fun. Take 'puka,' which literally means hole. Puka can mean everything from the top of a beer bottle, the goal of a basketball game—put it in the *puka!*— to, ah, a sexual kind of reference. A woman's . . ." He grinned.

She laughed. "Really?"

"*Puka.* That's it. The word for butt is good too. *Okole.* You have a fine, fine *okole*, Vivienne."

"I knew you'd know all that lingo."

They walked on, watching the surfers in the distance.

Quint cleared his throat. "Lambert called me at the paper to repeat his deal. Let me ask you again what is it he wants? If we're in this together, I need to know."

"I *might* have something he wants. Maybe I do. Maybe I don't. The answer is the same that I gave you at the Ala Moana Center. When it's safe for you to know, I'll tell you, I promise."

"He has been writing letters to my editors claiming I'm ghosting for traitors, yet he deliberately recruited me and threw us together. Why?"

Vivienne sighed. "Del and I have been arguing about your stories at supper from the day I arrived in Honolulu. You go out of your way to at least appear open-minded on the subject of the war. To me that means you're sympathetic to the doves."

"Why don't you just get on the plane and fly back to Vietnam?"

She sighed. "I'm living in a form of prison. Here's a good spot." She stopped and opened her case of watercolors and painting gear. As she started assembling her aluminum easel, she said, "You must never call me on the telephone, Jim. It's tapped. I will call you. If I don't call, you'll just have to wait and be patient."

"Be patient. Right."

"Promise."

"I promise." Meeting Vivienne was like stepping into an Eric Ambler spy novel. What was going to happen next?

She said, "Meeting you this afternoon is not good, but I had to talk to you."

"Just talk?"

She laughed. "That's all I had in mind until we were together on the front seat of your car." She put a pad of watercolor paper on the easel, and studied the beach spread out before them. She laid out a wash of pale blue, what Quint recognized as the beginning of a sky. She left a strip of white for the beach and some streaks of white for the high, thin clouds as well as some diminutive V's that would become seagulls floating in the wind.

As she worked, she said, "You can't lay light colors on dark in a watercolor. You have to plan your whites, whether they're clouds, houses, or sails. If they're not there in the beginning, you can't add them at the end." She worked quickly, laying on a thin wash of Hooker's green that would become the base of hills rising up from the beach.

Vivienne paused as she rinsed her brush. "In fact, if you think about it, the areas left blank are often the most telling part of a watercolor."

"The omissions."

"Colors not applied. Right. You work from light to dark. You finish with the shadows." Vivienne used Payne's gray to lay out the suggestion of the large boulders just up from the beach. She had left thin twists of blank paper that Quint could tell would become light reflected off the edges of the boulders. She said, "Up close, the strokes are as facts, individual and with little meaning. Only when you step back do the shapes and colors and highlights and shadows come together in an understandable image."

Jim Quint glanced up at the cars parked along the edge of the highway and saw a man watching them through binoculars.

Vivienne followed his eyes and saw the man. She said, "I suppose I should finish this off so we can get back." She added burnt umber to some of the Payne's gray on her palette, applying it as shadow under the boulders.

AS QUINT NEGOTIATED the traffic back to Honolulu, he felt dry-mouthed, giddy with recklessness. It was as though he had known Vivienne for years when the truth was he knew almost nothing about her. *Help me fight him. Together.* He was in lust, he knew. *As one. Swear it. Whatever the dangers.*

Quint said, "I remember when I was a kid I saw the movie *Zorba the Greek* with Anthony Quinn playing Zorba and Alan Bates as the proper young Englishman. The Bates character asked him if he had a wife. Zorba said, 'Do I have a wife? Of course I have a wife! I have a wife, kids, house, mortgage, the full disaster!' Zorba told Bates, 'You have a mind like a grocer. You weigh everything.' "

She leaned against him. Her smell was intoxicating. Her eyes were as quick as a bobcat's. "That's it exactly, Jim. We will be Zorba. We will live!"

In his mind's eye Quint could see Anthony Quinn, arms folded, dancing joyfully to spirited Greek music, telling the admiring Bates: *I dance!*

Quint leaned over and kissed Vivienne on the neck, which tasted salty from the sweat of their earlier sex. He murmured, "I don't know about you, but I think we've had enough get-acquainted talk for now. What do you say we go back to my apartment before I take you back? The front seat's okay for a spontaneous first time, but other than that it's best left for high school kids."

She took him by the hand. "We will not let him defeat us, Jim. We will prevail. No matter what it takes."

Quint heard himself say, "Whatever it takes." Despite saying that, Quint knew intuitively he was being drawn into a dangerous game that he did not understand. The amazing strip. Lambert's bizarre offer to swap his wife. Now this. No woman as beautiful as Vivienne would come on to a man with that much passion and energy unless she had good reason. Yet he knew he would not back out. Vivienne had seen to that on the front seat of the car. Lambert wanted him to desire his wife. Vivienne wanted him to desire her.

He did.

Of one thing Quint was confident. The origins of the erotic gambit that he had accepted almost certainly lay in Vietnam.

15

THE NEXT DAY, a bare two weeks after Eugene McCarthy's victory in New Hampshire, the Irish savior Bobby Kennedy made his heroic move on the eve of St. Patrick's day. Flanked by his wife, Ethel, and nine of his ten children and scores of New Frontiersmen, including Theodore Sorensen and Arthur Schlesinger, he held a press conference in a Senate caucus room to announce that yes, responding to the urging of his many supporters, he would, after all, run for the presidency. To hear the unembarrassed Kennedy tell it, everything was going to be hunky dory between him and Eugene McCarthy.

That night Jim Quint returned a third time to watch the Lambert residence from the flanking ridge. And as he had been the first time, Lambert sat in his chair brooding, sipping a drink as he stared down over the city lights. Behind him, on the deck outside her studio, Vivienne worked on her painting.

No sooner had Quint gotten settled into his spot than Lambert looked his way. Or had he? Pearl Harbor lay behind Quint. Perhaps Lambert was just looking at Pearl Harbor.

Again Lambert looked his way. Longer this time. He then stood and disappeared into the house.

A few seconds later he appeared on the deck with Vivienne. Without a word and with Quint watching through his binoculars, he grabbed Vivienne by the wrist, sending her palette flying. He spun her around and pinned her wrist between her shoulder blades. He ripped off her underpants and shoved her hard against the rail. He bent her over it and calmly unzipped his pants and entered her savagely. Vivienne screamed in pain. Quint could hear her clearly.

Was he screwing her in the anus? It appeared so. Keeping both of her wrists pinned between her shoulder blades, he took her brutally, punishing her. She screamed and continued screaming, crying out with each thrust of his pelvis.

Through his binoculars, Quint could see Vivienne's face. She was twisted by pain, humiliation, and rage.

As Lambert slammed her hips into the rail, he calmly looked in Quint's direction. Was he looking at Pearl Harbor or staring into the night? Or watching Jim Quint?

Should Quint run to the house like a love-struck adolescent and attempt a dramatic rescue? Del and Vivienne were man and wife, after all. For all Quint knew, Vivienne liked quickie anal intercourse. Or maybe it wasn't that at all. Maybe he just took her from behind.

Was this Lambert's way of encouraging Quint to help him get whatever he was after? Or was he was teaching a lesson to an unwelcome voyeur?

Quint put his binoculars back in its case and bailed off his limb. He hurried quickly back up the ridge. When he got to the double garage, he tried the door that led to the house. It opened. He went to Lambert's Mercedes and squatted, his hands trembling. Then he went around to the driver's side and took out his keys. Using the heel of his left hand to support his right hand, he slowly and carefully scratched in the silver paint, digging in hard and deep:

QUEER BOY

He circled to the driver's side.

BUTT FUCKER

If Lambert knew Quint had been watching from the ridge, he'd know who had—keyed his doors. If Lambert had just been looking at Pearl Harbor, let him wonder.

Quint left the garage. He strode back down Tantalus Drive to his car, the image of Lambert raping his wife, if that was what it was, burning in his mind's eye. He slipped into the car, seeing Vivienne's face. As he turned the key to the ignition, he remembered her scream.

Shaken, sweating heavily, mouth dry, but pumped high on adrenaline, Quint took a hard U-turn and drove too fast down Tantalus Mountain, heading for the Round Table.

AFTER THEIR LAST edition had been put to bed each afternoon, a regular group of reporters at the *Star-Bulletin* adjourned to the Round Table, a spot unofficially reserved for them in the Columbia Inn, the bar on the Diamond Head side of the newspaper parking lot. There they bitched, gossiped, and discussed the unending parade of disaster, heartache, and disappointment that they had to package for their readers. They laughed. They observed. They ridiculed.

It was unspoken, but mutually understood that the regulars were watching the passing of 1968 as a form of shared experience. They were educated, although not overly so. They were from largely working-class backgrounds. And they were by nature curious, which is why they had ended up as journalists. Although they would be embarrassed to admit it, Quint thought they were likely cynical because they were disappointed lovers of country. Mordant yes, but caring were the Round Table regulars. They were a kind of chorus singing the refrain of 1968.

There was a core of seven regulars, although on a given day the table could be larger or smaller.

The curly-haired Jerry Fortier, a wire service reporter gone to seed, was the editor of the editorial page—a professional at writing opinion that would offend nobody. Editorial writers were famous for a phenomenon called Afghanistanism, the practice of having strongly held opinions about faraway places over which the newspaper had no conceivable influence—in Afghanistan, say. Newspaper editorials were most influential in local issues and elections. *The New York Times* or *The Washington Post* might carry weight in Washington, not the *Honolulu Star-Bulletin*. The cultural civil wars of 1968 presented a special problem to the editors and owners of the paper. Should the paper ignore the war that was tearing the country apart, or should it take sides? Chinn Ho felt obliged to defend the Johnson administration, leaving Fortier as a kind of guerilla writer doing his best to slip a telltale phrase or statistic past the watchful eyes of Chick McGyver.

Phil Mayer, a skinny union enthusiast with a deep voice and a long morose face, was famous for a passionate speech he had once given urging the members of the newspaper guild to stand side-by-side with *tofu* makers and *shoyu* bottlers—*shoyu* being the Japanese word for soy sauce. Hawaii was a labor state and Mayer covered the unions, among which he had numerous contacts. Mayer cared so deeply and passionately about working people that his cynicism, famous among his colleagues, appeared limitless. No counter-culture New Left kind of guy, Mayer was an old-fashioned, bread-and-butter, better wages and medical benefits kind of liberal.

The loud, vulgar drunk Albert Barnhouse, given to flying spittle and braying laughter, covered cops. The cops had developed a lexicon of euphemisms to help them survive the brutality of their work, and some of this had rubbed off on Barnhouse.

Quint's quiet, sardonic friend, Steve Sanger, worked general assignment. He preferred being what he called a "general assignment dogface" because it let him see all three rings of the circus. Sanger was a quiet figure with a wry, ironic sense of humor.

The Japanese-American sexpot, Miki Hasegawa, a caring, committed liberal who still believed, wrote lengthy, serious tomes that few people likely read, but she got away with it because Chick McGyver was overwhelmed by the scent of her perfume. To her, the body count regularly reported by the paper was a barbarous indictment of a national policy gone wrong.

Babs Parsegian, the fat-thumbed, bespectacled reporter whose large-fronted body Sanger openly coveted, was an intelligent, high-spirited giggler whose specialty was soporific stories about boring bureaucrats. Scornful of the wave of young people arriving in Hawaii in search of sun, surf, and Maui Wowie, Babs reflected the values of the bureaucrats she covered.

And Jim Quint.

In Hawaii's multiracial Mulligan stew, haoles were regarded as perhaps a trifle slow off the mark. The Portuguese, one of the many waves of immigrants to the state, were the butt of racial jokes. Portugee jokes. Do you know how to tell if a Portugee has been through your backyard? Your garbage can is empty and your dog is pregnant. A Pake, pronounced pa-kay, was a Chinese. A Buddha-head was a Japanese. A Kim Chee was a Korean.

On St. Patrick's day, the jolly host and Irishman for the day, Tosh Kaneshiro, laced the draught beer at the Columbia Inn with green food coloring. In honor of the occasion, Kaneshiro had added a sprig of parsley to his little dishes of chicken and long rice—translucent rice noodles, a favorite *puu puu* of the regulars.

Kaneshiro passed out green paper hats for his patrons, a duke's mixture of racial and ethnic origin. The celebrants included Chan and Chun Irishmen and Micks named Woo and Park, Kawana and Kobayashi, not to mention Alcantara and Alvarez. In the end what difference did race make? The point of it all was to get loaded and have fun.

Among the *Star-Bulletin* regulars at the Round Table that day, the talk was about those Irish political combatants, Eugene McCarthy and Bobby Kennedy. The regulars cared deeply about what was happening to their country, but none of them had any idea at all how the country might best address problems of war and rebellion.

The AP had earlier moved a story from Wisconsin, giving the McCarthy reaction to Bobby's decision, "An Irishman who announces the day before St. Patrick's Day that he's going to run against another Irishman shouldn't say it's going to be a peaceful relationship." And an AP story pointed out that the Senate caucus room was the very same place where Bobby had served as counsel to the other McCarthy, the red-baiting Sen. Joseph R. McCarthy during the televised Army-McCarthy hearings.

The regulars agreed Bobby Kennedy was definitely one of Joe Kennedy's boys. But whereas John had been a charmer, Bobby Kennedy had a younger brother's edge to him.

"You really have to admire a liberal who started out by hiding under Joe McCarthy's skirts," Barnhouse said. He burst into braying laughter. "Gotta get all them Commies."

Mayer said, "You wait there, Abner. Bobby Kennedy's got courage and charisma. People believe in him. He's our only way out of this mess. We need him."

"Hey, he's a politician. He follows the fashion," Fortier said. "Mobs are in so he takes on the Mafia."

Sanger said, "Have you paid any attention to those teeth of his? He's got bright eyes and eager teeth."

"A political rat terrier!" Barnhouse said. "A yapping little barker!" *Har, har, har!*

"I was thinking more of Bugs Bunny," Sanger added.

Miki said, "You guys are just sore because he used his daddy's money to buy the New York Senate seat."

Mayer said, "I don't hold that against him. At least he's doing something with the Senate seat. You know he's there. He stands for something."

Har, har, har! Barnhouse, speaking without removing the cigarette that seemed almost glued to his lower lip, said, "But when the time had come for him to show some real balls, he let Gene McCarthy brave the odds and winter wind up there in New Hampshire. Then he casually elbows McCarthy aside. Without embarrassment!"

Fortier said, "Hey, hey, take it easy. He's a Kennedy. We're talking divine right here."

Mayer threw up his hands in disgust. "You two guys don't get it, do you? Go ahead, wisecrack, morons. The fact remains the country needs a leader. Just because Gene McCarthy entered the primaries first doesn't mean he could lead the first grade singing the national anthem. We need somebody capable of leading us out of this bullshit."

To Quint all the talk about McCarthy and Kennedy was verbal muzak. All he could think about was Vivienne bent over the rail, screaming in pain. She was a siren who had lured him into her mysterious struggle with her husband. She had pulled him into the primal zone of sexual desire. He wanted her passionately and he would do whatever it took to have her. He had committed. Taken sides. He had stepped aboard Neal Cassady's bus. No, that was wrong. The bus was an insular world for the Merry Pranksters, hermetic, a zone on wheels. The cultural guerillas traveled zonked, laughing at the straights outside.

Quint had joined a dangerous battle against the lethal Col. Del Lambert, regular army, U.S.A.

16

WAITING FOR VIVIENNE to call, Quint was rudderless. He took to driving by the entrance to the Lambert house at night like some teenaged kid caught in the heady grip of first love. He could barely catch a glimpse of the lights through the underbrush. Was Lambert home? Or was he in Saigon or Washington? Talk about the frustrations of Mt. Tantalus.

Then one day, she phoned. "Jim?" she said. She sounded tentative.

"Thought you'd never call," Quint said.

"It's okay to call?"

"Is it okay? What on earth are you talking about?"

"I wanted to call you sooner but couldn't because of Del. He flew to Saigon this morning for a quick trip. I'm calling from a pay phone."

Quint said, "I take it he knows about our trip to the North Shore."

"He got a report complete with graphic details," Vivienne said.

"Beginning with us on the front seat."

"Everything."

"What happened?"

"He sat outside brooding for a couple of hours, drinking Myers rum, then he taught me a lesson. Or his idea of a lesson."

"He bent you over the rail outside your studio and sodomized you," Quint said.

Vivienne paused. "So you're the one who keyed his car! Good for you. He thought it was you, but he couldn't be sure. It's been driving him crazy, not knowing whether it was you or a crackpot voyeur. He said it was like having to deal with Charlies. People out there watching."

Quint smiled. "Really?"

"Well, people wasn't the word he used. If we want to be alone, we have to go to your apartment."

"If?" Quint laughed.

"I shouldn't spend the night at your place. That would really set him off. His precious turf and all. You know anything about Vietnamese food? I can't take you to Vietnam, but I can cook you the food."

Quint asked, "Are you sure you want to risk another round of retaliation?"

Vivienne answered, "Del fancies himself a professional at the application of force. If he pushes me too far he risks losing what he's after, and he won't do that."

Quint thought about that. "What if he saw me on the ridge and did a number on you as a way of pushing us together? The heroic moron stupidly rushes in to rescue the pretty lady. Just what he wants to happen. See what I mean?"

Vivienne laughed. "Say, you do have a devious mind! Knowing Del, that's entirely possible. So are you going to pick me up or not?"

"I'll be there in about ten minutes."

"I'll bring my wok. I've been boiling beef ribs and brisket, and we'll need to take a quick trip to the market to buy a fish, some beefsteak, some pork, some squid, some dried lily flowers, and some dried Chinese mushrooms."

"And all that is for?"

"We'll make several dishes, so you'll have leftovers."

"I'll be right up," Quint said and hung up.

A few minutes later, as Quint drove down Ewa on Kalakaua he repeated her name out loud, "Vivienne. Vivienne. Vvvviiiv-vvvviennnnnnnnnneeeee!" She was beautiful. That he liked. She was smart. That he liked too. Yet he was also wary. He knew she wasn't telling him the whole truth. She was using him in some way he did not understand. She had drawn him into a dangerous game with her husband.

Quint didn't care about any of that.

VIVIENNE PUT HER stainless steel pot of ribs and boiled brisket on the stove and stored the mahi mahi, pork, and squid in the refrigerator. She filled bowls with hot tap water to plump up the dried mushrooms and lily flowers. Then she picked up a bottle of what looked like soy sauce. "Lesson number one," she said. "This is *nuoc mam*, a fish sauce which is maybe a little stronger than fish sauces used in the rest of Southeast Asia. We use this like the Chinese use soy sauce."

"Lesson one. *Nuoc mam*, fish sauce."

"Together with rice, soup is basic to most of our meals. We'll stop almost any time of day or night to have a bowl of *pho*."

"Vivienne soup. *Far*. Got it."

Vivienne grinned. "Pronounced *far*. Spelled p-h-o."

"Far spelled p-h-o. Lesson two."

She opened the lid to the pot she had brought with her. "I've been simmering beef ribs, a cinnamon stick, fresh ginger, onions, and peppercorns for the last six hours. This is for the stock. When we're ready to eat, I'll slice the steak into very thin slices. We'll put noodles and stock into a bowl, and heap some fresh bean sprouts on top of that. Then we'll lower some slices of steak into the hot stock until they lose their redness and sprinkle some fresh coriander leaves and chopped chilis on top. There we'll have our *pho*."

"All right," Quint said. "You make this for Del?"

Vivienne shook her head sadly. "It's easier to kill a stranger than someone you know. Del can tell you all about firepower and helicopter gunships, but he doesn't understand that you should learn to eat the food before you fight the man. When I first met him, he tried holding my hand when we were walking down the street." Her face tightened. "Bar girls touch men in public."

"Oops! Okay, what else are we having?"

"We're having *ca hap*, steamed fish. Before we steam the fish we'll smother it in lengths of soaked rice noodles, thin slices of pork and mushroom, threads of ginger and carrot, and soy sauce. When it's finished, we'll pour coconut milk over it and sprinkle chopped coriander and green onion on top."

"Hey, okay!"

Vivienne was pleased at his enthusiasm. "And finally, in addition to the rice, we'll have *muc don thit*—squid stuffed with pork. This is easy to make but delicious." She opened the door and retrieved the pork. "You can start mincing the pork. When that's done the mushrooms ought to be ready, and you can slice them into thin strips."

As they worked side by side at the counter in Quint's kitchen, Vivienne said, "I have an envelope I'd like you to mail to an address in Hong Kong for me, would you do that?"

Quint scooped some more mushrooms out of the warm water. "Oh?" So this was it, or at least part of it. She wanted him to be her mailman.

"I'm not supposed to go anywhere near a mailbox. You're my only way to communicate. They might be monitoring your mail too, so you should put somebody else's name on the return address. Put any name you want on the Hong Kong address. It'll get to my friend."

Quint hesitated. "Your friend being?"

"General Giap."

"What?"

Vivienne burst out laughing. "No, no, silly. A friend I went to school with in Saigon. She's like a sister to me. I want to let her know how I'm doing without having the letter read before she gets it. People in American prisons get to write letters, don't they?" Watching him, she said, "And no, it's not about the Lon Be film."

Quint had the spooky feeling that she had told the truth the first time. She was sending something to General Giap, or at least somebody working for Giap. Was this it then? Was he being sucked into some kind of spy game? Quint finished the last of the mushrooms and began peeling a hand of ginger.

She watched him, waiting for an answer. "You'll do it then?"

He started cutting the ginger into matchstick strips.

She said, "Return letters will be forwarded through an address in San Francisco. If you receive mail from Hong Kong either here or at the newspaper, it will be read before you get it."

"These the right size?" Quint held up the strips of ginger.

"That's it."

They worked in silence for a full minute.

Quint felt Vivienne's thigh brush against his. She smelled delicious. "Oh hell, yes, I'll do it."

"Oh, thank you, Jim." Vivienne gave him a kiss. "You know, I told you that it's not proper to put your hands on a Vietnamese girl in public. I didn't say anything about what they do in private."

"No?" He rested his hand on her rump and pulled her to him.

Her lips brushed his as she unfastened her skirt and dropped it to the floor. She snapped the band of her underpants. "I expect you'll want these off too," she said, her lips still against his.

"I think so," he said. He waited then cupped her butt with his hands.

"Yes," she breathed.

He did it again. "Take the top off."

She began unbuttoning her blouse with her tongue inside his mouth.

When she was naked, he scooped her up in his arms. "I think the food can wait."

"I agree," she said.

Quint took her into his bedroom and threw her onto the bed.

She looked up at him, watching him undress. "The two of us. Together."

"The two of us." He stepped out of his jeans and slipped inside the heat, and they had gentle sex, leisurely and sustained.

Afterward, they lay back covered in sweat. Quint ran a hand

across her wet breast. "Del offered to literally give you to me—for a price. I want you."

"And I want you, Jim."

"What do we have to do to make it happen?"

"We do nothing. We wait." She turned, pressing her body against his. "When the time comes for you to know the whole story, you'll understand."

He held her close. "But it does have to do with Lon Be?"

"Of course it has to do with Lon Be. What else?" She reached over and squeezed him. "And this has to do with?"

Quint grinned. She was using sex to change the subject. He didn't care. He turned her on her side and ran his tongue down her salty breast, feeling her shudder.

Later, after they ate their Vietnamese supper, Quint drove Vivienne back to the house on Tantalus. As he turned down the driveway, he said, "You've been working on a large canvas until midnight every night. I'm curious. Would you show it to me?"

She hesitated. "Sure. Anything for my favorite voyeur. Why not?"

Vivienne took him into her studio to show him the canvas that was perhaps four feet wide and five feet high. On it, in acrylics, she had blocked out three figures at a table—a man, a woman, and a child—with a crowded Asian street behind them.

Standing behind her, Quint said, "And this one will be about what?"

Vivienne stepped back, studying the canvas. She seemed deep in thought, then suddenly came out of it. Her eyes were bright. "Oh, I forgot." She went into her bedroom and came back with a large, well-stuffed envelope. She said, "Here you go Mr. Postman, I would like you to mail this to my friend at the Hong Kong address."

Quint took the envelope. He thought the war in Vietnam was grotesque, the foolishness of stubborn old men who refused to admit they were wrong. Yet working for an agent of General Giap was another matter entirely. He loved his country and yet. . . .

He looked at the envelope, weighing it. He said, "What if I open it and read it?"

Vivienne looked him in the eye. She said, "You really want to read it?" But that was not her real question. Her real question was: *You really want me?*

"I'll mail it for you," he said.

She cocked her head. "Unopened?"

"Unopened," Quint said. He was not lying. He was in love.

17

WHAT POLITICAL RADICALS and reactionaries of every stripe had in mind by way of media coverage—including such embryonic feminists as Babs and Miki—became clear to Jim Quint when Fred Fielding sent him to cover a convention of the American Legion. Whether or not his sanity had been affected by his service in Vietnam, Col. Del Lambert had been transformed by the military command on Oahu into a military cheerleader for the war. This was partly because of his rank and experience. Partly because he was an articulate and forceful speaker. And partly because he was a Lambert and this was Hawaii.

Quint entered the hall that morning feeling self-conscious, aware that suspicious legionnaires and their guests were staring at his hair, sandals, and mustache. He suspected what they were thinking—screwed again. He wanted to prove them wrong. It was not his job to judge causes. It was his job to report.

As Quint got out his pencil and pad, he spotted Del Lambert on the dais. But of course Lambert would be there—probably every day of the convention—a symbol of military determination and to answer such questions as the legionnaires might have. Pencil in hand, Quint pretended to listen attentively to the keynote speech by the national commander, a schoolteacher from Utah.

It was hard for Quint to keep his eyes off Lambert. He wondered if Lambert had spotted him. Yes, he thought. No. He couldn't tell for sure. Yes. No. The uncertainty of not knowing whether Lambert was watching him, much less of what he was thinking, was maddening.

The schoolteacher spoke about the verities of love of country and the American character; he was animated, passionate, and dramatic.

Quint imagined himself scribbling notes in the Crimea in a choking pall of smoke with muskets popping and cannons thundering, the combatants screaming, shouting, bleeding, dying, pushing forward—a vast confusion of horseless riders and riderless horses. Some colorful standards yet flapped in the breeze. Others lay trampled in the mud and blood. In such a passionate struggle, no hyperbole was excess.

In the high point of his speech, the schoolteacher, arms waving, thundered that in twenty years of teaching school, "always, without exception, my students with short hair were smarter, could run faster, and jump higher than my students with long hair!"

It was just what the legionnaires wanted to hear. The hall erupted in enthusiastic applause.

Quint was aware that the legionnaires around him, grinning in agreement, clapping their hands with gusto, were staring at him.

Suddenly, Lambert smiled. That had been a Lambert kind of declaration. He *was* watching Quint to see his reaction.

At the end of the speechifying, Lambert beckoned Quint to the dais with his hand. Quint ambled up to the front of the room to see what he had on his mind. Lambert said, "How are you going to write this, Jimbo?"

Quint shrugged. "The commander is a big boy. I'll let him say what he wants."

Lambert leaned forward, lowering his voice. "You know what this reminds me of, Jimbo? This is like the marines at Khesanh surrounded by Charlies. The people in this auditorium have got balls. They stand for something. And out there . . ." He gestured scornfully with his hand. "Snot-nosed chickenshits. American Charlies. Your people, pal."

Quint sighed. "Oh boy!"

Lambert's face turned even harder. "By the way, yesterday, you did the dirty deed with my wife. I made you an offer that was fair enough. Get me what I want and I'll give her to you. Turn her over: buns, boobs, and brains. She's yours. But no, you think you're going to get away with making a cuckold out of a Bird colonel in the United States Army? A Green Beret? A Lambert? It's not happening, Jimbo, no way."

A shot of adrenaline coursed through Quint's stomach.

"I know everything my wife does, pal. Everything. I know about your little talk at Ala Moana Center. I know about your front seat fuck and your trip to the North Shore. I know about the romantic evening at your place while I was in Saigon. I can give you a little leeway to build up interest, but I can't let you play hide the hippie sausage without giving me what I want. A deal is a deal. You'll have to be taught a lesson." He grinned broadly.

"And you're the guy to teach it to me," Quint said.

"You'll see."

Quint got back to the city room still pissed at Lambert and more than a little afraid of him. He sat down at his typewriter, thinking. The national commander had made the usual claims and assertions. Loyalty to country. Perseverance in the face of adversity. Understanding history. A great and powerful defender of democracy does not allow itself to be intimidated. Et cetera. Yawn! The line about shorthaired and longhaired students was the juiciest part of his speech.

Quint put the quote in the lead paragraph figuring Fred Fielding would give it the hook and send him a reproving note.

To his shock, Fielding read it, pencil poised, and, showing no emotion whatever turned and handed it to the copy desk. The copy editor read it, raised an eyebrow, glanced Quint's way then at Fielding, and went about his chore of writing a headline for it.

That night, there that quote was, in the lead graph of Quint's story.

The national commander of the American Legion opened the Legion's regional gathering in Honolulu today with a ringing declaration that in his twenty years of teaching school in Salt Lake City, "always, without exception, my students with short

hair were smarter, could run faster, and jump higher than my
students with long hair." The six hundred legionnaires gathered
in the Neil Blaisdel Concert Hall erupted in applause.

The next morning Fried Fielding again sent Jim Quint to the
convention. Quint eased into the rear of the hall, trying to be as
invisible as possible. Like he was going to get away with that.
Dream on, he thought.

Ominously, the legionnaires closed in on him. Quint's mouth
turned dry. He had visions of Paul Newman's Fast Eddie Felson
getting his fingers crushed in *The Hustler*. He glanced up at the
speaker's dais. Del Lambert, back for the second day of the convention, was surveying the floor from his seat at the dais.

A burly man with a crewcut, looking vaguely like Popeye the
Sailor Man, looked at Quint with narrowed eyes. "Are you the
reporter who wrote that story in last night's paper?"

Jesus, Quint thought, what had he gotten himself into? He was
aware that Lambert was watching the scene intently.

Quint eyed the exit. Should he make a break for it and save
his hide? That was impossible. He'd never make it. He didn't go
around sporting the peace symbol, but he knew that the legionnaires regarded it as the footprint of the American chicken. "That
was mine," he admitted.

The legionnaires moved fast. As Quint stepped back, startled,
he could see Lambert lean forward, grinning. They were upon
Quint instantly, a crush of middle-aged white men with big bellies
and short haircuts. But they were not sore at all. No, no, no.
They were jubilant! They slapped his back. They pumped his
hand with enthusiasm. They offered to buy him a drink.

Popeye beamed with approval. "We want you to know we appreciate your story. Ordinarily when one of us tells the truth it
never sees the light of day. To be honest, when we saw your hair
and your mustache yesterday, we thought, 'Here we go again,
another leftie hit man to do a number on us.' But no. You were
a straight arrow. You told the truth without pulling any punches.
We're truly grateful. Thank you."

When they told what they believed was the truth, by God they wanted to see it in the papers. To them, that was respect. It was all they asked. They didn't want reporters to condescend to them and make them appear more civilized and sane than they actually were. Their man had given the hairy, barbarian little chickenshits a verbal finger, and they wanted everybody to hear it.

Quint glanced up at the dais and gave Del Lambert a thumbs up.

Lambert had no idea why such attention was being lavished on Quint by the stalwart hawks of the American Legion, but he grinned broadly and gave him a touché gesture with his forefinger. It was at that moment that Quint understood that facts were a form of costume. Desire interpreted the facts. In the many qualities of passion—of women, students, radicals, Negroes, legionnaires and their supporters, and career military officers—lay Del Lambert's cultural firefights.

THAT NIGHT, WITH too much Primo under his belt, Jim Quint negotiated the late-night traffic on Kapiolani Avenue to Waikiki. He wasn't flat drunk—he didn't have the spins or anything like that—but it was a white-knuckler trip nevertheless. He gripped the steering wheel, told himself not to speed, and concentrated for all he was worth. He wasn't worried about getting busted on a drunk-driving charge; he had filled in for Abner Barnhouse on cops a few times and the people in the police department knew who he was. Cops didn't like spearing reporters for small shit. They wanted to keep their good will.

Finally, Quint made it home and successfully parked his Datsun in his assigned slot.

He went inside and took the preemptive caution of knocking back three aspirin to forestall a headache. He couldn't get his mind off Vivienne, and he knew it wasn't good to go to bed until the alcohol had worked its way through his system. He got out his bong and loaded the bowl with some Maui Wowie. He sat back on his small couch to mellow out and think. That's when he noticed the sliding glass door that opened onto his lanai was open. That was odd. Quint was good about keeping that door closed and latched. His small lanai—maybe twelve feet long by ten feet wide—was good for a modest barbecue and not much else. He had a table with a parasol over it and room for his domed barbecue and that was it. The lanai had a solid wooden fence around it, one of those designs where the boards are alternated on both sides of the rails. People couldn't see in, but the wind could blow through.

It was a warm, balmy night. He decided what the hell, he would move outside and sit in one of the aluminum folding chairs by his table.

He settled in, thinking. He reloaded his pipe. He lit up. It was good weed. Big, green, sticky buds. The aroma was wonderful. On top of the beer, the smoke was something else.

Suddenly, Quint realized that Del Lambert was standing in front of him. How long had he been there? Quint had no idea.

Lambert said, "I made you a good faith offer, but you didn't listen. I've got people watching my wife, you dumb son of a bitch. You screwed Vivienne three times, pal. Once in the front seat of your car like a goddam teenager. And twice more in this little chickenshit apartment. That's not to mention keying my car. And don't try to deny it, asshole. I know better. A peeping fucking tom hanging out in the shadows getting your cookies off! Where is your sense of honor, for Christ's sake? I offered you a quid pro quo. If you want the lady, earn her. Get me what I want, but there'll be no more poaching on my property or hanging out in the bushes. I want to make that abundantly clear. Do you un-derfuckingstand?!"

Lambert grabbed Quint by the hair and jerked him to his feet. He threw him against the fence, knocking the wind out of him. Lambert was upon Quint in a fury, hammering his stomach and face. He gave Quint a terrible blow to the side of his head. He hit him flush on his face.

Quint couldn't breathe. He couldn't shout. He couldn't defend himself. The blows kept coming. The pain, the pain! Lambert teed off on his crotch, a horrific kick. Quint, grabbing himself, fell to his knees, gasping, frozen by pain, his eyes wide with pain.

Lambert busted him flush on the chin. He was a soldier and knew how to fight, which was full bore, no punches pulled.

When Lambert had finished, Quint was on his hands and knees, vomiting.

Standing above Quint, looking down, he said, "I'll call you at the end of the month. In the meantime, stay the hell away from my wife if you don't fancy a broken jaw. All those wires and stuff. Having to suck your food through a straw. No damn good, pal. I say again, get me what I want, and you can have the devious, treacherous, lying bitch. Take her. She's yours. You hear me? You understand what I'm saying? An address or telephone number will do the trick."

Quint burbled an incoherent reply, nearly choking on blood and vomit.

"What's that? She trying to use you as a go-between is she?"

Quint shook his head.

"She will, give her time. That's why I invited you into this game, you fucking moron, to provide a weak link. When two people know a secret, it's no longer secret."

Quint vomited.

Lambert jumped back. "I'll tell Vivienne what I did here tonight and the dangers of you two letting anything like that happen again."

Then, mercifully, Lambert turned and left.

Quint managed to rise to one knee, still *whoooooping* for breath. He had blood all over him. With his testicles still throbbing with pain, he went inside and stared at himself in the bathroom mirror. He spit blood into the sink. He looked like one of those old photographs of Sandy Sadler after going fifteen rounds in one of his storied battles with Willie Pep. Jesus! Already Quint's left eye was swelling shut and his right eye wasn't a whole lot better. His lower lip looked like a burl on an oak tree. He headed for the kitchen and got out the ice. A devious, lying, treacherous bitch, Lambert had called her. Could Lambert be telling the truth?

18

JIM QUINT ARRIVED at work the next day with his left eye swollen shut, a shiner over his right eye, and his lips swollen like sausages. He told his colleagues that he had stupidly gotten into a fracas after emerging from a Korean bar late at night. He had flirted with the wrong woman.

Justified or not, Koreans were notorious for their hot tempers. Hanging out at one of their bars was out of character for Quint, and his friends didn't believe his story for a second. They weren't about to forego the fun of razzing him about what they concluded had really happened—he had gotten his end into the wrong man's wife.

Del Lambert had made his dubious point. Quint knew the swelling in his face would eventually subside, but that didn't mean he was any less in love with Vivienne. It just meant that he'd have to be more careful. For a while, at least, Quint thought it was smart to let sleeping dogs lie. Lambert said he'd tell Vivienne about the beating. Quint believed him. He did not fancy a broken jaw. He and Vivienne would both have to wait until Lambert called the next step of his game.

In the days that followed, Quint did his best to keep his mind off Vivienne and on the news. He was a newspaperman after all.

The polls all said that Eugene McCarthy was well ahead of Lyndon Johnson in the upcoming Wisconsin primary. Stories were surfacing that the administration was considering sending another two hundred thousand men to Vietnam at a cost of $10 billion in the coming year. What would this do to the economy, it was asked. Would the Federal Reserve be forced to raise interest rates? Would taxes be increased? Would Johnson just print more money? On top of that, allegations were surfacing that Defense Secretary Clark Clifford's generals had no idea of how long the war might continue. A year? Two years? When? Nobody could agree. In short, it looked like Johnson might have to keep the butter of his great society in the refrigerator for an indefinite period of time.

The pugnacious Secretary of State Dean Rusk was a resolute hawk. Vice President Hubert Humphrey, clinging pathetically to Papa Johnson's increasingly insubstantial shirttails, pretended to be one. But if media accounts of debate within the administration were accurate, closet doves were surfacing everywhere in the administration and on Capitol Hill, including Defense Secretary Clark Clifford himself. In the Senate, Richard Russell, the conservative chairman of the Senate Armed Services Committee, and a formerly reliable hawk, and Sen. Henry M. Jackson were reported to be expressing their reservations in private.

Everybody, it seemed, wanted out. But the problem remained, how to achieve peace with honor? Nobody screwed over Uncle Sam and got away with it. How was the country to withdraw from Vietnam without conceding defeat? Any politician who had ever read a history book knew what happened to reputations tarred by the brush of cowardice. Victory in war was widely regarded as a president's ticket to immortality. No president yet had suffered defeat. The rising count of young men being shipped home in black bags had one of two effects on their families and loved ones. There were those who wanted a vigorous prosecution of the war out of a need for revenge and vindication, and those who were enraged that their husband or son had been sacrificed in such a dubious cause. Almost nobody was neutral.

The president announced that Gen. Westmoreland would be returning to the Pentagon to become the army chief of staff. His deputy, Gen. Creighton Abrams, would replace him as commander in Vietnam. Was this a signal of a coming change of policy? Nobody knew, or at least nobody was talking.

One radical possibility, that Johnson might just say to hell with it and withdraw from the presidential race, had been broached at the Round Table for the last two weeks, but put aside as being impossible. Johnson had an intimidating reputation. He was an alpha male in the extreme. He was powerful. He was indomitable. He was a punisher and bully. Nobody crossed him and got away with it. Not politicians. Not journalists. He was like a macho Hispanic boxer, who lowered his head and kept punching, oblivious to the punishment he might be taking. Johnson's manhood was on the line.

Two days before the April 2 primary in Wisconsin—and still no call to Quint from Lambert—Quint received a letter with a San Francisco postmark that he knew was from Vivienne's mysterious correspondent.

Later the wire services began moving a stunner. Lyndon Johnson had gone on television at 9 P.M. Eastern Standard Time to tell his amazed countrymen of his irrevocable decision to withdraw from the race for the presidency. Just like that, without warning or fanfare, he quit. For most people, the far-out notion that *el gran toro de Texas* Lyndon Baines Johnson might throw in the towel and cry *no mas* was so out of character as to be unthinkable. But there it was.

At the time, Eugene McCarthy was delivering yet another colorless speech at Carroll College in Waukesha, near Milwaukee, which was one hour behind Washington time. At 8:44 P.M., the hall erupted in tumult and the reporters charged the stage with the news. The political David who had fought the odds and brought down the towering Goliath from Johnson City was given a chance to make a speech of a lifetime. The moment was incendiary. Here was an opportunity to ignite the passion of his followers and lead the charge onward and upward to victory.

But Eugene McCarthy apparently lacked the fire. He simply said, "It's a surprise to me. Things have gotten rather complicated." That said, he quietly left the stage, abandoning a hall filled with cheering supporters sure he would be president.

JIM QUINT LEFT the Columbia Inn that afternoon with a slight buzz on. Quint didn't feel like hanging around bullshitting about Johnson's amazing decision, so he negotiated the traffic to his diminutive pad near the Ala Wai canal on the backside of Waikiki. When he stepped inside, the phone was ringing. He grabbed the receiver. It was Del Lambert.

"Hey, Jimbo. How's everything hanging?"

Quint said, "It's still there."

"How's your face?"

"Swelling went down. No broken bones or missing teeth."

"And your balls? That was like punting a couple of apricots with the top of my foot. Fun!"

"They're okay too," Quint said.

"I'm a professional at dispensing violence. The trick was to make my point but leave your face pretty for Vivienne to admire. At least you paid attention to my lesson."

"Yeah, right," Quint said.

"Enough death and disaster to keep those papers moving? I take it you've been getting the news on the wire service machines about that big ol' Texas quitter! Can you believe that? I just have to tell you, pal, that has to be wonderful for the morale in Nam. The boys out there getting shot while their commander in chief turns chickenshit on them."

"Maybe Johnson had brains enough to know when he was licked," Quint said.

"Have you had anything to eat yet, or have you been spending the afternoon getting loaded at the Columbia Inn?"

"I'm pretty tanked."

Lambert said, "Listen, why don't you come up for supper tonight? When the tapes come in from the mainland, we can watch Johnson's resignation speech on the box. He'll be looking like a big, sad old dog with somebody standing on his ear. I got the best damn brandy the PX has to offer."

Quint couldn't help himself. He wanted to see Vivienne. "Well, sure, I don't know why not. If it isn't any imposition on Vivienne."

Lambert laughed. "Imposition? Oh, no, no. She'll be all for it. We both know that. Just hop in that piece of crud you call a car and come on up. You never know what might happen."

"I'm on my way."

"I thought so," Lambert said. "Bring the address."

"What address?"

"Or phone number. Either one will do."

"I don't know what you're talking about."

"Aw fuck, Jimbo. Don't give me that crap. What do you take me for?" Lambert hung up.

19

JIM QUINT DROVE up Tantalus Drive for his second evening with Del and Vivienne Lambert thinking that whatever else happened in 1968 the stunning political reversal of fortunes that day would rate a check on any cynic's calendar of memorable days. He had read most of the amazing wire service stories that had been arriving all afternoon, but his mind was not on Lyndon Johnson. What did Col. Del Lambert have in mind for Quint and Vivienne that evening? Another strip and kiss? That seemed anticlimatic. If not that, sweet Jesus, then what?

Or maybe sexual didn't cover the mystery of the unfolding drama. Sexual was only part of it. The labyrinth of the human imagination was complicated. So too was Quint's situation.

He was intensely curious about what Lambert would make of the news arriving from the mainland. Would this turn of events mean a dramatic change in American policy toward the war? Hard to tell.

It occurred to Quint as he rounded a corner and spotted the lights of Del Lambert's house up ahead, that Lambert might be right—the obsessed and self-conscious combatants were groping in the darkness of ignorance and denial. The territory of the sexual and the political were tangled in more complicated and obscure ways than most people imagined or were willing to concede: desire, pride, competition, control, domination, submission, and all those mysterious, unfathomable fetishes and practices that so afflicted human imagination.

Quint parked his car and took his time walking up the curved flagstone path. He would not retreat. Could not. He took a deep breath and punched the bell.

Del Lambert looked enthusiastic as he answered the door. "Jimbo, come on in! Welcome to my house and mine."

Behind Lambert, Vivienne waited in a tight black miniskirt and a nearly translucent white blouse.

"Hello, Jim," she said.

Watching Quint's eyes, Lambert turned to admire his wife. "What do you think, Jim? No bra and a see-through blouse. Very fashionable. Like those chocolate nips? Sexy stuff."

Vivienne's eyes clouded. It was one thing for Lambert to throw Vivienne together with Quint and watch the result as a form of erotic sport. Vivienne had been raised to be modest. Chocolate nips? Her eyes clouded. "He embarrasses himself, not me."

Quint said, "You have a beautiful wife, Colonel."

Lambert said, "All you have to do is take a walk down Waikiki, and you'll see a whole lot more than she's showing. If it's okay for hippie girls to walk around half naked, why not Vivienne? I figure she might as well be in fashion. I know you've been thinking about her. I know what that's all about. I couldn't get her off my mind the first time I laid eyes on her."

Quint wanted to change the subject. "I take it you've been listening to the radio this afternoon for all the wonderful news."

"Yes, I have," Lambert said. He sighed deeply. "Lyndon Johnson. Just ran up the flag just like that. Turned in his piece. Embarrassed himself. He and Lloyd Bucher. Here, you want my ship, take it. Here, you want to win the war, do it without me. Take my balls and play ping-pong with them. Two maximum chickenshits in one year. Hard to believe."

"President Guns and Butter," Quint said.

"President No Balls."

"You like Gene McCarthy or Bobby Kennedy any better?"

Lambert laughed. "Neither Eugene McCarthy or Bobby Kennedy will ever be elected president of the United States. The country will vote for whoever will lead us to victory. People want strength in a leader."

"Happy Hubie then. He's a jolly warrior."

Lambert scowled. "Humphrey is a mama's boy who has spent the last four years clinging to Papa Johnson's shirttails. I can live with Richard Nixon. He knows how the world works. He understands that war is an extension of politics."

"Or the other way around."

"That too. One thing Nixon isn't and that's a quitter, which is a good sign. He nailed that pecker Alger Hiss, didn't he? Hiss had been delivering State Department secrets to Joe Stalin and Nixon knew it. He never gave up until he took him under."

"With the help of Whittaker Chambers," Quint said.

"Nixon will promise to end the war, of course; he'll have to do that to get elected. But one thing he's not is a quitter. And he understands the consequences of defeat. We cannot allow ourselves to be defeated if we hope to remain a world power."

"World power," Quint said. "Can't forget that."

Lambert shook his head sadly. He thought a moment then perked up. "Of course, I predicted this in a way, didn't I? I told you this was going to be some kind of year. The civil war is getting worse. You got an idea of how people feel at the American Legion convention. They're getting fed up with posturing Negroes and the little chickenshits in the streets. I was there. I saw it."

AFTER SUPPER THEY adjourned to Lambert's book-lined library for more talk about the war, Eugene McCarthy, Bobby Kennedy, the polls in Wisconsin, the radicals, the draft-card burners, the incendiary mood of the country, and Lyndon Johnson's decision to quit.

For Quint, the uncertain, provocative mystery of the emerging triangle, a tangle of human desire, loomed above everything. It was a mystery only to him. Vivienne knew precisely what her husband was after. Lambert was clearly proceeding according to some kind of plan that, however twisted or deviant to other people, apparently made sense to him. He was the inspired author of the script. It was as though Quint, a character in whatever demented fantasy that gripped Lambert's imagination, was an actor awaiting the lines and cues.

But Vivienne was another story. She knew exactly what Lambert was doing and why.

As Quint watched Lambert pour brandy, he said, "No offense, Del, but it has always struck me that while you soldiers make a big thing out of pledging your fealty to God and country, the truth is you understand and appreciate it the least."

"Oh, you think that, do you?" Lambert said. "You like the brandy?"

"Yes, good stuff. A commitment to democracy means an acceptance of ambiguity and all the messiness that goes with it."

Lambert smiled. "We're restless in the face of ambiguity, I'll grant you. We want form and structure. Polished buckles. Shined boots. Barracks all spiffed up." He leaned forward, his eyes intense. "Tell me, Jimbo, if push came to shove who would you trust to put his life on the line to protect your right to mouth off, a guy with shined boots and a haircut or a sport wearing sandals and beads around his neck?"

"Good point," Quint said. "What do you think, Vivienne?"

Vivienne said, "I would want soldiers who know right from wrong, soldiers who have the courtesy not to insert themselves into somebody else's fight."

Lambert didn't like that one damn bit.

Vivienne pressed forward. "Or even soldiers who are smart enough to know when they're in a fight they can't win."

Lambert looked at his wife with heavy, lizard's eyes. "You think the VC are righteous patriots, do you, Vivienne?"

"You asked the question," Vivienne said mildly.

"Lucky you kept your mouth shut at the INS interview." Lambert stood. "Before we watch Johnson I want to give you both something to think about. I've got it all set up outside. Come on."

As he followed Lambert onto the deck, Quint slipped Vivienne the letter from San Francisco, and her face lit with delight. "Thank you for being civilized," she whispered.

LAMBERT STOOD AND led the way onto the wide deck overlooking the city where he had erected a screen and a slide projector. On the table by the slide projector in front of the screen
was a small, carved wooden box decorated with elaborate designs
on what looked like ivory and a sleek pistol designed like a
German Luger. The three of them sat in darkness on the wide
screened lanai overlooking Honolulu. The crickets trilled. The air
smelled sweet. A gentle, warm breeze washed across their bodies.
Below them, the city lights were grand.

Lambert paused, thinking. "Tell me, Jim, do you know anything about air rifles?"

Quint shrugged. "I had a BB gun when I was a kid."

"You any good?"

"Well, I don't know. I grew up on a Montana farm. Nothing
to do except torment squirrels and tweety birds."

Lambert scowled. "I don't mean a fucking Daisy BB gun. I'm
talking about a high-precision German-made competition weapon
that fires one point seven-seven caliber pellets per second from a
rifled barrel at seven hundred feet."

Quint blinked. "I don't know anything about competition guns,
that's true."

"Weapons. They're weapons."

"Weapons," Quint said.

"I first got acquainted with them at the Citadel. I was the
captain of the shooting team. We beat the fuck out of the cadets
at West Point and VMI and the midshipmen at Annapolis. It's
now in the Olympics. Great sport. I got this idea of a combination
slide show and demonstration of what an air pistol can do. Nice
warm night. Let's have a little fun, what do you say? You game?"

"Do we have a choice?" Quint asked.

Lambert laughed. "Sit, you two. Sit, sit. I'll run the slide
show." He gestured toward two aluminum deck chairs with web
seats and backs. He picked up the pistol. "This little pistol is a
Beeman, German-made. They make them with CO_2 cartridges,
but they don't have any pop. Each time you shoot, the pressure

gets weaker. What's fun about a Beeman is that you can pump up enough pressure to sink a pellet an inch deep in a pine tree. Not bad." The pistol had a pump on the bottom of the barrel. Lambert gave it a half dozen quick pumps. Grinning to himself, he aimed it at the deck and fired.

Whack! The pellet disappeared into the wood. "See what I mean. But if you don't give it any pressure it won't have a lot of pop. Here, let me show you." Lambert gave the pistol a leisurely quarterly pump and aimed it at the screen. He pulled the trigger and the pellet looped toward the screen and bounced off, falling to the deck.

Lambert opened the carved box and took it to Quint. He opened it wider. Inside were a packet of cigarettes and some large green marijuana buds. Lambert grinned. "Maui Wowie. Surprised?" He smelled the buds, inhaling deeply. "Mmmmm." He handed the box to Quint. "Take a whiff."

Quint did. "Nice."

Lambert sat in the third chair and began rolling a joint. "The bud in Nam isn't as good as this. Full of seeds and stems."

"Like Mexican butt rush," Quint said.

Lambert held up a bud. "But this! This is a proper bud. Whoever grew it had brains enough to yank the male plants. No seeds."

"*Sensemilla,*" Quint said.

"There you go." Lambert finished the joint. He lit up and took a drag, holding his breath. He passed it to Quint. Quint took a hit.

"Her too," Lambert said.

Vivienne looked alarmed. "I've never done this."

"Do it," Lambert ordered.

Vivienne hesitated, then took a tentative draw. She began coughing.

Lambert released the smoke from his lungs. "You'll get the hang of it, sweetness. You think you and your hippie friends are the only ones who smoke, Jimbo? The grunts in Nam do it to survive the horseshit. Hard to blame them." He took another hit, and passed it to Quint. "Nice night isn't it? The warm air. The city down below." Still holding smoke in his lungs, he said, "I looked up your military record, Jim. Easy enough to do. At least you went in. I respect you for that. You were drafted and wound up at Fort Holabird, Maryland, learning how to interpret reconnaissance photographs. As you probably figured, I'm a graduate of the Bird too." He released the smoke. "Good weed. Vivienne?"

Lambert waited while Vivienne took another drag on the joint, which was close to becoming a roach. Holding it with her fingernails to keep from burning her fingers, she took another tentative draw, again coughing, but less this time.

Lambert took the roach and set about rolling another joint. "The real fun was in the classic spook courses. There were courses in photography. Courses in clandestine listening devices. Courses in surveillance techniques. Courses in locks. The whole smear. The classes in battlefield interrogations were especially wonderful. The idea was Americans wear the white hats, see, so instructors couldn't teach us practices employed by unrespectable black hats. How they got around that problem was telling us in gross detail all the god-awful things the Japanese and Germans did to their prisoners to get them to talk. This was the T-word, torture, baaaad, baaaad shit. But we don't do those things, see. We've got morals and a conscience and all that. The instructors couldn't even wink."

Lambert lit the new joint and took a drag. "One of the most effective techniques, a mixing of the threatening and the sympathetic, went by a variety of names. I like to call it strawberries and dingleberries." He exhaled. "The deal is, Jimbo, now that I've dealt you in on the action, I've got two people to break. Either one of you can give me what I want."

Stoned, Quint and Vivienne sat in silence.

Lambert watched them with lizard's eyes. Finally he said, "One of the first things an intelligence operative learns is the importance of knowing the daily routines of the enemy. Take you for instance, Jimbo. Every day at three o'clock you go over to the

Columbia Inn and sit around a round table bullshitting with your friends. Including you, there are seven regulars at what you call the Round Table."

He picked up the Beeman and gave it four quick pumps. Then he picked up the control of the slide projector and punched it on. He tapped it again and on the screen popped a middle-aged, curly-haired man entering the Columbia Inn. "This is your friend Jerry Fortier who writes those editorials nobody reads." Lambert snapped a quick shot at the screen. He giggled. "Square between the eyes. I told you I know how to shoot." He tapped the control again.

Up jumped a skinny man with a long face leaving the side entrance of the *Star-Bulletin*. "This is your friend, Phil Mayer, the wannabe Wobblie." Lambert gave the pistol a quick three pumps and snapped off a shot. A hole appeared in the middle of Mayer's forehead. "Pow! Got 'im. Deader 'n fuck. Great sport, eh, Jimbo?"

A man with a high forehead, pointed nose, odd mouth, and huge belly made an appearance, climbing out of his car. Lambert recharged his pistol. "This is the loud, vulgar drunk Albert Barnhouse, who covers cops. A human tanker. If I shot him in the gut, he'd squirt Primo. Bang! You're dead." He put a neat hole in the side of Barnhouse's neck.

Quint watched this, floating.

Next on the screen was a grinning man with a balding head wearing a blue and white flowered aloha shirt, jeans, and desert boots. "Your special pal, Steve Sanger, the only guy Frank Fasi will talk to." Lambert took a thoughtful hit on the joint, studying the image on the screen. He put the joint down and re-pumped his pistol. "What would you think if somebody just fucking wasted your friend Steve just for the hell of it? Just because it could be done." He took a slow, deliberate aim and snapped a hole in Sanger's left eye. He looked at Quint with a lazy smile. "I just bet that would piss you off, wouldn't it? No damn telling what you would do to catch the bastard who did it." Lambert looked at once dreamy, drifty, and amused. Then he perked up. "You think women are exempt? No, no, no." He recharged the pistol.

A curly-haired woman with a large bosom and thick rimmed eyeglasses took her turn on the screen, walking down the sidewalk toward the Columbia Inn. "Here we've got Babs Parsegian." Lambert put a hole in the side of Babs's head. He cranked the pump. "And one more. Sexy Miki Hasegawa who writes those lengthy, serious pieces that take up half the newspaper."

Miki Hasegawa, a sensual looking Japanese-American did look sexy walking to the Columbia Inn with Quint, looking up at him with large flirtatious eyes. Lambert drilled a hole in her heart. He turned off the projector. "Hey, here you go. Plenty of this left." He passed the joint to Quint.

Already stoned, Quint took another hit. Holding his breath, he looked down at the city lights.

Lambert checked his wristwatch. "Oops, almost eleven. Time to watch the news." He pumped the pistol with a carefully measured quarter stroke. He aimed the pistol at his wife's chest. Without a word he snapped off a shot, and quickly re-pumped the pistol.

Vivienne howled in pain, grabbing her breast.

Quint jumped to his feet.

Lambert aimed the pistol at Quint's face. "Ah, ah, value your eyes? You don't think I'd do it? Try me." He grinned. "Smart does it, Vivienne? Right on the nip. I gave it enough pressure to make you feel it, but not enough to break the skin. That's why I bought you that blouse. Wanted to be able to see my target, a nice, brown bulls-eye."

Vivienne looked up at him, tears welling up.

Lambert cocked his head. "Chickenshit stunt, you say. Pissed you off? Lesson learned. Both of you. You know every time I get stoned, I think I'm a reincarnation of George Patton. There was a man who knew what life was all about. Patton would tell you that to understand the meaning of the Vietnam War, you have to pay some attention to history, back to Franklin Roosevelt's refusal to listen to Winston Churchill. Patton anticipated the Communists. He knew what they had in mind after the war. He wanted to kick ass and keep on rolling while the ass kicking was good but Ike said no. The Russians were our allies. People were tired of war. The country was worn out. Well, by God, look at what happened. And look here? Another hit left in this roach."

"You need a clip," Quint said.

Lambert shook his head. "If a man can't take the heat, he shouldn't be smoking a joint. By God, I sound like Harry Truman." Amused, Lambert held the roach by his fingernails and took a last drag. With smoke in his lungs, he said, "All you reporters can think about is how many people were killed the day before. Well, let me tell you there's far more to war than any goddam body count. If you expect to learn anything about a military struggle, you have to understand its origins. You begin with territory and turf, which is what war is all about. One or the other of you two will either give me what I want or both of you will learn more about warfare than you ever dreamed. A good soldier has discipline. You two have been thrown in together. Let's see if you've got any discipline. I tell you what I'm gonna do, Vivienne. If you sit straight at me, hands at your side, I'll see if I can't hit the center of your other tit. If you flinch, I try for Jim's eye. It might not put it out, but it could do some real damage. Face me, girl, let's see what you're made of."

"Hey!" Quint said.

Lambert aimed the pistol at his face. "Shut up!"

"It's okay. It's okay, Jim. Let him do what he thinks he has to do."

Lambert smiled. "Well, that's a good little soldier. Hands down. Sit up straight. Chest out."

Vivienne did as she was told.

Lambert aimed the pistol at her breast, making her wait, "Fun, huh, Jimbo?"

Quint was amazed by Vivienne's remarkable calm.

Vivienne bit her lower lip and pushed her chest out farther, challenging him.

Lambert pulled the trigger.

She stiffened, but remained silent.

Lambert put the pistol down and clapped. "All right. Discipline. The little lady's tough as nails."

"Tough as the Vietcong?" Quint asked mildly.

"Oh, yes. She's got the stuff." Lambert grabbed his pot box. "You think you could sit there like that, Jimbo?"

"No," Quint said.

"I agree. She's not the link that'll give first. That will be you. What do you say we smoke another joint while we watch the news? Only way to watch a man castrate himself." He looked at Vivienne, whose eyes were glistening with tears. "Oh, go ahead, rub your tits if you want."

Vivienne shook her head. "No need. They don't hurt." She stood, regarding her husband as though he were an animal in a zoo. "There's no feeling as good as winning. Isn't that what you're always telling me, Del?"

20

THEY SETTLED INTO Del Lambert's study to watch the resignation on television, but they were ten minutes early. Lambert gave the air pistol two quick pumps. Leaving it in his lap, he rolled another joint and insisted they all smoke.

Quint murmured to Vivienne, "You okay?" He was still amazed by her bravery. He suspected she was tough as nails, but now he regarded her with renewed respect.

"Rub them," Lambert told her.

"I told you they don't hurt," she said.

"She's stubborn as hell, Jimbo. You'll learn that." Lambert took another hit and passed it to Quint. "You know we've got a lot of down time on our hands there in Saigon. Nothing to do but sit around and drink and smoke dope and play cards. In addition to that, I've been reading. Here, I want you to listen to this. I memorized it just for you. 'The goal of man and society should be human independence: a concern not with image or popularity but with finding a meaning in life that is personally authentic. We would replace power rooted in possession, privilege, or circumstance, by power and uniqueness rooted in love, reflectiveness, reason, and creativity.' Who is that, do you know? Jim? Jim?"

Quint shook his head no, wishing Lambert would shut up.

"That's Tom Hayden's Port Huron Statement, a manifesto he wrote for the Students for a Democratic Society in 1962—the hippie Declaration of Independence. Isn't that a kick? Jim?"

Quint was having a hard time staying focused. "A real blast."

"That's the same SDS that passed out leaflets in Waikiki urging soldiers to frag their officers in Vietnam. Quite a leap. Jesus! By the way, I am aware that you two can't keep your minds off one another. After we watch Johnson resign, I'll take the two of you to the bedroom so you can give one another such succor and comfort as you please. Give Vivienne a chance to give herself some relief. What do you say to that?" He looked at Quint.

Quint said nothing.

"My treat. I require just one thing before you go home to-night."

Quint took a hit on the joint. Holding his breath, he said, "And that would be?"

"That Vivienne tell you about Genevieve. We'll take this one fact at a time until we eventually arrive at the truth."

"No," she said.

"Or Jim goes home with one eye." He aimed the pistol at Quint's face.

"Genevieve is my sister," she said.

Lambert said, "A Charlie."

Vivienne narrowed her left eye. "You don't know that."

"I've got a damn good idea," Lambert said. "Your pretty lady's sister is a VC, Jimbo. Vietcong. You see what you're getting yourself into? You're way in over your head. Thinking through your dick can do that."

On the tube, Chet Huntley gave way to an image of a grave President Johnson, sitting behind his desk in the oval office.

Lambert said, "Oh, oh, here we go." He put the pistol down.

LYNDON JOHNSON HAD originally become president only because the prince of Camelot was felled by an assassin's bullet. Whereas the handsome John Kennedy had been stylish and elegant, Johnson was an old shoe of a figure, something for which he had never been truly forgiven. He had long been an admirer of Franklin D. Roosevelt, who had seen the country through the Great Depression, and as senate majority leader he had been a famous arm twister and dealmaker. As president, he had modeled his great society after Roosevelt's New Deal. There were men who had achieved power without loving it so obviously as Johnson. He relished it. He gloried in it. He had pursued it with passion and determination.

The country, deprived of the charming John Kennedy, had never warmed to Lyndon Johnson's Texas drawl, but now, what had once been a lack of enthusiasm had turned into raw hatred. Television comics mimicked the way Johnson pronounced Negro. Try as Johnson might, and as well intentioned as he was, Negro in his mouth always came out "nigra," somewhere between "knee-grow" and the ungracious, inflammatory N word.

Johnson's hopes for a legacy of a great society had been dashed by a foreign misadventure that was out of his control. He routinely manhandled Congress with his determination. He would politically screw a senator without a twinge of regret. He would literally yell at a congressman. He would call up a newspaper reporter or network correspondent and chew him out. But the war. The goddamned war. Other presidents had used war to secure a place in the history books. Lyndon Johnson had ended up impotent and humiliated, trapped in the White House.

Johnson stared gravely out at his countrymen with sorrowful, squinty little eyes, looking unloved, and suddenly aged in defeat. The deepening lines in his forehead looked like great cracks of mud. His huge earlobes looked ridiculous. His long, solemn face was morose and haggard. There were few sights more sad and pathetic than a neutered bully. The old fire and resolution were gone. He looked like an old hound with false teeth.

Johnson began his speech with those five familiar words in that awful accent that had become a national joke. He had started out as a Texan with a cracker accent, and a Texan with a cracker accent he would finish. To change his accent now would be to relinquish all pride.

He touched his large beak with his hand. His fleshy lips began to move. "Good evenin', mah fellah Amuricans, Ah come to you tonight . . ."

AFTER WATCHING JOHNSON'S humiliation, Del Lambert punched off the television set in disgust then sat for a moment shaking his head. Then, he said, as if he could hardly believe it, "He quit. The son of a bitch just quit. Our commander in chief."

"He did that," Quint said.

Vivienne said, "Maybe he didn't think war was worth fighting or it can't be won. Let somebody else deal with it."

Lambert blinked. "What did you say?"

"I think you probably heard me the first time."

Lambert said, "Here I thought the night was going pretty well, then you had to go and pull a stunt like that. I know you're a Vietnamese citizen, Vivienne. But while you're holding a green card, a guest of the United States, and you live in my house, you will, I say again, will keep such opinions to yourself."

She shrugged. "You don't even know who you're fighting. How do you propose to win?"

"It was the shot on the tit that's bringing all this out. I understand that." Lambert stood. "Well, shall we do it then? A little time alone for you two peaceniks?"

"We'll take what we can get," Quint said.

Holding hands, Quint and Vivienne followed Lambert through the house.

Lambert opened the door to the master bedroom, and they stepped inside, standing in the darkness. Lambert flipped a toggle switch, bathing the room in light. "Well, this is it, Jimbo."

Quint looked around at the bedroom that was dramatic in the erotic sense, being organized around a king-sized bed under a ceiling mirror. The headboard was made of a red hardwood, twisted with a wild grain and studded by knots, knotholes, knobs, and polished burls; the same wood was used to top the night stands that were the preserved feet of elephants. From above the headboard, the mounted head of a white mountain goat with enormous curved horns looked down with baleful, brown eyes. Other than an ebony vanity covered with Vivienne's things, the shelves were all built into one wall along with a walk-in closet. At the window overlooking Honolulu was a wide, broad couch made of tropical hardwood streaked with green, yellow, and red, and upholstered in black leather. The cherry wood floor was scattered with oriental carpets. There were no canopies, lace, or pink here. The room was Lambert. Nothing suggested Vivienne.

"Well, what do you think?" Lambert asked.

"I like the goat," Quint said. "They've got those in Montana."

Lambert walked over and pressed down hard on the mattress with the palm of his hand. "Vivienne swore to love, honor, and obey me. I own her by right of legal document. If you want her, you have to either give me what I want or summon up the nuts to take her. Like it or not there, Jimbo, you've gone and got yourself ass-deep in the Vivienne War. I won't let you have her without satisfaction. You can regard me as Ho Chi Minh if you want." Lambert gave a good-natured laugh. "Isn't that a kick? I like it."

"Real sport," Quint said.

"Who knows, maybe you'll even learn something?" Lambert sat on the bed and bounced up and down. "King-sized. Plenty of room for you two to have a good time. Don't be bashful. Come on over." He motioned with his hand.

Quint and Vivienne walked to the edge of the bed.

Lambert said, "All in love are we? Anxious? Eager to get on with it? Jim loves Vivienne. Vivienne loves Jim. Freethinking hippie longhaired prick and his Vietnamese beauty. Another man's wife. You're together with my blessing, remember. This is what your leftie professors like to call a 'moratorium' in the battle. Don't let anybody ever say Del Lambert isn't a gracious host. An officer and a gentleman."

"Right," Quint said.

Softly, Vivienne said, "You want us to think of you as Ho Chi Minh. You think you're as honorable as Ho?" She looked disbelieving.

Lambert strolled over to the full-length mirror on the bathroom door. "I thought about the best way to do this. I came up with a hell of an idea. Very creative." He tapped the mirror with his forefinger.

Vivienne blinked.

"I know you've been wondering what this is all about, Vivienne. Why would I install a two-way mirror on the door to the john?" He grinned broadly. "I did it so I could watch the sport. I even hooked up a mike and some speakers under your bed so I could talk to you while you have fun. Sort of like a color commentator." He looked at Jim. "You get to have your fun while I watch and then go home twisting with envy, knowing that anytime I want I can throw her on her back and have my way. She's mine, not yours. You want her do you, Jimbo?"

Quint licked his lips.

Lambert said, "Vivienne, tell me again what the Buddhists say about unhappiness."

"Unhappiness is caused by desire," she murmured.

"You two have a good time now." Lambert hopped off the bed and turned off the lights, plunging the room into darkness. Then he flipped on four spotlights mounted on the ceiling. These bathed the wide bed in a dim light. Saying no more, he disappeared into the bathroom and closed the mirrored door behind him.

Quint drew Vivienne close and held her.

Eerily, from the speakers beneath the bed, Lambert said, "You know, it was Vivienne's name that got me to thinking about my deal with you. *Vivre* is the French verb to live. That has to be the origin of Vivienne. Vivienne is life. She comes from life. She gives life. She is sweet. She is beautiful. She is desirable above everything else. Life! She is to be appreciated and embraced. You speak French?"

"A little Spanish."

"The French verb 'to live' is *vivre*. The Spanish equivalent is *Vivir. Vivre!* There's some Vietnam in Vivienne too. Viv-ienne. Vie-etnam."

Watching Quint, her eyes large, Vivienne quietly slipped out of her skirt, followed by her blouse.

From under the bed, Lambert's voice said, "Atta girl. You've got a real pair there. Show him what you've got. Remember, Jim, she's yours for keepsies if you give me what I want, physically take her by force, or convince me that I'm wrong. Those are your only options."

Quint looked at the mirror. "Change your mind?"

"Convince me that I've committed my imagination and energy to a way of life that's finished." He grinned. "But that's like talking to Ho Chi Minh. Ain't gonna happen. You equate length of hair with amount of brains. I agree with the American Legion commander. I say the reverse is true. You do want Vivienne, don't you? She's territory. Loyalty. Victory. She belongs to old Ho Chi Lambert, and you want her. I ask you again. You do want her, don't you?"

"I want her," Quint said.

"You give your readers the ignorant blathering of those kids without knowing anything yourself. You can forget your Karl Marx and Chairman Mao and Bob Dylan. Now you get to learn how the real world works. No firepower in fancy theory. All those professors and radical kids are doing is firing blanks, all noise and smoke and no damn bullets."

"And how is that?"

"Everything ultimately grows out of reproduction and competition, Jimbo. Procreation and violence are at the heart of everything. Sex. Creativity. The push for territory. The drive for power. Demonstrations of prowess. No theory there. Look around you. Bugs. Birds. Fish. Everywhere the same. If a man wants something badly enough, he'll take it. He who has, defends. That's why I'm putting you two on the bed tonight. That's where it all starts. Charlie Darwin figured that out a hundred and fifty years ago. It's not pretty. It's not uplifting. In fact, it's downright ugly. But it's the truth. Hell, even that big horned sheep up behind the bed knew that when he was alive. That's why I put it up there behind the bed. To remind me that procreation and violence are the yin and the yang of universal desire."

Vivienne slipped off her underpants.

"Beautiful," Lambert said. "Mine."

"Jim's," Vivienne said loudly. "All you have is my name on a piece of paper."

"I own you, a fact you insufficiently appreciate, but go ahead you two. Have some fun. I'll shut my mouth and watch."

"Ignore him," Quint said softly.

"I agree," Vivienne said. She began massaging her breasts. She had a large, ugly welt at the corner of her left nipple and an even worse bruise on her right nipple.

Quint began undressing. "Those still hurt?"

She said, "They'll be okay."

"How did you have the courage to sit there like that and take those shots without flinching? I could hardly believe you did that."

Vivienne smiled, "Del finds it difficult to believe I'm tougher than he is. What he doesn't understand is that I'm defending my country. He's not defending his. The difference is crucial."

Quint drew Vivienne's slender body gently next to him and kissed her.

She broke the kiss momentarily and said, "Really hold me. Don't worry about my breasts. I want to feel the burning."

Quint held her as tightly as he could, mashing her breasts against his chest.

She flinched, sucking in her breath. "Yessssssssss," she breathed. "The bastard."

Their tongues tangled like desperate snakes. Her mouth tasted sweet. They lay back on the bed.

Quint said, "Genevieve is the one who . . ."

Quickly, Vivienne clamped her hand over his mouth. She gripped his hand and slid it under the pillow.

Quint felt an envelope.

Vivienne whispered. "We will fight him and we will win." She slid her hand up his thigh. "He said we should enjoy ourselves. No sense disappointing him."

"Or ourselves."

"Most of all ourselves." She took him in her hand.

Avoiding Vivienne's sore breasts, Quint laid a trail of kisses down her slender body. In Quint's experience Asian women had little or no body hair and their skin was softer and silkier than European women. Velvet was sandpaper compared to Vivienne's skin. She was small and delicate and unimaginably warm. She squirmed beneath him.

"That's very nice, yes," she murmured.

He reached the pubic hair on Vivienne's mons veneris and rested his hand on the softness of the V.

She put her hand over his. "We are together," she whispered.

"Yes."

Lambert said, "My offer still stands, Jimbo. Give me what I want and she's yours."

She whispered, "No matter what he does we will not yield."

"We will not," he breathed.

"We will not surrender."

"Never," he said.

Vivienne pulled him into her.

Lambert said, "Okay, you're home. Go for it! Both of you. Enjoy. Everything begins and comes together down there in the sweet, sweet V between milady's lovely legs. The coming together in the V down below. The vaginal V. Vortex. Visceral. Volatile. Vital. Victory, Jimbo!"

Beneath Quint, Vivienne stiffened. Quint didn't care if she was working for the Vietcong. He wanted her. He pushed hard against her, thinking *Vainglorious. Venal. Veneer. Vile. Vixen. Vampire. Verboten.*

They relaxed in one another's arms. So warm she was. So very beautiful. Vivienne clung to him. He wanted her so very, very much. Floating in the sweet ebb, Quint thought:

Victim. Vessel. Vouchsafe.

21

*W*HEN AN INCOMING journalistic round—a major story—was on its way, the wire services used an alarm bell to alert editors who were off drinking coffee or bullshitting. A ringing bell on the A wire meant that something bad-ass had happened. A bridge had collapsed. A fire had consumed an apartment building. A killer had run amok. The Chinese were spilling over the border in a presumed invasion of Vietnam.

The green streak final, named for the green streak that ran up the side of the page, sold mostly on the street in Waikiki. At a little before Jim Quint's 2 P.M. deadline for the green streak final of April 4—7 P.M. Central Time on the mainland—the alarm bell began ringing on the A wire of the Associated Press. For most disasters, the bell went off in a modest series of three *bings*, followed by a pause, then three more. The object was to get people's attention, not overdo it. But this was different: *BING, BING, BING, BING, BING, BING!*

The reporters and editors toiling in the city room all looked up. The *binging* continued, unabated. Somebody on the mainland was leaning on the button. Wake the fuck up out there in newspaper and radio land!

BING, BING, BING, BING, BING, BING!

Carl Zimmerman bent over the A wire, reading the copy as it inched out of the machine. "Jesus Christ!"

BING, BING, BING, BING, BING, BING!

Fielding, editing furiously at the city desk, turned, scowling. "Well, what is it?"

Zimmerman looked up and licked his lips. "Somebody shot

Martin Luther King, Jr. in Memphis, Tennessee. He died in the hospital." He continued reading.

BING, BING, BING, BING, BING, BING!

If the city room had been deserted for any odd reason, the paper would have gone to bed minus the news of the assassination of the Rev. Dr. Martin Luther King, Jr. If that had happened, the green streak final would have been famous among newspapermen for what it had *not* included—a sinful journalistic omission. But the *Honolulu Star-Bulletin* was a newspaper famous for handling breaking news in the clutch. It was the *Star-Bulletin's* Riley Allen who covered that breaking story of all breaking stories in Hawaii on December 7, 1941, by racing out to Pearl Harbor and collecting the amazing details of the Japanese ambush of the Pacific fleet at anchor. Amid the confusion of contradictory accounts, rolling smoke, and screams of dying sailors, Allen had kept his cool and got the story right with few mistakes, winning a Pulitzer Prize in the process. He was the right man in the clutch and then some.

BING, BING, BING, BING, BING, BING!

Fielding blinked. "Somebody shot King?" He laid down his copy. "Turn off that damned bell."

Zimmerman doused the bell and read from the story, "He was on the balcony of his room on the second floor of the Lorraine Motel in Memphis. He was getting ready to go eat with some friends when a single shot was fired from across the street."

The reporters and editors all gathered around the A wire, reading the story that continued inching out in sketchy details. The wire service reporters were still trying to find out what happened at the Lorraine Motel. When they learned more, they would send a top to the story. That was standard AP practice. If a wire service reporter couldn't immediately think of a just right top to a story, he was trained to keep on trucking, brain racing, fingers dancing on the keys, and slug it, *led to cum*. Lead, in the sense of the opening paragraph, was spelled "led" so it wouldn't be confused with lead, from which the metal slugs were made in linotype machines. Thus told what to expect, the editors out in the boonies, including Honolulu, could start thinking about how to play the story.

Meanwhile, the wire service reporters were giving their client papers backgrounders and sidebars as quickly as they could rustle up the quotes. For a wire service writer, covering an assassination was like a football player making it to the Super Bowl. It was a dream of a lifetime. All the skills of wire service reporters were on the line: their ability to keep cool, their ability to separate facts from hyperbole in an emotional maelstrom, their ability to write quickly and clearly. These were not Shakespearean skills, but they were not to be denigrated. The best of wire service reporters were very, very good. Some were so quick they could describe a boxing match blow by blow as they followed the action at ringside.

On March 20, AP told its clients that Martin Luther King, Jr. had gone to Memphis to support a strike by black sanitation workers who wanted the same deal as the white transit union: a $1.70 an hour plus union recognition and a dues check-off on their paychecks. The Negroes in Memphis began a boycott of white businesses. King, who was preparing a poor people's campaign in Washington to be held in April, had left Memphis but returned on March 28, to lead a nonviolent show of force. As he led twelve thousand marchers down Beale Street, a shop window was broken, followed by another and yet another. In the end, fifty store windows were broken, sixty people were injured, a sixteen-year-old identified as a looter was shot and killed, and there were more than two hundred arrests.

The sidebar on King's involvement in the Memphis strike contained a quote from his speech the previous night at the Mason Temple. He talked ominously about threats and what might happen to him "from some of our sick white brothers."

"Well, I don't know what will happen now," King had said. "We've got some difficult days ahead. But it really doesn't matter with me now, because I've been to the mountain top. And I don't mind. Like anybody, I would like to live a long life. Longevity has its place. But I'm not concerned about that now. I just want to do God's will. And he's allowed me to go up to the mountain, and I've looked over, and I've seen the promised land. I may not get there with you. But I want you to know tonight that we, as a people, will get to the promised land. And so I'm happy tonight. I'm not worried about anything. I'm not fearing any man. Mine eyes have seen the glory of the coming of the Lord."

Gathered around the AP machine, Quint and his companions read the quote in eerie silence. King had felt it coming. His own death. A called shot.

There were no cynical remarks or baiting of Fred Fielding by Steve Sanger this time. This was serious business, and Sanger was as stunned as Quint, Jerry Fortier, Babs Parsegian, Miki Hasegawa. Even Abner Barnhouse remained mute.

THE PACKAGING OF the King assassination was a job for the city desk and the copy desk. Two hours passed and the action quieted down, but with a steady stream of stories still coming over the wire service machines. At last Quint and the regulars headed for the Round Table. The tube was running above the bar, and Ken Kashiwahara, a local reporter, was giving the details of the King assassination as they were coming over the wire. On the mainland, the network famous faces would be delivering the story of the King assassination, but here, owing to Hawaii's isolation, Kashiwahara got the job. Kashiwahara, a Japanese-American reporter with a resonant, articulate voice, had the ability to maintain a completely bland face while barely moving the lips of his small, round mouth. He had the same remarkable skill as Barbara Walters of coming off like a serious, earnest ventriloquist. It was widely predicted in Honolulu that Kashiwahara would one day make the network bigs, as would Al Michaels, the fast-talking voice of the Hawaii Islanders.

Suddenly, Howard K. Smith was on live and Kashiwahara got bumped.

Quint and his friends sat for a contemplative moment as they waited for Tosh Kaneshiro to bring them their Primos. Quint braced himself. Abner Barnhouse, originally a farm boy from southern Illinois, was eternally tanked.

Their Primos delivered, Barnhouse took a sample. Subdued in the city room, he now quickly loosened up. "Well, by God, Martin Luther King took the big one on our time, how about that?" By 'our time,' he meant before the deadline of the green streak final. The worse the news, the more newspapers sold. If King had fielded the bullet an hour later, the *Honolulu Advertiser* would have gotten the profitable breaking headline.

"Abner!" Babs said.

"Mighty white of him, I'd say." *Har, har, har.*

Mayer glared at him. "Shut up, Abner!"

"Second that. Zip it, Abner," Fortier said. He clenched his jaw. "My God, what next?"

Mayer looked gloomy. "We can't take a whole lot more of this, that's a fact."

The national reaction to King's murder was swift and predictable. There was immediate violence in Boston, in Hartford, Connecticut; in Winston-Salem, Durham, and Charlotte, North Carolina; and Jackson, Mississippi. In New York, Mayor John Lindsay had gone to Harlem in order to calm things down only to have his bodyguards push him into a limousine belonging to borough president Percy Sutton. But the night had barely gotten started.

Stokely Carmichael, brandishing what looked like a small pistol, addressed a crowd of four hundred people at the corner of 14th and U Streets in northwest Washington. "Go home and get a gun! When the white man comes, he is coming to kill you. I don't want any black blood in the street. Go home and get you a gun and then come back because I got me a gun."

A reporter noted murmurs in the crowd. "I got my gun. You got your gun?"

But another erstwhile black leader offered dramatics of another sort. The Rev. Jesse Jackson, wearing a bloody shirt, was telling reporters that he was the last person to speak to King. Unfortunately for Jackson, this flight of fancy was contradicted by King's assistant Hosea Williams and other aides. They said when the fatal bullet struck that Jackson was one floor below, on the ground floor. King's chief aide Ralph Abernathy was actually the last man to cradle the martyred civil rights leader.

Watching this, Abner said, "Now there's a blue gums with a future. The Reverend Jesse Jackson. Mark my words. Never let the truth stand in the way of a good story. The man should have become a newspaper reporter."

Fortier looked disgusted. "We said shut up, Abner."

Mildly, Miki Hasegawa said, "This is not the time for it, Abner, truly not."

"Guy has the presence of mind to get himself a bloody shirt before he starts mouthing off. Tell me, you're talking leadership there." *Har, har, har!*

Babs Parsegian said, "If you want a pitcher of beer dumped over your head, keep it up."

Tosh Kaneshiro tapped Quint on the shoulder. "You got a call, Jim."

Quint retreated toward the rear of the bar and the pay phone on the wall. He snatched the receiver that dangled on the end of the cord. He knew intuitively who it was likely to be. "Hello."

"Jim?" It was Vivienne. Quint could hear traffic in the background. She too was speaking from a pay phone.

"Me, Vivienne."

"Are you okay?"

"Of course, I'm okay. Why shouldn't I be?"

"It's complicated."

He said. "How about you? How are your breasts?"

"Bruised. Sore. We will never yield," she said.

"We will not," Quint said.

"I love you." Vivienne hung up.

No sooner had Quint got settled in with his companions at the Round Table than he was paged again.

This time it was Col. Del Lambert. "Well, there, Jimbo. They tell me Vivienne just made a call from a pay phone. You reassured the little lady did you? Ask her about her sore tits? Tell her it'll be okay. You'll protect her. If you really want to help her out and yourself at the same time, you'll press her to tell you what

I'm after and give it to me. The right address or telephone number will turn the trick. Do that and we can end the Vivienne War with a negotiated settlement. No more using her tits for target practice. She's yours. The other thing I wanted to talk about was the King assassination. Let's see if you're learning anything. Once again, Jimbo, you tell me what war is all about."

"Turf."

"There you go. I got. You want. Struggle begins with sex and works its way up. All kinds of turf are at stake in the war you're covering, Jimbo. Pissed off Negroes want. Stubborn as hell whites won't yield. That's just one front." Lambert's voice suddenly hardened. "Liberty, equality, fraternity," he said scornfully. "These kids aren't baby Gandhis, Jimbo. The little snot-nosed sons of bitches are motherfucking Jacobins. I take that back. Bolsheviks. Wake up for Christ's sakes!"

"I say again. I have no idea what Vivienne has that you want, Colonel Lambert." That was a lie. Quint did too know. It had to do with the CBS film.

"But I have what you want, Vivienne. That much is clear."

"I have to go now."

"You ever read John Reed's *Ten Days that Shook the World?* No? Read it. Keep a stiff dick, Jimbo."

Quint hung up, wondering if he too were being followed. He also wondered if Tosh Kanishiro's pay phone might not be tapped.

MARTIN LUTHER KING, Jr. was assassinated on a Thursday. By the following Monday, the nation was caught in a frenzy of posturing and hyperbolic encomiums to the fallen civil rights leader. King was a good guy, yes—it was difficult to find anybody who did not agree that content of character should precede color of skin—but Quint found it hard to believe that he had somehow surpassed Jesus, St. Francis, and Gandhi in a single night.

The way to greatness was apparently to get assassinated. Those who now asserted the magnificence of John F. Kennedy had a curious lapse of memory when it came to his monumental fuck-up in approving the invasion at the Bay of Pigs in Cuba. And if it was true, as published rumor had it, that he had ordered the assassination of President Diem in Vietnam and had connived to do the same to Fidel Castro, his own demise was a kind of rough justice. It was not an ennobling thought to have, but the possibility did occur to Quint.

At a minimum, the murder of King demanded rioting by blacks as a show of respect if not justified sport, and so by Friday morning plumes of smoke rolled up from Washington, the worst fire since the British burned the capital city in 1814. Jesse Jackson appeared on three different television stations Friday morning wearing his bloody shirt—never mind that a chicken or suckling pig rather than King had surrendered its life fluids for the dramatic prop. Under the circumstances, nobody dared call Jackson a fraud.

By Friday afternoon, the fires and rioting mobs inched closer to the White House, drawing to within two blocks of the perimeter fence. Riot troops took up positions on President Johnson's lawn, establishing machine gun nests. On the Hill, Guardsmen built machine gun nests on the steps of the Capitol. Ninety-five hundred troops patrolled Washington, establishing a curfew from 4 P.M. to 6:30 A.M., and special buttons were installed on the telephones of congressmen and senators; by punching the buttons they could find out which sections of the city were safe for them to travel.

The hyperbole was like oxygen to the flames of emotion. In Minneapolis, a black man vowed to kill the first white man he saw, who turned out to be his neighbor. He shot him dead with three bullets. The weekend body count was mercifully small, a mere four were killed in Washington, two in Detroit, and scattered corpses in Memphis and Tallahassee, Florida. Chicago, Pittsburgh, Hartford, Trenton, Newark, and Baltimore were all set upon by rioters.

By Monday morning, fifteen thousand National Guard troops patrolled Washington. There were six hundred guardsmen in Columbia, South Carolina, two thousand in Wilmington, Delaware, and four thousand in Pittsburgh. In all, sixty-five thousand riot troops saw duty in a hundred and thirty cities. By all appearances the rioting would not last hours or days, but weeks. Only then could the final numbers of dead be totaled and the cost of the riots be calculated.

Jesse Jackson was not the only opportunist to seize the moment. Bobby Kennedy, saying that Lee Harvey Oswald had "set something loose in this country," toured the burned-out ruins on U Street. Federal troops, mistaking Kennedy's entourage for another rioting mob, put on their gas masks and readied their rifles.

22

AFTER DEL LAMBERT'S stoned treatise on the nature of war and violence and the assassination of Martin Luther King, Jr., Jim Quint began paying more attention to Lambert's new American civil war. If Lambert was right, there was no clear opening round such as the action at Fort Sumter, but rather growing social and political discontent—goaded by the increasingly unpopular and expensive war in Vietnam—that had culminated in the wildly explosive and unpredictable year of 1968.

King's murder triggered a racial firefight that slammed through urban slums, leaving thirty-nine people dead across the nation, all but five of them Negro, and twenty thousand people under arrest. Everywhere it seemed the old order, now popularly called the Establishment, was under attack.

Quint read John Reed's *Ten Days that Shook the World*, an enthusiastic journalist's account of the October 1917 Bolshevik Revolution in Russia. While Quint felt Lambert's comparison of American street protestors with Marxist Bolsheviks was wildly overdrawn, the enthusiastic American radicals had clearly appropriated the revolutionary lingo. On his beat, Quint encountered daily the same practices that Reed had described in his novel— radicals passionately announcing this or that "white paper" on behalf of the "workers" whoever they were. Until Eugene McCarthy, these words and phrases, appropriated by students and intellectuals, had become the standard socialist rhetoric of class struggle.

While regarding themselves as the romantic vanguard of the new revolution, the students really couldn't connect with the working class. Quint himself had watched this frustrating failure. He had covered a demonstration of striking garbage collectors at the state capitol when student radicals showed up in an attempt to show their solidarity. The garbage collectors, huge Hawaiians and Samoans, had sent them packing.

Looking back, Quint felt the cultural struggle was clearly visible in the 1963 civil rights marches in Alabama and John Kennedy's assassination in November of that year. While popular opinion had raised Kennedy to the status of a revered martyr, antiwar activists had quickly forgotten that he had been a preeminent cold warrior. It was Kennedy who had made the famous declaration at the Berlin wall, "Ich bin ein Berliner."

A year following the Alabama civil rights marches, Mario Savio had appropriated King's tactic of nonviolent demonstrations for his Berkeley Free Speech Movement. Having spent the previous summer in Mississippi, Savio later said that he had seen small groups of people in the minority work their will over a tyrannical majority. He returned to the University of California to lead the first open student rebellion, sparked and fueled by discontent over Vietnam.

Now, in the first week of April 1968, the unyielding storm of protest triggered by Vietnam had gone international. Brandishing Chairman Mao's *Little Red Book*, Daniel Cohn-Bendit, aka Dany the Red, led the assault against overcrowding and segregation of the sexes at the Sorbonne in Paris. In West Berlin, Red Rudi Dutschke led protests against the Axel Springer magazine empire, accusing it of reviving reactionary sentiment in West Germany—a movement that erupted in violence after Dutschke survived three bullets fired by a twenty-year-old house painter, an erstwhile fan of Adolf Hitler.

The revolt popularly called Prague Spring had actually begun the previous October, when two thousand students from the Prague Polytechnical University marched on the presidential palace to protest the lack of heat and light in their dormitories. In the dead of winter, the police struck back with clubs and tear gas.

Now a forty-six-year-old party official named Alexander Dubcek led a movement to oust the Communist party's conservative first secretary, Antonin Novotny, and was himself chosen as Novotny's successor. Dubcek proceeded to announce the return of freedom of speech and set about to rehabilitate the victims of previous Stalinist purges.

For a brief, sweet moment in Prague, democracy blossomed, but everybody knew it wouldn't last; eventually Soviet tanks would rumble into Prague as they had in Budapest in 1956. The Americans, stuck in the morass of Vietnam, would do nothing.

THERE WAS ONE new front of Del Lambert's cultural civil war that Quint enjoyed following, that was the one opened by the emerging villain of uptight America, the fun-loving radical Abbie Hoffman. Hoffman and his pal Jerry Rubin had founded the Youth International Party, more popularly known as the yippies— hippies with a Y in place of the H. The Yippies were making it clear that they were going to give the Democrats a hard time at their August convention in Chicago.

The high-spirited Hoffman and Rubin had begun their spirited campaign in March when Helen Running Water, a white girl in an Indian costume, presented Deputy Mayor David Stahl with an application for a permit to camp out in Chicago's Grant Park. Miss Running Water's yippie sponsors had scrawled their request on a page torn out of *Playboy* magazine—the one featuring the Playmate of the Month. In reference to Mayor Richard Daley, the yippies had added under the model, "To Dick, with love, the yippies."

Fred Fielding did not think these antics were in any way clever, but the managing editor, Hobe Duncan, secretly amused, knew how to sell newspapers. As the spring wore on, the *Star-Bulletin* treated its readers to a series of bizarre yippie plans intended to shock and dismay the country. The yippies taunted the humorless Establishment, saying they were going to assemble ten thousand nude protesters to float on Lake Michigan. They were going to dump LSD in the Chicago water supply. Yippie women were going to spike the drinks of delegates with LSD and show them the sexual time of their lives. A separate group of "hyper-potent" yippie men would take care of their wives and daughters.

How Fielding suffered when the mischievous Carl Zimmerman, knowing the reaction to come, ripped another yippie proposal from the AP machine and handed it to him. With each outrage, Fielding clenched his jaw. He compressed his lips, turning them white. Quint and his Round Table friends called this his LeMay look, after Gen. Curtis "Nuke 'Em Back to the Stone Age" LeMay, commander of the Strategic Air Command.

QUINT AND VIVIENNE lay back on Quint's bed with the glass slats of his bedroom window turned at an angle so they could feel the balmy air flow with feather fingers across their bodies. They could see the yellow moon. They were sated from sex and feeling good, but after the beating Quint had taken from Lambert following their earlier transgression, they were clearly courting danger.

Vivienne turned on her side and rested her chin on the heel of her hand. "I want to tell you the story of a man who was out chopping wood in the forest. A Zen *koan* actually. You game?"

Quint kissed her lightly. "Sure," he said.

"A tiger jumped from the bushes. The man dropped his ax and wood and ran for his life. The tiger chased him to the edge of a cliff. He looked down and in a river far below a crocodile looked up at him. But wait! He spotted a root growing on the side of the cliff."

"Okay!" Quint said.

"He grabbed the root and jumped, holding on. There he hung. Above him, the tiger swiped at him with its claw. Below him, the crocodile waited with its jaws open. Just then he saw a ripe, wild strawberry growing on the side of the cliff. He tried to reach the strawberry, but couldn't. It was just inches from his fingertips. He'd have to surrender his root to get it." She fell silent, watching Quint.

Quint waited.

"It tasted so sweet," she said.

23

*A*BBIE HOFFMAN AND Jerry Rubin led the satirical wing of the student front; Columbia University's Mark Rudd commandeered the confrontational wing pioneered by Mario Savio. The passionate challenging and defending of turf at Columbia University replaced the assassination of Martin Luther King, Jr. as the principal domestic drama coming across the wire services in April.

As the Prague Spring unfolded in Czechoslovakia, so too did the events at the Ivy League campus situated on Morningside Heights overlooking the Hudson River on Manhattan's Upper West Side. Between Columbia and the impoverished blacks in Harlem lay the thirty-acre Morningside Park, a boot-shaped demilitarized zone stretching from 110th to 123rd Streets. Columbia wanted to build a gym on the park, which was public property; to do that the university had to appease the Harlem community, and so proposed to build an $8.4 million gymnasium at the top of the sloping property and a facility for the Negroes at the bottom—at one-fifth the cost.

The Students's Afro-American Society, led by Cicero Wilson, called this "Gym Crow." The university offered to throw a swimming pool into the deal. Wilson was a tough city kid. He was a native of the Brooklyn slum of Bedford-Stuyvesant. He would have none of it. He wanted action.

Twenty-year-old Mark Rudd, chairman of the Columbia chapter of the Students for a Democratic Society, led the assault against the on-campus recruitment by the CIA and Dow Chemical, which manufactured the napalm used in Vietnam. The SDS objected to Columbia's affiliation with the Institute for Defense Analyses, which did research in weapons and counter-insurgency warfare, and to the university's ban on indoor demonstrations.

Earlier in the month, Columbia President Grayson Kirk, then sixty-four, personifying "the generation gap," had declined to link arms and sing "We Shall Overcome" at a memorial service for Martin Luther King, Jr., which showed, perhaps, that he was the wrong man in the wrong place.

On April 22, the SAS and SDS held a demonstration with bullhorns, placards, banners, and the other accoutrements of revolution. Wilson was in fine, if scary form, saying, "You people had better realize that you condone Grayson Kirk with his rough riding over the black community. But do you realize that when you come back, there might not *be* a Columbia University? Do you think this white citadel of hypocrisy will be bypassed if an insurrection occurs this summer?"

The week was consumed by heated rhetoric. Kirk complained of "inchoate nihilism." Rudd replied with, "up against the wall, motherfucker, this is a stickup."

The police moved in with shields and clubs. The radicals, both black and white, responded by taking over buildings on campus, which had been their goal all along. Blacks occupied some buildings. Whites took others. University administrators filed a complaint of trespass. Fearing the blacks, who were taking in members of the Harlem community, some allegedly with guns, they asked the police to throw out the whites but leave the blacks alone. The cops refused, saying they would throw both groups out or none; they would not administer the law on the basis of race.

Finally, on April 30, one thousand New York policemen marched in military formation and emptied all five of the occupied buildings. The blacks, given to the most grandiose and hyperbolic threats, left peacefully. The whites, led by Rudd, engaged the police in pitched battle, matching rocks, chairs, and bottles against punches, kicks, and billy clubs. In the end there were 722 arrests and 148 injured, including 28 policemen.

WHILE COLUMBIA UNIVERSITY and campuses across the country were twisted by rage and riot and with the expected urban burning season coming up, Eugene McCarthy remained aloof and intellectual, quoting obscure passages of Walt Whitman's poetry and declining to campaign in the Negro slums. When asked at Harvard University what he had done for Democratic voters, McCarthy said all anybody had to do was check his voting record, but the students were apparently less interested in how he voted than how he *felt*.

If numbers of delegates won in Kennedy-less primaries meant anything, April had been Eugene McCarthy's month. In the first week, McCarthy beat the lame duck president 56 to 35 percent in a primary in which Bobby Kennedy had not entered. On April 10, he forced an election for delegates to the Connecticut primaries and won 44 percent of the votes. Two weeks later, he won 71 percent of Pennsylvania's non-binding primaries. On April 30, in the Massachusetts primary—where it was too late for Kennedy to enter—he won again.

Kennedy, meanwhile, was igniting passion with emotional, furious speeches calling for an end to the war that was ripping the country apart. Screaming women ripped off his clothes at near hysterical rallies, and the crowds swelled along with his poll numbers. On May 7, Bobby won the New York primaries with 42 percent to 30 percent for the state's governor; McCarthy got 27 percent. The next week, he crushed McCarthy in Nebraska, 51 to 31 percent.

Then, for the first time in twenty-two years that a Kennedy had lost any kind of election, McCarthy beat Kennedy in Oregon, 44 percent to 37. But then Oregon was a curious state; its senior senator, Wayne Morse, was one of only two senators to vote against the Tonkin Gulf Resolution that the president subsequently used to expand the war at will. But never mind Oregon, California was coming up. California was the prize, a bonanza of delegates to the convention in Chicago. Whoever won California would be the one to challenge Hubert Humphrey, who was popularly regarded as being to Lyndon Johnson what Charley McCarthy had been to Edgar Bergen.

After his defeat in Oregon, Bobby Kennedy had headed south, and at Fresno, he said, "My family eats more tomatoes than any family I know, and my wife and children all wear cotton clothes." Reminded of that quote by Babs Parsegian, Abner Barnhouse said, dryly, cigarette stuck to the crud on his lower lip, "He forgot to mention guacamole. Isn't that what they use in Fresno instead of Vaseline?"

Kennedy had done everything imaginable to avoid debating McCarthy. He had stalled and stalled, making up every kind of excuse imaginable. His schedule was tight, he said. There wasn't enough time to tend to all the details. And so on. In the end, he agreed to just one debate, saying studies had shown that nobody paid any attention to the second debate between his brother and Richard Nixon in 1960.

DEL LAMBERT CALLED Jim Quint at his *Star-Bulletin* desk on May 1. "Hey, Jimbo, how are you doing?"

"Hanging loose."

"Don't give me that shit. It's been a month since you've dipped your wick into my wife—with the exception of one little quickie there. After the beating I gave you the first time, that took some real balls, I admit."

"Am I to expect another ambush?"

"Aw no, I'll let it pass. As long as you don't pull a stunt like keying my car again. Say, hasn't this been a helluva month? Martin Luther King, Jr. and Columbia University! The Negroes had themselves some fun and young Mr. Rudd made a real show of it. Cicero Wilson strutting around pretending he has a brain. Just what do you think those Negroes are going to do come summer? God, bless America. And those pipsqueak pretenders will be out parading their placards and banners. At least the fucking Bolsheviks had real hair."

Quint said. "I take it you've been following the story out of

Prague. The Czechs want their freedom back. The Soviets say they can't have it. That's not such a bad turn of events, is it?"

Lambert ignored that. "Say, Jim, the reason I'm calling is I'd like to invite you to a party at my house to watch the California debate between McCarthy and Bobby Kennedy. They say it'll be carried live in Hawaii. Clark Clifford and General Wheeler will both be there so you should find it entertaining. Maybe you can give them some ideas on how we can pull the troops out of Vietnam without embarrassing ourselves."

"Right."

"Afterwards, you can get your horns trimmed with my wife if you like. Invitation's open. Big ol' bed. Bounce, bounce, bounce. The hippie chickenshit and the pretty Vietnamese lady. Compliments of Ho Chi Lambert. Just like before."

Quint said, "Sure, I'd like to show your wife a good time, Colonel. She's obviously starved for a little affection and some good sex. You know the saying, a hard man is good to find."

Mildly, Lambert said, "By the time I'm finished with you, bub, we'll see who's the hard man. In the meantime, remember, I'm easy enough to deal with. Get me what I want and you got yourself Vivienne seven nights a week. You can fuck 'till your cock drops off. One of the most beautiful women on the island and you dither. Hard to figure." Lambert hung up.

24

JIM QUINT PARKED his car down the hill that night out of consideration for Del Lambert's high-powered guests. As Quint walked up the winding road to the house, he saw a truck from Aloha Pacific that he knew from an article in the *Star-Bulletin's* style section was the fanciest of the fancy caterers on Oahu. Their chef literally took over the host's kitchen for the day, presumably shouting orders like a culinary field marshal, and produced some of the most exotic Asian-Pacific cuisine to be found outside of San Francisco. From bartenders to waiters, Aloha Pacific, the best on the island, was class all the way.

Vivienne ushered Quint into her house and as he stepped inside, he caught a waiter in an aloha shirt observing him from the corner of his eye. Had Quint seen him before? Did he have some special reason for watching Quint that way or was he just curious? Quint didn't know.

Del Lambert introduced Quint to Secretary of Defense Clark Clifford and Gen. Earle G. Wheeler, chairman of the Joint Chiefs of Staff, saying he was Vivienne's friend. Clifford, a fatherly-looking Washington lawyer with a handsomely rugged, lined face, was an old friend of Lyndon Johnson, who, the previous November, had given him Robert McNamara's job as head of the Pentagon. Clifford was an up-front hawk, and Johnson had made the change amid suggestions that McNamara had gone soft on the war. Johnson had a great society that he wanted to install as his legacy. He wanted to win the war, dammit.

Now, after Tet and the rest of that shocking spring, here they were on the Saturday night of the debate in Los Angeles between two doves for president, Eugene McCarthy and Bobby Kennedy. On rare occasions, when potential Neilsen ratings merited live telecasts from the mainland, Hawaii got to see the action live. Tonight Quint would get to watch the debate live in the company of the secretary of defense and the chairman of the Joint Chiefs of Staff. Pretty high cut of the hog.

Both Clifford and Wheeler wore white aloha shirts, Clifford's with orange blossoms, Wheeler's with green. They had worn the shirts as a political gesture to show they were just human after all; they didn't need the crutch of a bemedaled uniform or power suit. If either of them regarded Quint with suspicion because of his mustache or hair, they didn't show it. Quint was a nobody, and they were running the war in Vietnam. To them, he was an odd specimen of insect who stuck to their domestic flank like a bloated tick.

Quint had seen them only on television or in newspaper photographs, always with Wheeler in his uniform with the fruit salad on his chest and Clifford in his power suit. At a distance, they were like gods or dieties, players in a great international struggle to prevent the toppling of Communist dominoes in Southeast Asia. These men, and a handful of others at the top of the government, were determined to hold the line at Vietnam.

Up close, separated from the legend of public identity, they were mortals. They carried with them the glow of fame, almost exuding power. They unconsciously gave off little clues with body language, a slight tilt of chin, the prideful curve of spine, the easy way they moved about. They were aware that they were being watched. In public places, their names were whispered as they were identified. They were special people, a famous soldier and a celebrity bureaucrat. They were deferred to. They were triumphant males, having worked their way to the top of both military and civilian hierarchies in competition with other ambitious men. Career building was a test of guile and will, and they were winners.

Lambert said, "Jim covers the radicals and war protesters for the *Honolulu Star-Bulletin*."

Eyeing Quint, Wheeler, pretending not to notice Quint's long hair, took a sip of Scotch and said, "Really? What are they saying about us these days?"

Quint said, "Nothing that would be good for your blood pressure, but if they saw you tonight they'd call you a flower soldier. I like your shirt, more inviting than ribbons and stars."

Clifford grinned. "You know, Jim, ordinarily we only get to talk to people who agree with us, or want us to think they do. You don't mind if we pick your brain a little?"

Quint laughed. "No, no. Not at all. If I even have one to speak of. And not that I can tell you anything you can't read in the *New York Times*. But I suspect that's why Del invited me. I'm just a provincial newspaper reporter though, not a Weatherman or anything like that."

"He'd probably surrender a testicle to be able to interview one though. Right, Jim?" Lambert said.

Vivienne, dressed in a fashionably short black cocktail dress glided up, accompanied by a waiter, bearing a platter of puu puus which this night had been prepared by the celebrated chef of the Ala Moana Hotel.

She touched her husband on the elbow, the respectful wife, and said, "I hope you're all having a good time. If there's anything you need, just let me know."

Clifford said, "We've just been introduced to your reporter friend. He called Earle a flower soldier. The chairman of the Joint Chiefs of Staff!" He looked amused.

Vivienne smiled. "You show some respect now, Jim." Then both she and Lambert moved off to attend to their other guests.

Wheeler said, "I take it you've been following the primary action, Jim."

"Hard not to."

Clifford looked mildly amused. "Which candidate are you for tonight, Jim, Clean Gene?"

"I'm a Republican actually. I like Rocky."

He blinked.

"Just kidding. Yes, I like Gene. A bit colorless, I'll give you

that and maybe lacking the clichéd fire in the belly. I suppose
Bobby's got the fire, but it's hard to forgive him sitting there with
his thumb up his butt while Gene took on the president in New
Hampshire. I have to ask myself which one really has the *cojones*
and who is *la boca grande*."

"And Humphrey?"

"Preaching the politics of happiness and joy strikes me as a
stretch with the kind of year we're having. There's precious little
happiness or joy remaining in Vietnam, begging your pardon,
that's not to mention Martin Luther King, Jr., and the rest
of it."

Clifford seemed not to take offense. "How about Nixon or
Rockefeller?"

"My parents are Democrats so I turned out to be one too.
Maybe when I get older and have something to defend, I'll switch
to the Republican party. Or maybe when I grow up. That possibility remains." Quint gave them a self-deprecating grin.

Clifford laughed. "Who do you think will win the primaries?"

"Bobby Kennedy and Richard Nixon."

He looked surprised. "Not the vice president?"

"Not unless he promises to pull you people out of Vietnam.
It's hard to imagine him letting go of Lyndon Johnson's apron
strings."

"I take it you don't like the war?" Clifford asked.

"I like football okay," Quint said. "Baseball too."

"Talk to us," Wheeler said. "Tell us what you think about the
war."

Wheeler seemed amiable and sincere. Quint said, "I can tell
you what I think, but that's not a reflection of what you're up
against on the domestic front. All you have to do is pick up a
newspaper. You've got Gene telling you what's wrong. You've
got Bobby joining the chorus. You've got radicals all over the
place. You don't want to know what I really think."

"Try us," Clifford said.

"We're big boys," Wheeler said. "People are always criticizing
us for surrounding ourselves with people who tell us what we

want to hear. There might be something to that. Our subordinates all have their careers to think about. No sense making us sore for no reason."

"Better for them to go with the flow," Clifford said.

Quint glanced at Vivienne. He didn't want to be so boorish as to piss off her guests of honor.

"Did you serve in the military yourself?"

"I was drafted and trained as a photo analyst. You know the stuff, poring over high altitude reconnaissance photography trying to pick out the tanks and missile silos. Spent my time right here at Ft. Shafter. Good duty. Got out as an E-5. I had a journalism degree so the *Star-Bulletin* hired me."

On hearing that Quint had served in the army, they seemed suddenly more interested in his opinion. Clifford leaned forward watching him. "Talk to us."

Quint said, "First, you should understand that I don't hate the military or think you're all fascist assholes or any of that. I know better, and I credit you with good faith, at least most of you. But I view war as an extension of politics that can be misguided just like anything else."

Clifford rolled his eyeballs, pretending to plead the heavens. "They sure as hell can."

Wheeler gave him a wry look. "The expression is 'right on!' "

Quint said, "One of the first things I did when I came to Hawaii was read James Jones's novel *From Here to Eternity*, which, as you know, was about life in the garrisoned army between the wars. The Depression had stripped back the defense budget to almost nothing. Morale was low. Life in the barracks was petty and boring."

"Sergeant Burt Lancaster screwing his commander's wife on the beach," Clifford said. "Deborah Kerr with those soulful eyes. The waves crashing in. The soaring music."

"Pretty racy stuff in those days," Wheeler said.

Quint said, "Pearl Harbor changed all that and then the Cold War. Now you've got money and high-tech weapons and an enemy who has obliged you by professing to spread their crappola to every country on the planet. Those of you who are in the regular army are professional soldiers. You train and train and train, but in the end fighting is ultimately what soldiering is all about, not training to fight. You're naturally not going to back off an opportunity to take on General Giap. A war means an opportunity for officers to get promotions. For you to sit around in garrison all the time is like a writer with no editor or publisher. He writes and writes and writes, but nobody gets to read his stuff. None of this makes you evil or awful. It just is. You know, every afternoon when I grab a fresh paper, I check out my stories. I see my name up there, 'by Jim Quint,' and I get this little rush of pride. I'm a good writer, or at least I think I am. You see what I'm getting at?" Quint hesitated.

Clifford said, "Keep going."

"I think most people understand that intuitively. That's not at the heart of their objection, but it does make them wary of your pronouncements about the light at the end of the tunnel and all that."

"I'd like to strangle the S.O.B. who came up with that phrase," Wheeler murmured.

Quint said, "People don't see this as a defense of the U.S. which is their definition of a good and proper war. The boys who kept the Germans at bay and defended the West Coast against the Japanese were heroes because they laid down their lives for their countrymen. As a country we were faced with a clear and present danger—or at least we thought we were after Pearl Harbor and Japanese incendiary balloons landing on the West Coast. People just aren't buying into the domino theory that we're somehow preventing a bamboo curtain from being erected around Southeast Asia. If they see something that looks like a duck, and walks like a duck, and quacks like a duck, why then they conclude that it is a duck."

"What do they think this duck is?" Clifford asked mildly, although he knew the answer.

"A civil war. Somebody else's war. And when Lyndon Johnson makes grand speeches about those freedom-loving Vietnamese allies of ours, he isn't fooling anybody. Everybody knows the Vietnamese don't have any tradition of freedom. People are willing to support people fighting for political freedom, which was Kennedy's original policy, but they have to do the fighting themselves, not us. The kids marching in the streets aren't any different than those who gave up their lives on Omaha Beach or on Guadalcanal. If the Soviets sent their tank divisions west tomorrow afternoon, they'd overwhelm your enlistment offices just like they did after Pearl Harbor."

Clifford sighed. "But they won't fight somebody else's war."

Quint said, "Even worse, somebody else's war prosecuted by old farts who refuse to admit they're wrong because it might cost them political power, begging your pardon. The fury won't subside, because they don't want to be killed by hubris. If their homeland is threatened, the same kids who're carrying placards and banners in parades will break into enlistment offices to join up."

Clifford laughed. "We asked a question. You gave us an answer, which is precisely what is giving succor to Ho Chi Minh. The truth lies in firepower. Firepower talks, bullshit walks. That's the way of the world."

"Good war or bad, we will win," Wheeler said, his voice was suddenly suffused with passion and resolve. "We've got air power and firepower. If we have to, we'll flatten the bastards. Winning is a question of will, and they should never underestimate our resolve. It's a mistake."

At that point, Del Lambert arrived with a waiter in tow—the same guy who had been eying Jim all evening. "Well, the three of you look like you're having a deep conversation. You give them your 'get out of Vietnam now,' pitch, Jim?"

"Why yes, he did, Colonel," Clifford said. "We've heard it all before, and Jim is right, we are stubborn old farts who refuse to give up. We know the costs of yielding territory to bullshit dictators, and we won't be making the same mistake again. It will not happen. Nyet!"

Wheeler said, "If we'd kept the Germans in place in 1939 and the Russians in 1945, our boys would never have had to give up their blood at Bastogne and the Russian tanks would never have rolled into Budapest in 1956."

Lambert said, "A couple of men who know their history. What did I tell you, Jim?"

Quint shrugged. "Maybe you're right, Mr. Clifford, but your argument might also be too complicated for the public to understand."

Quint excused himself and moved on, leaving Lambert with Clifford and Wheeler. Vivienne had caught a moment alone and was looking down at the city lights through a large window. Quint went and stood beside her. He said, "Are we in for more games tonight?"

"Almost certainly." She gave him a shy smile. "The thing to do is enjoy ourselves, Jim. Ignore him. He's crazy, so we just ignore him and take what we can."

Just then Quint caught sight of the waiter again. He was interested in Quint. This was not sexual, he didn't think. He had no reason to believe the waiter was gay.

Later, after the guests had gone, Quint sat alone on the rear deck while Lambert set up the next act of his game. Quint knew from the look in Vivienne's eyes that they had a long night ahead of them.

As she and Lambert headed for the bedroom to make whatever preparations had to be made, Vivienne murmured to Quint, "Courage. We'll get through it."

25

VIVIENNE AND QUINT stood face-to-face, naked. The evening of her ambush strip signaled their arrival in the combat zone. The night of voyeur sex, they rode the streets of the besieged capital of human desire listening to their instructor tell them of the dangers and the rules of engagement. Now they were entering the jungle, listening to spooky rumbling and gurgling in the darkness. They did not wear boots, fatigues, or helmets. In this place, where men and women grappled with urgent demons, sweaty in the night, the soldiers wore only skin and, here and there, a patch of hair. Their mouths were dry. Their imaginations raced with the expectation of the coming action. Their adrenaline pumped.

In Quint's hand, the cool feel of metal.

They wondered what was coming next.

From behind the mirror, Del Lambert said, "Stiffen 'em up, Vivienne."

Vivienne kneaded her outsized nipples between her thumbs and forefingers.

"Okay, put 'em on her, Jim. They don't have to be tight, just firm enough that they'll stay in place and we know she can feel 'em a little. It's the erotic symbolism we're after here. Jim, you told me the radicals were engaged in a form of public theater. I agree, but it is a theater for the masses, given over to posturing and half-truths. Well, this is the opposite, private theater. Here, we deal with total, disconcerting truth."

Vivienne said, "Go ahead, Jim."

The stainless steel chain had nipple clamps on either end. These clamps were like metal clothes pins; a small ring at the base slid up the clamps tightening them onto milady's nipples. With Vivienne looking down at her chest, Quint fastened the clamps, squeezing the brown flesh.

Quint said, "Vivienne?"

She glanced up, meeting his eyes. She smiled. "They're okay. Don't worry so much."

"They look sexy on those spikes of hers, don't they, Jim? Close your eyes, Vivienne. I want him to watch your face while he gives the chain a little tug. If they come off, they're too loose."

She stiffened.

"Go ahead, Jim."

Quint gave the chain a tug.

She stiffened.

Quint grabbed her and held her in his arms.

Lambert yelled, "Ah, ah, none of that I-want-to-hold-you-and-love-you-and-protect-you crappola. Save that for later."

Quint let her go.

Vivienne whispered, "Thank you, Jim."

Lambert said, "Remember last month, I recited to you from Tom Hayden's Port Huron Statement of the Students for a Democratic Society? That's from 1962, and I propose to use it much as a preacher might quote from the Scriptures. It is a kind of hippie scripture, isn't it? It goes to the heart of the rhetoric that you people rehash in your stories, so I'll repeat it for emphasis. *We regard men as infinitely possessed of unfulfilled capacities for reason, freedom, and love. Men have unrealized potential for self-cultivation, self-direction, self-understanding, and creativity. It is this potential that we regard as crucial and to which we appeal. The goal of man and society should be human independence: a concern not with image or popularity but with finding a meaning in life that is personally authentic.* Freedom. Love. Self-understanding. Creativity. The personally authentic."

Quint glanced at the mirror, seeing himself and Vivienne with her dark brown nipples clamped in stainless steel. "Are you sure those aren't too tight?" he whispered to Vivienne.

"They're okay," she breathed.

Lambert said. "I want you two to lie down now and listen while I tell you what tonight's little adventure is all about. This is not just a horny exercise. There's a point to it, a didactic fuck."

They lay on the bed together, and Vivienne slipped into Quint's arms. She was exquisitely warm and soft. He could feel the chain pressing against his chest.

"The hippies you write about are always talking about trips and tripping out. Isn't that what Timothy Leary was doing up there in Harvard, going on LSD trips? Tripping out? One trips, leaving behind uptight rules and oppressive conventions. This is a form of surreal travel, a liberating mental journey, an exploration of the suppressed interior world of dreams and nightmares. A prying into unsettling secrets. Do I have that right, Jim?"

"Trips, tripping, tripping out, yes," Quint said.

"I'm going to send you two on a trip of your own, right there on the bed—a metaphorical ride through the wilderness. Other than estrogen, testosterone, and adrenaline, no chemicals or drugs are needed, just courage. A ceremony of deliverance."

"Deliver us from what?"

Lambert sounded surprised. "Why, I've already told you, from posturing and half-truth. From pretense! Animals you are. If Woodrow Wilson had been able to separate himself from the mush of what-ought-to-be, he wouldn't have been promising people a war to end all wars. But that's another story. World War I. World War II. We've started numbering them like Super Bowls. I've stashed something under the pillow. Vivienne, I want you to retrieve it now and give it to your would-be lover."

She looked sharply at the mirror. "Would-be?"

"Ah, a little rebellious are we? Do as you're told."

Vivienne slipped her hand under the pillow and retrieved a black leather strap or paddle a little more than a foot long and maybe three inches wide. Licking her lips, she handed it to Quint.

Quint looked at the mirror. "What's this?" He knew what it was.

"It's an erotic spanking strap. It's too wide to cut or anything like that, but it makes an evil slapping sound once you get the hang of it. Very horny and wicked. It's stiff enough that you can control it. You don't want the blows to be too hard, but not too soft either. Give yourself a pop in the palm of your hand. You'll see what I mean."

Quint did. He was right on both counts. The strap was easy to control. And it delivered more sound than actual sting. With Vivienne sitting cross-legged on the bed with a chain looped between her clamped nipples, he had more than a good idea what was coming next. That made the slapping sound all the more sexy. There was no denying it. "I thought you were supposed to be teaching us about Vietnam?"

"This *is* about Vietnam, Jim. The horseshit on the front page of the *Star-Bulletin* is all patina. Veneer. In the long run, it hardly matters. It is diversion, ready-made issues for drunks in bar rooms. Tonight, we're after the genetic grain beneath the surface. I want you on your hands and knees with your rump up, Vivienne. Give him a sexy target."

Vivienne hesitated, then got on her hands and knees.

"Push it up there, Vivienne. We're after honesty here. Nobody here tonight gets away with lying."

She pushed her rump higher.

"She likes doing that for you, Jimbo. She knows it turns you on. It turns her on too. This is not abasement or humiliation of any sort. It's sexy for reasons that are mysterious only if you never give them any thought. No reason for either of you to be embarrassed about anything. We're being open minded and creative here, Tom Hayden all the way. A little hippie moment. What do you say, Jim?"

Quint ran his hand over her butt.

Lambert said, "Ah, ah, hands off until it's time. You know the rules. I'm Uncle Ho, remember, I set the rules of this little war of ours. You do as I say."

"I love you," Vivienne whispered.

"Have you ever wondered how it is that people caught in the grip of a dictator endure what amounts to political slavery for years without doing anything about it? You'd have thought that somebody would have popped Papa Doc Duvalier or Fidel Castro years ago. They say Joseph Stalin killed twenty million of his own people to ensure that he stayed in power, but in the end he died of natural causes. And you've read the accounts of Mao's cultural purges going on now in China. Okay, Jimbo, I want you to pick up the strap and give Vivienne a little pop on the butt. Not too hard. We'll match the pain of pops with the strength of the truth. They're directly related."

Quint hesitated.

Vivienne whispered. "Go ahead, Jim."

Quint picked up the strap and gave her a gentle tap.

Lambert burst out laughing. "Oh, for Christ's sake, that's ridiculous. Nothing sexy about that. Make her feel it."

Quint gave her butt an audible slap.

Vivienne moaned softly.

"Put your hand down there and check her out."

Quint put his hand between her legs. She was awash.

"Is she wet?"

Quint nodded.

"Nobody has touched her down there. Not once. Yet, nature delivers. She's ready for sex. Why is that, do you think? Do you suppose she's an anomaly among females, somehow different? Only Vivienne feels that way, not other women? Only you're worked up, not other men? You're some kind of an anomaly? Please, spare me."

Quint licked his lips.

"Ahh, avoidance. The closer to the truth the greater the denial, which is why most of the talk about Vietnam is horseshit. The truth is the submission has turned her on. Nobody likes to admit that. It's a dirty little secret. It's scary. Yet here it is, we can both see it. She yields. She submits. She obeys. *And she likes it.* The control is *sexy.* This is the River V, dirty as the Ganges, wide as the Nile, coursing its way through the core of all living things. So what are we to make of it beyond getting our rocks off?"

Quint's hand strayed to Vivienne's butt.

"Ah, ah, I said hand off!"

Quint yanked his hand back.

"The masses can't handle ambiguity. They're social animals who want certainty. They want to belong, so they've divided themselves into bullshit camps, Republicans and Democrats, hawks and doves, establishmentarians and anti-establishmentarians, old farts and the young. All over the planet you see the elemental deal repeated. They willingly swap freedom for control, but nobody wants to admit that. We live our lives by mutually agreed upon lies."

Vivienne whispered, "It's okay, Jim."

Lambert said, "I didn't hear that, Jim. What did she say?"

"She said, 'It's okay, Jim.'"

"Ah, that's what I thought. We're not torturing Vivienne here. This is done with her consent. She's giving herself to you, freely and of her own will. She likes it. There's no denying the truth. And the more open and forthright we are, the more erotic it becomes. The farther you travel, the sexier the truth."

"Don't be afraid," Vivienne whispered.

Lambert said, "Strip away the rhetoric and the foolishness and this is what life comes down to: sex, violence, and the mysterious V. We start with elementary, primal truths, our dirty little secrets, and work our way up to what we pretend is the sophisticated and complicated. We wear clothes to cover up fat and droopy tits. The function of politics is to cover up the truth."

Quint was mesmerized, both by his target and Vivienne's reaction.

"Why do you think adolescent males get off on Conan the Barbarian? We are warriors. We capture and defend the V. It consumes our imaginations until the day we die."

Quint was so hard he felt like he was going to explode.

"We don't listen to the whining of pussies and wimps back on college campuses. We have our manhood on the line. We will not yield. Lyndon Johnson talks about peace with honor. Bullshit. It's peace with our balls intact."

Quint watched Vivienne's hand move between her legs. She gripped herself.

"If General Giap and Ho Chi Minh think we will listen to the blathering of kids in the street, they're wrong. They're deceiving themselves. Vietnam is not an exercise in realpolitik. We're talking gonads and hormones here. This is the territory of V."

He struck her again.

Lambert said, "Ah, ah, don't stop. If you stop now, you'll disappoint her. Vivienne has turned herself over to you. None of that horseshit rhetoric for her. She wants passion. She wants to live. Follow the truth, Jimbo. See where it goes. The only experience that comes close to the intensity of orgasm is the moment a fire fight ends and you are still alive."

Quint gripped his balls with his left hand as he struck her with his right. She moaned softly.

"She belongs. She is owned. She feels. She soars."

Vivienne looked up at him. Their eyes held. He struck her again. She cried out. She rolled over, legs spread. She arched her torso, her brown eyes suffused with passion and desire.

Quint entered her as hard as he could. Accepting the thrust, she made a noise in her throat. Looking up at him, she grabbed him by his hair.

She was so very, very warm. Quint could not believe he was so hard. He was overcome by desire and attacked her with all the fury he could muster.

Lambert said, "Yes, sir, the territory of the V! Fuck her, Jimbo. Fuck her hard. Fuck is the unembarrassed, honest word, straightforward and to the point. No horseshit euphemisms."

The V was awash. She was so nice. So very nice. And those eyes looking up at him!

Lambert said, "Yes, Jimbo. Yes. Do it to her."

Quint and Vivienne fucked in passionate union, oblivious to Lambert watching them, until Quint stiffened and Vivienne arched her torso beneath him.

Lambert applauded from behind the mirror, clapping his hands with boisterous enthusiasm. "Well, look at you two get into it! That was a wild ride. A real trip. Didn't I tell you? I forced you to do what you wouldn't have done on your own. I thought that would do the trick. More passion, more desire. More desire, more unhappiness."

Quint held Vivienne tightly. He had entered new and unexpected territory, wild, primal, and not a little spooky. And Lambert was right. He wouldn't have done that on his own.

Lambert said, "She loves you completely, Jimbo. Totally. She'll do anything for you. You like that passion? The yielding. The reddened ass. Those beautiful eyes looking up at you. The sharing of the truth. The crazed fucking. You want to do it again sometime? You only have to turn her over. Am I lying, Vivienne?" Lambert paused, waiting for an answer that didn't come. Then he said, "The lady's silence tells the story. I figured if ordinary sex wouldn't convince you, I'd take you into new territory. It worked too, I can tell it. You want Vivienne forever with me out of the way? I've said before and I'll say it again. You know how to earn her. I'm a man of my word. My offer still stands."

26

THE NEXT MORNING, Jim Quint, not hearing from either Del Lambert or Vivienne, went numbly about his work, interviewing oceanographers at the University of Hawaii about a developing new trend in science. Back in the city room, Quint wrote what he thought was an incisive, thoughtful feature, and, predictably, Fred Fielding furrowed his brows upon reading Quint's copy. He stared at him across the city room. "The spaceship earth! What the hell is that?"

Quint said, "It's a metaphor coined by Buckminster Fuller so the unwashed masses will get the idea, Fred. Here we are living on this self-enclosed globe hurtling through the void, a kind of spaceship. There is only so much air and water on the planet, only so many trees and it has to support a huge, growing population. We need to preserve, not destroy. We need to recycle so we don't destroy ourselves. We need to limit reproduction so as not to consume resources too fast. We need to be more concerned about the quality of our air and water."

Fielding rolled his eyes. "Ecology? What does that mean? This is not an academic journal, *The Bulletin of Atomic Scientists*, or something. This is the *Honolulu Star-Bulletin*. You have to explain obscure lingo to your readers. You know that."

Quint said, "Ecology means the science of the relationship between organisms and their environment."

"This is news?"

"That's what the scientists are telling me. No free lunch, they're saying. This is going to cost time and money to take care of."

"I don't get it." Fielding looked at the story again and frowned. "And 'environment?' What the hell does that mean?"

"The circumstances or conditions that surround one," Quint said. "This city room is a kind of environment. So is the island of Oahu."

"Right. And you think this is a story?"

"I'm supposed to cover radicals and science. This is science."

"The spaceship earth? Ecology? The environment? Are those words even in the dictionary?" Fielding shook his head sadly and spiked the story with conviction.

Quint maintained a continuing fantasy that someday Fielding would dramatically spike the palm of his hand. "I don't even get to explain ecology and the environment," he said. "That's it?"

"That's it," Fielding said.

"Did you really read what those people are saying?"

Fielding continued editing copy without looking up. "We've got real news to cover, Jim. It's depressing to think that the taxpayers are paying those people's salaries. I won't go into how much we're paying you to write stuff like this. When we say science, we mean science that means something to our readers. How does it affect their lives? Give me something that affects people's lives, then you've got a story."

IT WAS THE consensus of the Round Table that, after all the hoo rah, the debate between Eugene McCarthy and Bobby Kennedy had been a pathetic letdown with both candidates disappointing their fans and encouraging their critics. McCarthy as usual had been dry and too intellectual by half. He had stepped on the first verbal land mine, suggesting that to avoid a "kind of apartheid in this country," ghetto residents should have the opportunity to move into the country.

Kennedy, going for the crotch, had deftly pulled a number out of thin air, and used it like a bony knee: "You say you are going to take ten thousand black people and move them into Orange county?"

Barnhouse, recalling the quote, said McCarthy's proposal was

"Sort of like chocolate swirl ice cream, only if you run your tongue across the dark spots, it gets blown off."

The Round Table's prediction that Bobby Kennedy would win the debate big time was confirmed by the polls.

"Of course people like him," Barnhouse said. "People are fascinated by ferrets. They like the energy and those sharp little teeth. And they know from his having all those kids that he loves to fuck. They know you can't trust a man who isn't getting his end in."

Phil Mayer said, "You're a real deep thinker, Abner. We're in trouble here. You better hope that the system somehow pulls through and delivers a candidate the public can believe in." He bunched his face in disgust and took a puff on his cigar.

Barnhouse said, "So Clean Gene won in Oregon. Everybody knows people of that state have mold on the brain. They have a university whose athletes call themselves ducks. And so what if Bobby wins the California primary? You actually think those primaries mean anything?" *Har, har, har!*

"He's right," Fortier said. "It'll all be decided in smoke-filled rooms. We're talking Marlboro men here."

"Marlboros?" Barnhouse gave Fortier a look of reprimand. "Cigars, Jerry. Teenagers and girls smoke Marlboros. Politicians drink their whiskey straight, fuck knotholes in oak trees, and smoke big old stogies." *Har, har, har!* "Cigar smoke plus bullshit ass-deep to a tall squaw."

Mayer said, "Laugh on, Abner. Like the country doesn't have enough clowns who see this all as a joke. This isn't funny, pal."

Quint felt Hubert Humphrey had announced too late to enter the primaries, so he was sucking up to the party leaders who controlled 60 percent of the convention delegates, almost all of whom were under the political thumb of Lyndon Johnson. Like the war or not, Happy Hubie was forced to abase himself at Johnson's feet if he wanted to move into the White House.

When Quint brought up the episode of spaceship earth, his amiable companions agreed with Fielding. In a year twisted by military misadventure, riot, and assassination, it was hard to believe that a concern with clean air and water was a story with a future. The scientists liked it because it promised to be a mother lode of research grants, Quint understood that but he remained resolute, for which he was cheerfully ridiculed. The ridicule was a form of sport. Everyone was subjected to it at one time or another. Quint himself didn't know if the issue had legs or if it was half-baked nonsense intended to cadge more research grants from the government. However, Quint intuitively thought it was a problem that wasn't going away. Growing population. Limited resources. There had to be a reckoning somewhere down the line.

Quint said, "People are fucking like minks all over the planet. We're faced with finite resources. Only so much coal and oil and the rest of it. That's not to mention our ability to feed everybody."

"There's the green revolution," Miki Hasegawa said mildly.

Barnhouse said, "See there. No sweat. The miracle of fertilizer! We can all crap in little plastic bags and save it for the gardens of people in India. All those tomatoes! If we work it right, we can all have two cucumbers in every garage." *Har, har, har!*

Quint continued, "And the pollution! There's so much crap in the Hudson River people can almost walk on it."

"A nation of Jesuses," Barnhouse said. "Skipping merrily from turd to turd. Talk about progress!"

Fortier said, "Aw, fuck the Hudson River. What do we care out here in Honolulu? The board of tourism says we're living in paradise."

"The longer we wait to do something about it, the worse it's going to be. Think about it."

Mayer shook his head sadly. "Jim, why don't you rewrite another press release from Project Mohole? That's science isn't it? Riveting stuff."

"Go ahead, laugh. There's more to Mohole than meets the eye."

"Yeah, like a drill bit more than a mile beneath the earth's crust."

Quint said, "I've talked to several geologists at the university.

They say there's plenty of places where the earth's mantle is thinner. Yet they've got the Mohole drilling platform anchored over deep ocean. Why would they want to do that, except to waste money?"

Mayer said, "You know, Jim, sometimes I think you need one of old Abner's smartnin' pills. What's the point of taxing people if you don't piss away the treasury on armies and research projects that don't make sense? They're blowing all that money in order to provide you science writers with another fascinating story to put people to sleep. You'd bitch if you were being hung with a new rope."

"Right," Quint said.

"Or you could write another cheerful story about global cooling. Get all that depression out of your system. Fielding likes those doesn't he? Thinks they give readers goosebumps. They sure do send a shiver up my spine, I can tell you. Brrrrrrrr." Mayer pretended to shiver, giving Quint a sardonic grin.

Sanger said, "Fielding probably had a pair of ice skates when he was a kid. Looking forward to playing hockey on Pearl Harbor."

Mayer looked amused. "Guaranteed nobody will be worrying about the spaceship earth when the planet freezes over."

"That's when hell freezes over," Babs said.

"We'll call it snowball earth," Barnhouse said. *Har, har, har!*

27

DEL LAMBERT FLEW to Washington two days after the McCarthy-Kennedy debate, so Vivienne and Jim treated themselves to a day together. If Lambert found out, he found out. Quint decided to take his chances. Vivienne didn't like hanging out in the sun. White-skinned American women were famous for destroying their skin in the name of a tan. In Asia, the reverse was true—the whiter the skin, the greater the status—and by Southeast Asian standards, Vivienne was very light skinned.

Quint wasn't especially enamoured of beaches either. The exception to this was an occasional afternoon he and Vivienne spent belly surfing on the modest waves at Kailua Beach. Quint had once belly surfed one of the horrific surges at Makapuu, but was dumped so hard on the beach he thought he was going to break his neck; after that he left Makapuu to young men who were stronger and more foolhardy than he.

From Honolulu, there were two ways to the North Shore to watch the surfers—the direct way, through Pearl City, central Oahu, and Haleiwa, and the leisurely way, across the Pali and up the windward side. Quint and Vivienne headed across the Pali. With a white Chevrolet car following them around the curving road, they headed on North Shore up the windward shoreline. They stopped at the village of Kaaawa for lunch at a rustic eatery named Big Buddha's. Big Buddha's was all bamboo and rattan with small thatched roofs over the tables on a lanai that overlooked the ocean. The specialty of the house was sautéed sea turtle. They had found themselves a table when Quint noticed that the man who was following them had decided to come in out of the heat and have himself a drink at the bar while he waited for them to finish their meal. A sensible move.

Quint said, "That man was at the party at your house, Vivienne. He was a waiter for your caterers, but he seemed more interested in me than taking care of his guests."

"One of Del's helpers."

Quint said, "I think I'll have a chat with him."

Vivienne didn't want Quint to talk to the man. "Jim, please."

"It'll only take a minute."

She chewed on her lower lip.

"Would you like an iced tea?"

"That would be nice."

Quint ordered Vivienne an iced tea, then walked up to the man and took a rattan stool next to him. Watching him, Quint ordered a Primo. The man was in his mid-thirties with his light brown hair cut short. He wore a light blue aloha shirt with yellow flowers, walking shorts, and sandals. He eyed Quint casually, looking unconcerned, and took a sip of Primo.

"Nothing like a cold beer on a day like this," Quint said.

"It's hotter than the sheriff's pistol, that's a fact."

"Or the rifle in Memphis."

The man grimaced. "Wasn't that something? What a year this is turning out to be."

"So who do you think will win the election now, Bobby, the Hump, or the Nix?"

The man considered that, looking thoughtful. "It'll be the Hump versus the Nix with the Nix winning by a nose. I don't think the voters can imagine the Happy Warrior dealing with Vietnam. People don't like it that he's been Charlie McCarthy to Johnson's Edgar Bergen."

"And they can imagine the Nix?"

He said, "Half the country might be laughing at the little pecker, but the Nix takes himself seriously. The French have a saying for it, *L' Homme Serieux*. The serious man. Charles de

Gaulle is an example of that. Always serious. People will never elect a president who goes around saying, 'By Golly!' Lou Costello says 'By Golly!' Look at John Wayne, Gary Cooper, and Charlton Heston. Serious guys. *L' Homme Serieux.*"

"Ah, so you speak French then?"

The man smiled. "I know the phrase."

Quint said, "Who are you?"

He blinked. "I beg your pardon?"

Quint said, "You were a waiter at Lambert's party. Now you've been following me around. Since when does a waiter follow people around? You're no waiter. I want to know who you are and why you're following me."

He pursed his lips. "Somebody better keep an eye on you, don't you think? And your lady friend. For your own good."

"Oh? Why is that?"

"I'm Roger, by the way." The man offered his hand and they shook.

"Do you have a last name?" Quint asked.

The man thought a moment. "How about Lobry? Will that do?" He glanced toward Vivienne, then back at Quint.

"So what kind of name is Lobry?"

Lobry looked amused. "French. I'm from Quebec Province, an officer of the Royal Canadian Mounted Police."

Quint raised an eyebrow. "Chasing a lost moose in Hawaii?"

"How about the Sûreté chasing Union Corse heroin smugglers operating from Vietnam? I'm scouting recruits. An American journalist with a Vietnamese girlfriend would make good cover."

Quint frowned. "Oh for Christ's sake, quit the games."

Lobry studied Quint for a moment. "Tell me, Jim, do you love Vivienne?"

"Yes, I do."

"I mean really love her." Lobry signaled for another beer.

"Why yes."

"And what about her? Does she love you?"

"I think so, yes."

Lobry seemed satisfied by that answer. "Well, good. It's nice that you have one another," he said. "People need that. What do you really know about her? Her past, I mean. And about Lambert for that matter?"

"I think he's probably crazy."

Lobry grinned.

"Said he can't sleep. Gripped by rage. Post-battle stress syndrome."

Lobry burst out laughing. "He told you that? What else did he say?"

"He says he's been after the CBS film of the Lon Be massacre for three years. He thinks Vivienne's sister knows where it is. He wants it."

Quint's companion looked amused. "I bet he does."

"Are you telling me he's not suffering from battle fatigue or whatever they're calling it these days?"

The waiter arrived with the beer.

"You didn't answer me."

Lobry said, "Lambert might very well be a head case. I have no idea. All things considered, there's probably a good argument for that."

"But it hasn't been made," Quint said.

"I didn't say that either."

Quint decided to take another track. "Vivienne says she hasn't talked to her sister. She thinks she's probably dead."

"You believe that?"

"To be honest, I don't know what to believe."

Lobry pointed to Vivienne with his glass of beer. "Let me be honest with you, Jim. I have no interest in you whatsoever except as a curious example of someone who has gotten himself involved in something he doesn't understand. The reason I'm following Vivienne is to make sure she lives to see another day."

"You think somebody's going to kill her?"

"Del Lambert might be thinking about it. He might very well try to kill you too. I wouldn't put it past him."

Quint looked alarmed. "But her health is more important than mine."

"You have to understand, Jim, I'm not any kind of guardian angel or anything. Just a guy doing my job. I don't hold anything against you, but orders are orders."

"Lambert says he's been after the Lon Be film for three years. If Vivienne is his only link to Genevieve and the film why on earth would he want to kill her?"

"Good question." Lobry took another sip of beer.

"But you're not going to answer it."

"I don't think so. By the way, I read your stuff in the *Star-Bulletin*. Good writer."

"Are you telling me I should learn more about her?"

"In your shoes, I sure as hell would," Lobry said. "Ask her again what happened at Lon Be, but not today after she's seen you talking to me. If you learn anything you think I should know, I'll be around. Just give me the word."

"How will I know what it is I should tell you?"

"Believe me, you'll get the picture."

Quint said, "Okay so who are you really working for?"

Lobry poured directly to the bottom of his glass, watching the head form up. He sucked up some of the head before it spilled over the edge of the glass. "You can pour your beer down the side of the glass or just dump it in the bottom. The truth is kind of that way. You can kind of ease into it or dump it in the bottom. You get a little foam or a whole bunch. Either way it eventually settles down."

Lobry took a sip, studying Quint. "Life goes on. The beer still tastes good. Crisp. Refreshing. Bittersweet. Still has some fizz to it. Isn't that what life's all about?" He took another sip. "Mmmmm. Primo. Number one."

28

J IM QUINT FOUND it increasingly difficult to listen to the Round Table banter every afternoon, much less participate. Quint thought about Vivienne and Lambert and the mystery of Lon Be almost every waking moment. Why on earth would the Vietcong not have long since destroyed the film?

Tuesday was the day of the California primary, therefore a big day at the Round Table. As Quint opened the door to the Columbia Inn late that afternoon, he was welcomed by a grotesque round of *har, har, har* laughter by Abner Barnhouse, who had gotten a head start on another bender. The object of his merriment turned out to be a bumper sticker that had appeared in California.

FIRST ETHEL, NOW US.

Quint's thoughts were interrupted by Jerry Fortier, Babs's poke, who showed up at the table. Fortier ran his fingers through his curly hair and hopped aboard a stool. He adjusted his glasses and signaled for a Primo. The regulars all could tell by the look on his face that something had happened.

"Well?" Mayer asked.

"Well what?" Fortier pretended to be innocent.

Mayer scowled. "What do you think, Einstein? What's going on? Talking to you is like talking to a tree."

Only half listening to the Round Table bullshit, Quint drifted off again. He couldn't help it.

Fortier said, "Bells in the city room. Got everybody scurrying. They're thinking a rump edition of the green streak."

Bells? That woke Quint up.

Babs leaned forward, her substantial front threatening to topple Primo bottles. A rump edition was a partial run to include a breaking story from the mainland. "Oh?"

Quint and his companions were all obviously thinking the same thing: Something maximum crappy must have happened in California.

"This one's good," Fortier said. He accepted a Primo from Tosh Kaneshiro and poured himself a glass. He took a sip, making everybody wait.

Bells in the city room? They were all curious.

Finally Phil Mayer slammed his hand down on the table. "Okay, goddamn it. Out with it. What fucking bells are you talking about?"

Fortier said, "As we speak, surgeons in a Manhattan hospital are attempting to remove two thirty-two calibre bullets from the stomach of Andy Warhol. Totally ruined his election night."

Barnhouse said, "The Campbell Soup man? What happened?"

Fortier took another sip of beer. "The stories are still coming in, but Warhol was apparently shot by a woman named Valerie Solanis, one of his acquaintances. Ms. Solanis, as she likes to be addressed, is the founder of SCUM."

Andy Warhol? The Society for Cutting Up Men?

The regulars all blinked, waiting for Fortier to continue.

Fortier said, "The lead story said Miss Solanis is seeking the complete elimination of the male sex. She thinks that would result in an 'out-of-sight, groovy, all-female world.' "

Babs said, "Are you serious or are you making this up?"

"Andy Warhol, shot by the founder of SCUM? Bullshit," Mayer said. He was disbelieving. "By an art critic, I could believe."

"You think not?" Fortier said. "The SCUM woman, yes." He eyed Babs with suspicion and scooted his stool away from hers. So did Mayer and Sanger.

"Assholes," Babs said.

Fortier took another sip of Primo. "Here, see for yourselves." He laid a strip of wire service copy on the table. "First step toward an out-of-sight, groovy world. The all-female world started today. Mark it on your calendar."

Babs snatched the copy, reading it. "He's right. The woman who founded SCUM shot Andy Warhol."

"Jesus, is he going to live?" Barnhouse asked.

"They don't know," Fortier said. "It's touch and go."

Sanger said, "I suppose this means we're going to have to let the women into our tea party or they'll shoot us. No more goosey, goosey."

"Groovy!" Babs beamed.

Sanger leered lasciviously. "Which groove are you talking about?"

Abner Barnhouse cocked his head, eyeing Quint. "What's the matter there, Jimbo? You're looking off your feed. We've got SCUM mounting a third front and you're just sitting there."

"Looks like he's in love," Sanger said. "Got that vacant look in his eye."

Quint supposed he did have a vacant look in his eye. "I was thinking about passion and turf."

"Thinking about your pee pee," Mayer said.

Quint retreated into his thoughts, vaguely aware of the shift in subject from SCUM to Gov. George C. Wallace of Alabama and his wife Lurleen. Wallace, unable to succeed himself as governor of Alabama, had fast-talked Alabamans into electing Lurleen as governor in 1966. This transparent con enabled Wallace to launch his new American Independent party from the governor's mansion.

You should know I'm doomed.

The consequences of doing nothing are closing in on both of you. One of the most beautiful women on the island and you dither.

"Hey, you!"

It was Steve, trying to shake Quint out of his trance.

"Yeah, yeah, I was listening. You're talking about lust and groovy Babs."

Babs adjusted her spectacles. One member or another of the Round Table was poking her or thinking about it. She was flattered. Quint liked Babs okay, but he couldn't figure her as a sexual object. She did have a handsome pair under her blouse, that was true. But she wasn't Vivienne. Beside Vivienne, all women were ordinary.

Babs said, "We're talking about the First Husband of Alabama, Jim, not Steve's unobtainable fantasies."

Barnhouse said, "George Wallace is like a fat girl running for prom queen. How will old Happy Hubie steal his votes short of calling him a nigger lover?"

As usual, Barnhouse had gone straight to the heart of it: To Wallace's followers in the South, state's rights was a code, meaning the right to have Jim Crow if they wanted. In 1967, doing his best to mask his racism, Wallace had gone north to recruit working-class whites from north of the Mason-Dixon who were frightened and angry at the cultural changes around them. It was the Democrats who stood to be screwed by the American Independent Party, not the Republicans.

Sanger ran the palm of his hand over his balding forehead. "Maybe Bobby could co-opt him. Name him as his running mate before the primaries in the South. That would be fun. President Ferrett Face and Vice President Coon Dog."

Barnhouse said, "Coon Dog, that's good. Say did you hear the one about the first Negro astronaut? They're waiting for the launch, see, five, four, three, and so on, then the countdown guy says, 'Moon the coon!' Mission control scrubs the count. Hey, hey, hey, knock that crap off. So they do it again, five, four, three, two, one . . . The guy says, 'Trigger the nigger!' Mission control instantly erupts with protest, but the guy says, 'Too late, the jig is up.' " *Har, har, har*! Barnhouse nearly fell of his stool with laughter. He squinted his eyes from the smoke curling up from his cigarette.

Mayer looked disgusted. "Jesus, Abner!"

Miki Hasegawa, who had been sitting quietly, looked vaguely ill. "Abner, give us a break and keep those kinds of stories to yourself. You're the guy who has been moaning and groaning about black people rioting."

Quint was thinking he was madly, wildly in love with Vivienne. He wanted her forevermore. He wanted to grow old and die with her and all the rest of the romantic fantasy. Roger Lobry had said he should learn more about her. What?

Quint caught Mayer watching him. "By God, Quint is off his feed. You're right, Steve, he does look like he's in love."

Sanger said, "Shows all the signs of it. Sitting there like a stump. Preoccupied look on his face."

Mayer arched an eyebrow. "Who's the unlucky lady? A hooker just got out of prison? A hippie with boils?"

"The wife of an army officer, I think," Sanger said.

Quint frowned. "Asshole."

Mayer perked up. "Really? Bayonet practice on an officer's wife?" Mayer loved gossip. "The officer know about this?"

"An affair with a military wife? A longhair like me? Sure!" Quint was an unconvincing liar.

Barnhouse said, "If the officer catches you at it, he'll probably want to put you through a little boot camp. Kick ass time. Teach you the meaning of honor and discipline. You ever think about that? K-Y-P-I-Y-P."

Quint thought a moment. "Okay, I bite. What does K-Y-P-I-Y-P mean?"

"It's a military acronym for the best way to avoid the clap or in this case the wrath of the lady's husband. Keep your pecker in your pants." *Har, har, har*!

29

As Andy Warhol lay in the hospital recovering from a four-hour operation in Manhattan, voters in California made known their preferences in the Democratic primary. A *Los Angeles Times* poll said that by a margin of two and a half to one, California Democrats thought Kennedy had won the debate on the previous Friday, and he was highly favored to win the election and with it a substantial block of convention delegates.

The first polls had closed at the deadline of the *Star-Bulletin's* green streak final, and the results continued all afternoon and evening, showing Kennedy leading and getting stronger. Jim Quint didn't want to spend the night at home alone thinking about Del and Vivienne Lambert, so he ate his dinner at the Columbia Inn and stayed on with the regulars waiting for the California vote to be totaled, getting more and more sloshed. It wasn't just that Quint had allowed himself to get sucked into a dangerous game, but what if Del's cockeyed idea of a Vivienne War meant putting the regulars in harm's way? How could Quint possibly explain to his friends what was going on?

At 11 P.M., the Honolulu television stations would get tapes of the network news; until then, the regulars had to watch the locals do their thing. At 8 P.M. Ken Kashiwahara, Linda Coble, and other local television newscasters interrupted the programming with the final numbers from California. Bobby Kennedy had scored about 50 percent of the vote. Hubert Humphrey was looking at 30 percent. Clean Gene, the man who crumpled in the clutch, had collected about 20 percent; the Don Quixote of 1968 had tilted his last windmill.

Quint stayed on, lingering with Steve Sanger, Phil Mayer, and Abner Barnhouse, who was so bombed he could hardly stay on his stool. Still Abner knocked them back, Primo after Primo, until his huge gut slurped and gurgled like a tank car every time he moved.

At ten o'clock, midnight in Los Angeles, Ken Kashiwahara passed on the details of Kennedy's acceptance speech. Kashiwahara gave his viewers video clips of Kennedy giving campaign speeches in California as regulars listened to his acceptance speech live on the radio. A network reporter described the action.

Kennedy, interrupting his frenzied supporters who were singing, "This Land is Your Land," began by expressing his high regard for Don Drysdale, who had thrown a shutout that night. "I hope we have as good fortune in our campaign." Kennedy had all kinds of good things to say about Eugene McCarthy, whom he had figuratively kneed in the balls, thanking him for breaking a political logjam. He said McCarthy had made "citizen participation a new and powerful force in our political life." He invited McCarthy's followers to join his campaign "not for myself, but for the cause and ideas which moved you to begin this great popular movement."

Listening to this, Barnhouse said, " 'Ideas that,' not 'ideas which,' ferret face. A Harvard man!"

"Would you just listen to what he has to say?" Mayer said.

Miki Hasegawa gave Barnhouse a look. "I agree, Phil. Please, Abner."

"Control yourself, Abner," Babs Parsegian said dryly.

"The rest of us want to hear what he has to say even if you don't," Mayer added.

Then Kennedy thanked everybody. His brother Teddy and the rest of the Kennedy clan. The blacks and Mexicans. His dog Freckles. This was followed by the obligatory summing up. "We are a great country, an unselfish country, and a compassionate country."

Barnhouse said, "An unselfish and compassionate country." He slapped his mighty paunch. *Har, har, har!* "I think I need another beer."

"That's precisely what you don't need," Mayer said.

In the live sound behind Kennedy's image the regulars could hear them going bonkers in the ballroom.

The network reporter said, "Now Senator Kennedy is giving his followers the V-sign, for peace and victory. He pushes his hair back from his forehead. He turns and retreats to the kitchen, his evening of triumph at an end."

The regulars lingered for a few minutes, then suddenly, a news flash jumped on the bottom of the screen: THIS IN FROM LOS ANGELES. SEN. ROBERT KENNEDY HAS BEEN SHOT. REPEAT, ROB-ERT KENNEDY HAS BEEN SHOT. WE WILL BE BRINGING YOU DE-TAILS AS THEY BECOME AVAILABLE.

They leaped up and lurched for the door. Mayer, Sanger, and Quint led the way, with Abner Barnhouse trailing, his mammoth gut bouncing. They sprinted across the parking lot to the guard at the entrance to the stairs leading upstairs into the *Star-Bulletin's* city room. Mayer threw open the door, and they raced up the concrete stairs. Mayer yanked open the second door, this one opposite the door to the darkroom. The bells were still ringing.

BING, BING, BING, BING, BING, BING, BING, BING!

Joe Arakaki, the night city editor, was standing over the AP machine, looking stunned.

BING, BING, BING, BING, BING, BING, BING, BING!

They gathered around him and watched the copy inching out.

BING, BING, BING, BING, BING, BING, BING, BING!

Bobby Kennedy had stopped in the kitchen to shake hands with a dishwasher. The best story of the shooting was a verbatim account, moved by the wire services, of an eyewitness, Andrew West, a radio reporter for KRKD in Los Angeles, who had trailed Kennedy from the podium to the kitchen:

"Senator Kennedy has been shot. Is that possible? Is that pos-sible? Is it possible, ladies and gentlemen? It is possible he has— not only Senator Kennedy. Oh my God. Senator Kennedy has been shot, and another man, a Kennedy campaign

manager—and possibly shot in the head. Rafer Johnson has ahold of the man who apparently has fired the shot.

He still has the gun—the gun is pointed at me right at this moment. I hope they can get the gun out of his hand. Be very careful. Get that gun. Get that gun. GET THAT GUN! Stay away from the gun. Stay away from the gun. His hand is frozen. TAKE AHOLD OF HIS THUMB AND BREAK IT IF YOU HAVE TO. GET HIS THUMB! ALL RIGHT, THAT'S IT, RAFER, GET IT, GET THE GUN, RAFER. Hold him, hold him. We don't want another Oswald."

Sanger looked numb. "Looks like we've got another Oswald whether we want one or not."

Mayer, staring at the wire service machine, said, "Andy Warhol was just a warmup. Spencer Tracey thought he had it bad at Black Rock. This is a bad, bad, day in the U.S.A."

Sanger said, "Make that a bad, bad year."

The first AP reporter on the scene noted that five feet from where Kennedy had fallen, somebody had scrawled five words on the kitchen wall: "The once and future king."

Finally, the bells having stopped, the regulars read that Kennedy had indeed been shot in the head, but he was still alive as he was taken to the hospital. An unidentified man was being held for the shooting.

30

*B*OBBY KENNEDY'S FUNERAL was carried live in Honolulu. The Round Table regulars gathered at the Columbia Inn to watch Teddy Kennedy give a eulogy for his brother in St. Patrick's Cathedral in New York. The country buzzed with what Phil Mayer called the "predictable oh-my-God-what-is-happening-to-us" posturing as the Kennedy family prepared to bury Bobby. A nutball Arab had murdered Robert Kennedy because he was sore at Kennedy's having said he would continue American support of Israel if he were elected president. Sirhan Sirhan was a joker in the deck. Amid the fury of domestic politics and the war in Vietnam, nobody, but nobody was paying any attention to the Israelis and Arabs.

The regulars all thought the Israelis had taken care of the sorehead Arabs the year before, having kicked the manure out of the Egyptians in just six days. Besides, Kennedy's comment was probably just idle talk anyway. Kennedy didn't mean to cause a lot of hard feelings among Arabs. All he wanted was for Jewish liberals to contribute to his political campaign.

Jim Quint had always regarded Teddy as a lightweight whom the Massachusetts voters had elected to the Senate as a courtesy to the Kennedy family. Now he watched as Teddy, standing tall, speaking forcefully in his Boston accent, his wide, square-jawed face resolute, said, "There is discrimination in this world, and slavery and slaughter and starvation. Governments repress their people, millions are trapped in poverty while the nations grow rich, and wealth is lavished on armaments everywhere."

Teddy looked out over the assembled mourners.

"The answer is to rely on youth. Not a time of life but a state of mind, a temper of the will, a quality of imagination, a predominance of courage over timidity."

As Quint watched, he wondered what obsessive Del Lambert, no lover of what he regarded as a generation of chickenshit draft dodgers and war protestors, would be thinking if he was watching Teddy's eulogy.

Teddy said, "A young monk began the Protestant reformation. A young general extended an empire from Macedonia to the borders of the earth. And a young woman reclaimed the territory of France. It was a young Italian explorer who discovered the New World. And the thirty-two-year-old Thomas Jefferson who proclaimed that 'all men are created equal.' "

A man at the bar slapped his thigh. "Right on, Teddy!"

"Yes!" his companion cried.

Both hawks and doves in the Columbia Inn were caught in the emotion of the moment, and Quint suspected that must be the reaction across the country.

"My brother need not be idealized, or enlarged in death beyond what he was in life—to be remembered simply as a good and decent man who saw wrong and tried to right it, saw suffering and tried to heal it, saw war and tried to stop it."

After Gene McCarthy proved it could be done, Quint thought.

"Those of us who loved and who take him to his rest today pray that what he was to us and what he wished for others will someday come to pass for all the world." Teddy struggled to control the emotion of the moment. "As he said many times, in many parts of this nation, to those he touched and who sought to touch him: 'Some men see things as they are and say why. I dream things that never were, and say why not?' "

Thus Teddy Kennedy sent his brother to his rest. Quint felt it was an impressive performance and then some. Teddy had done what Eugene McCarthy had failed to do at Carroll College the night Lyndon Johnson announced his decision not to run for reelection. He had demonstrated that he was no lightweight little brother. He had the stuff. He had stepped forward to claim the torch of his fallen brothers with a forceful, memorable speech. If he did not do something monumentally, unimaginably stupid, Teddy, not Bobby, would be the Kennedy to reclaim the White House.

As they carried Bobby's body from St. Patrick's Cathedral, a television reporter broke in to announce that the suspected assassin of Martin Luther King had been apprehended in London's Heathrow Airport on his way to Brussels. Working from an FBI photograph, the Royal Canadian Mounted Police had searched through 200,000 passport applications before they found one with a resemblance to the suspect. Detective Chief Superintendent Thomas Butler and Detective Chief Inspector Noel Thompson, known as the "Terrible Twins" for their tenacity in pursuing criminals, took James Earl Ray into custody. Ray, traveling under a passport issued to Ramon George Sneyd, was carrying a loaded pistol.

As reporters, the Round Table regulars were used to thinking about the news in terms of cycles and timing. Bad news was ordinarily released on a Sunday because weekend newspaper staffs were small and Monday was a skinny paper. Thursday papers were fat because of food ads touting weekend sales. And so on. There was only so much space on the nation's front pages—that's not to mention time available on the network news programs where, increasingly, Americans got their news. All politicians and bureaucrats knew the difference between a bad news day and a good news day. Timed news was managed news. Everything else was unpredictable and so potentially dangerous.

To the regulars it was incomprehensible that the FBI had inadvertently announced the arrest of James Earl Ray at the exact same moment when the nation was paying its last respects to the fallen Robert F. Kennedy. Could it not have waited another forty minutes?

Here was a director of the FBI who had for years denied the existence of the Mafia because he was afraid his agency couldn't deal with the Sicilian crime families. Bobby Kennedy, for all his faults, at least had the courage to take on the mob. In doing so, he had shown Hoover up. The director of the FBI didn't like upstart poachers. The consensus at the Round Table was that J. Edgar Hoover was an envious moron if not an unmitigated bastard.

31

THE ASSASSINATION OF Robert Kennedy opened a summer season of escalating confusion, rage, and fury. Neither Democrats nor Republicans had any idea how to douse the domestic firestorm, and American commanders in Saigon were telling reporters on the side that they were fighting the war with their hands tied behind their backs.

Oblivious to irony, blacks resorted to violence that Martin Luther King, Jr. had sought to avoid. Parts of Detroit and Baltimore and Washington's 14th Street corridor still lay in ruins from the violence in the summer of 1965. Now, one by one, more urban slums went up in flames. And with school out for the summer, the restless armies of youthful protesters had emerged from their dorms and apartments, joints in hand, looking for a tan and a little action. No radical deserving of sweatband or Joan Baez hair wanted to leave 1968 without exceeding the violence and mayhem of 1967. These precious moments of youth were not to be squandered.

A week after Bobby Kennedy was buried, Quint drove to the Unitarian Church on the Pali Highway to interview the Black Panther firebrand Stokely Carmichael. Quint had not heard from Lambert since the night of strapping Vivienne's rump. Was it possible that Lambert was closing in on the Lon Be film and the secrets it held? It was hard to imagine any public figure would want to be interviewed by a reporter with so much on his mind, but that was Carmichael's bad luck.

Carmichael had been a radical black activist for several years, but now, two months after the murder of Martin Luther King,

Jr. there was a bull market for charismatic Negroes skilled at anti-honkie rhetoric. Judging from the stories on the A Wire of the Associated Press, Carmichael was making speeches just about everywhere, airfare paid by white liberals abasing themselves from presumed guilt.

Given the history of slavery and race relations in America, Quint didn't think guilt was entirely out of order, but the white sponsors of black power advocates had a way of overdoing it that he found a bit much. It was like they were monks lining up to be flogged for their sins.

There were presumably places in the United States—cities with substantial populations of Negroes—that would have been more productive destinations for a prophet of black rebellion, but who in his right mind was going to turn down a trip to Hawaii? Carmichael was an enthusiastic revolutionary. The stupid honkies wanted to be called names, he'd call them names with enthusiasm. It would be his pleasure.

Carmichael had spoken at several locations that day, but the pastor of the local Unitarian Church, a bearded, serious man, famously guilty and given to sermons that were pseudo-scholarly analyses of rock and roll lyrics—once devoting two Sundays in a row to Bob Dylan—had called Quint to arrange a one-on-one interview. The pastor was groovy cubed. He wanted the whole state to know what Carmichael had to say about the evil white people, not just gatherings of fellow liberals at the university and his church.

Carmichael was a tall man, light skinned and good looking in a non-African way. Also, he spoke fluent Standard English, all of which brought out the latent racist in Quint that Quint struggled earnestly to suppress. Quint figured there was a white man in the woodpile of Carmichael's heritage somewhere. He also suspected that most well intentioned whites probably thought like he did, including the humble Unitarian pastor, but they would never admit it except with a knife at their throat. That didn't mean the country was doomed, but it would probably be a long march to racial harmony.

Carmichael obviously felt that if the honkies who'd sprung for his ticket wanted to be verbally flogged, he'd give good measure, the racist motherfucking hypocrite honkies. By his reckoning, blacks were surrounded by honkies and pigs. They were all racists, including his hosts.

He said the guilt mongers were phony assholes, pretending to give a flying fuck what happened to the brothers. George Wallace at least had the balls to say what he honestly felt even if he did mask it in his horseshit about state's rights. Lyndon Johnson was a plain old racist Texas prick, trying to buy time with some horseshit civil rights legislation that did nothing to address the real problems. Enemies like that blacks could deal with. The hypocrites were the worst.

As Quint scribbled Carmichael's more inflammatory lines in his notebook, he couldn't help but admire him in a grudging sort of way. Carmichael knew that in the current social climate he could get away with saying anything he wanted, however outrageous. Quint didn't like ignoring obvious questions, but he did what he had to do.

Carmichael was clearly having fun. No matter how outrageous or inflammatory his assertion, the honkey reporter scribbled every word. No professional black radical scolding the odious honkies ever mentioned King's assertion that content of character should come before color of skin. But never mind. What King had said meant little if anything. The fact that a redneck white had murdered him meant everything.

It was hard for Quint to disagree with Carmichael's charge that the Kerner Commission's report on relations was an exercise in futility. "As if low income housing and the creation of a couple of million jobs is going to do anything. Right!" Carmichael rolled his eyes.

It wasn't until the end of the interview that Carmichael hit Quint with a request that Quint agreed was also justified, but spelled trouble when he turned his story in to Fielding.

Carmichael looked Quint straight on and said, "I note that in the newspapers here in Honolulu, we are called Negroes. We don't want to be called Negroes. We're finished with that honkie shit. We want to be called black. You call yourselves white. We want to be called black."

Quint hesitated.

"Any problem with that?" Carmichael asked.

Quint shook his head. "Makes sense. No problem. I'll do it." Quint did agree with him. And it was true, the current style made no sense. But to tell Carmichael no problem? What a liar Quint was!

"I appreciate it. Thank you," Carmichael said.

This thanking of the honkie reporter was Stokely Carmichael's way of sealing the deal with a ration of guilt, never mind that he could see that Quint agreed with him. But if Quint hadn't agreed, if he had tried to argue with Carmichael, Carmichael would have dumped on him big time with the Unitarian pastor and his friends nodding their heads in vigorous agreement. Like it or not, Quint would have to do his best to use black instead of Negro in his story.

But Quint drove back down the Pali Highway with Vivienne on his mind, not Stokely Carmichael. When he got to the city room, he found a note that had been left for him by a delivery service.

Jim, Del left for Saigon this morning. If you have the time, come and see me. Don't call. Love, Vivienne.

Quint glanced at the clock. The city desk wanted to use the Carmichael interview for its Sunday edition. Plenty of time to write it later on. No reason not to take some time out for Vivienne.

LOOKING PENSIVE, VIVIENNE stood beside Quint as he studied the painting. She had completed the male figure at the café table. Having looked at his face in the mirror every day for twenty-seven years, Quint no longer really saw it, yet the man in the painting was clearly him. He had originally grown his handlebar mustache because he was self-conscious about his full lips. As rendered by Vivienne, they were sensual. His hair was a rich, brown tangle. His blue eyes were having fun with his companions. He was flattered and proud that Vivienne saw in him the man at the table in her painting.

She had obviously spent a lot of time on the little girl. Quint didn't have to be told that Vivienne had looked very much like that child when she was that age. He assumed Vivienne had used a photo of herself to work from, but he never saw it. It struck him as unlikely that she could have imagined so accurate an image. This was not maybe or almost Vivienne as a child. It was she. There was no doubting it.

The mother of the child, the man's partner, was next. As she had with her rendering of Quint, Vivienne began with the feet and worked her way upward. Everything from the shoulders up was still blank.

"What do you think?" Vivienne asked.

"What do I think? Wow!" Quint said, "I like this scene a lot. Me. My lady. And my little girl. Looks just like you. Big bowls of *pho*. I think I'm falling in love with the artist."

"Really?" Vivienne looked pleased.

"Are we visiting Saigon in this painting or is it permanent?"

She laughed. "Could be just a visit."

"The war is over though. That much seems clear. It's a lazy day. People are having fun."

"The war is over and people have resumed their lives, yes."

"I hope you make yourself look as good as me."

"You want to see how I look?"

Quint grinned. "You bet!"

WHEN THEY GOT to Quint's apartment, Vivienne ripped off his shirt, sending buttons flying. "You. Oh, you," she murmured.

"Horny lady. I like that." He pinned her wrists behind her, kissing her.

"We're doing it, Jim. We're beating him. We're defeating him. Us against him and we're winning." Her tongue worked urgently against his.

The phone began ringing.

Annoyed, Quint answered it. "Hello."

Del Lambert said, "Surprise!"

Quint slumped. "Nothing you do is ever a surprise, Colonel."

"They postponed my trip to Saigon. Say, Jim, I was wondering, have you seen my wife today?"

Quint frowned. He mouthed *Del* to Vivienne. "No, I haven't."

Lambert's voice turned hard. "Don't lie to me, you dumb son of a bitch. I've got people outside your apartment right now. Are you listening, Jim?"

"I'm listening."

"You need to pay attention to me, Jimbo, once you commit to one course of action, you seal off other possibilities. This is true of any military operation, whether it's the invasion at Normandy or the assault on Pork Chop Hill. Delay and your options narrow. The same logic holds for a political campaign. As the campaign progresses candidates will become locked into a strategy, however bad. They lose options. Hubert Humphrey is convinced that he can't win the nomination if he loses Johnson's patronage. The longer he waits to decide whether he wants to be his own man, the more difficult it becomes for him. Watch the news. I'm making a called shot here. See if I'm not right. I say again, are you listening?"

"I'm listening."

"You know what you're doing, pal? You're helping Uncle Ho Chi Minh run the clock against the United States of America. Tell me you're listening."

"I'm listening."

"Do you know what that makes you?"

Quint cleared his throat.

"Well do you? Remember Westmoreland's speech at the Pacific Club? You laughed, remember? Well, I'm tired of fucking around. If you want to spare both yourself and Vivienne some serious harm, I mean some really bad shit, you'll goddamn it deliver for me and deliver fast. You still want her, don't you? You haven't changed your mind about that?"

"I still want her."

"Well for Christ's sake make me happy, and maybe we can have a negotiated settlement here. I don't want to see people seriously hurt, but I've come to the end of my patience."

Lambert hung up.

"What did he say?" Vivienne said.

"He says I'm helping Ho Chi Minh run the clock."

Vivienne looked puzzled.

Quint said, "It means stalling until the game is over. We need to talk."

"Talk?" Vivienne buried her mouth at the base of his neck and began sucking.

He grabbed her by the hair and turned her onto her back. "Why you little vampire you."

JIM QUINT GOT back to the city room with plenty of time to write his Stokely Carmichael story. Quint knew what was expected of him and he delivered. He wrote a right-minded "color" piece, meaning it had no real news hook and was larded with unnecessary detail about Carmichael's personal appearance—to prove that he'd actually talked to him—and short if not completely devoid of honest questions asked. Not once had Quint truly challenged any of Carmichael's assertions, no matter how hyperbolic or demented.

Quint threw in some of Carmichael's more outrageous quotes as a form of seasoning. Each quote was a righteous slug of Tabasco. *We honkies be bad. Oh, my goodness how bad we are!* After he turned the article in, Quint went to the back shop for some more of Yamani's coffee before he returned to his desk to await the inevitable fireworks that would follow his transgression of using black instead of Negro, as decreed by the *Star-Bulletin's* stylebook.

The *Star-Bulletin* was in the middle of a transition from the old-fashioned "women's" section with all the stuff about engagements, weddings, recipes, and stories about how to lose weight and get rid of cellulite fat. The enthusiastic new editor, a lanky hank of hair married to a smoothie lawyer, was looking into the larger and presumably more liberating concept of "style." Occasionally that meant cadging "legit" stories from the city desk, rather like hanging a necktie on a manikin. The editors were all enthusiastically pretending that women no longer wanted to read about engagements, weddings, and how to avoid cottage cheese thighs.

Quint knew Carmichael would be sore as hell if his story wound up in the style section. Here was an articulate, pissed-off black man airing a big time beef. He wanted to be taken seriously.

Fielding put the story in front of him. The decision was his. If he edited it himself, it stayed city side. If he put it into the tray, it was headed for the style editor. He picked up his pencil. So far, so good. Quint reminded himself for the umpteenth time that Fielding was not a bad person at heart. He was not evil. He was not uncivilized. He was simply uncomprehending and afraid of the tumult and upheaval that was tearing the country apart. He felt he was somehow being left behind and he wanted to preserve a way of life he thought must have been better than this turmoil.

Fielding glared at Quint, his mouth tight. "Black? What is this? These people are Negroes."

Quint took a sip of coffee, noting that Steve Sanger was watching him with a grin. He said, "Carmichael asked me to call him black, not Negro. I agreed. Couldn't see any good reason why not."

Fielding rolled his eyes. "Oh, well, he did, did he? Has it ever occurred to you that the *Honolulu Star-Bullentin* is our newspaper, not Stokely Carmichael's? We write our stylebook, not him. If he wants to change the way we do business, he can apply for a job."

Quint knew he was in for a struggle. "I think Carmichael's got a good point," he said. "Doesn't hurt to listen to him or to change our ways once in a while. We call ourselves white, why shouldn't we call them black? Everybody knows which is which. I don't see the big deal."

"We all ourselves white because Caucasian takes up too much space, that's why. White is shorter. Pure logic."

Quint held his ground. "Logic? Black and Negro take up the same amount of space. Be thankful they don't want to call themselves African-Americans. Then I could understand your complaint."

Fielding's mouth tightened. His voice rose, taking on an edge. "They're Negroes, Jim. Negro is a straightforward term used by anthropologists to describe a race of people who evolved in Africa. It's not good. It's not bad. It just is. I don't understand their objection. Are they embarrassed at being Negroes? That seems curious. By whatever name, they are the same. Calling them black instead of Negro won't change anything. When they wake up tomorrow morning, they'll see the same skin, the same hair, everything the same."

"They'll see black," Quint said. "They see us, they see white. That's the point."

The managing editor, Hobert Duncan, who could hear the fuss over the windowed partition that surrounded his office, had been listening to the debate. He stood and looked through the glass. His slightly pudgy face bunched into a frown.

"We have our stylebook," Fielding said. As far as he was concerned, that ended it. Was Quint going to argue with the stylebook?

"They're calling them blacks on the mainland," Quint said. "What's it hurt, really? You'll get used to it. Our readers will adjust. No harm done."

Fielding ground his teeth. He narrowed his eyes and said, evenly, "Jim, I don't care what they do on the mainland. I'm the city editor of the *Honolulu Star-Bulletin*. They are Negroes. In this newspaper, they have always been Negroes. They will remain Negroes until the name of their race is officially changed in the Encyclopedia Britannica."

Hobe Duncan, grimacing, stepped out of his office. "I agree with Jim. From now on, they're blacks."

Fielding blinked. "What?"

"Jim's right. It won't hurt us to call them black. We have to live with them. Life goes on."

"The stylebook clearly says . . ."

Hobe looked annoyed. His round face was flushed. He didn't like having to play referee. "I don't give a damn what the stylebook says. It's our stylebook. We wrote it. We can change it. I hereby decree that the stylebook is amended. End of the argument."

Duncan stepped back into his office and closed the door. Period. Full stop. A small step in the long march of racial accommodation. Quint viewed this as a small, but necessary change in the evolving handbook of national style—one of the central issues in the cultural revolution.

Quint thought, *Right fucking on, Hobe!*

Duncan was an off-again, on-again, participant in the discussions at the Round Table. On occasions like this, Quint wondered just how he had risen to become managing editor. Having common sense and a willingness to yield when the circumstances called for it would ordinarily have disqualified him for that kind of responsibility. His success ran contrary to Quint's observation that newspaper owners went out of their way to appoint small-minded assholes to positions of authority.

32

*T*HE NEXT AFTERNOON, Jim Quint passed on meeting with the Round Table regulars and picked Vivienne up. Followed as usual by the ubiquitous Roger Lobry, they drove toward Pearl City, riding in silence. They passed Ft. Shafter and Tripler Army Hospital, a large pink building on a hill to their right or mauka by local reckoning, then circling the East Loch of Pearl Harbor; the Arizona Memorial, a stark white shell over the azure blue, was clearly visible in the distance. They stopped at a delicatessen in Pearl City to get the ingredients for their picnic—a bottle of California zinfandel, French bread, a pint of marinated Greek olives and feta cheese, some ripe mangoes, and a quart of colorful, fresh primavera pasta salad.

At Haleiwa Beach Park, they spread their tablecloth on a picnic table under a palm tree, and Quint opened their bottle of wine. The view of the surf and beach was grand, the day was warm, and a gentle wind blew off the Pacific. There were surfers here too, but not as many as at Waimea and Sunset Beach. The olives were especially delicious, and Quint savored the salty chunks of marinated feta cheese. They ate, saying little. Quint could tell that whatever Vivienne had to say wasn't easy for her. He waited. Better to let her tell it in her own way without prompting from him.

Vivienne helped herself to some more pasta salad. "I guess it's time."

"After all we've been through, I think so," Quint said.

She sighed. "Hard to know where to begin." She looked rueful.

"From the beginning wouldn't hurt."

"After the Lon Be massacre, Del and his investigators obviously concluded I was their only link to Genevieve who had been an eyewitness to what happened—or at least they thought she was an eyewitness—and was a link to the CBS film. Del tracked me down in Saigon. He married me as a way to find the film. He knows Vietnamese families are close and assumed I'd eventually find a way to contact Genevieve."

Quint grinned. "And you did. Through me."

"Del thinks Genevieve is an active member of the Vietcong, but he doesn't know that and neither do I. The Pentagon thinks it would like to have CBS show the film of the Lon Be massacre on *60 Minutes* before the Democratic National Convention in Chicago. I've been monitored constantly since I arrived in Honolulu—everything from my mail to my telephone conversations."

"Roger Lobry said he was following us to prevent Del from murdering you. If you're his only link to Genevieve why on earth would he want to kill you?"

Vivienne smiled grimly. "What I think they've finally figured out after three years of interviewing survivors is . . ." She stopped.

"Is what?" Quint leaned forward. Vivienne was still holding something back. "What did they figure out?"

Vivienne bit her lower lip, looking at him with worried eyes.

"If the film is of such great propaganda value to the Americans the Vietcong would have destroyed it by now. The only other possibilities are that the VC are just plain stupid, which I don't believe, or they haven't thought about the consequences of what would happen if it were ever shown on American television, which seems like a stretch."

Vivienne sighed. "Sometimes not knowing everything is what's best for you. Have you ever thought of that?"

"I'm a newspaper reporter," Quint said. "We reporters don't like secrets."

Vivienne said, "I'm a woman in love. We women in love protect our men. You have to trust me. Are you still with me, Jim? Look at me."

Quint realized that Vivienne's emotional grip on him was total. He would have followed her into a burning building. "Oh, damn, yes. I'm still with you, Vivienne."

33

THAT NIGHT JIM Quint went to bed at midnight and lay there thinking about Vivienne and her sister Genevieve. Genevieve was possibly a Vietcong. Had Genevieve participated in a slaughter of her own village? Quint found that hard to believe. And how could Genevieve remain loyal to people who had murdered her family? If it had been Quint's family, he would have wanted the entire world to know what happened, no matter who did it.

Suddenly Quint felt a presence. He opened his eyes. When they were adjusted to the dim light, he saw a man in a flowered aloha shirt sitting on the floor leaning against the wall. He heard the click of a cigarette lighter and a glow.

Del Lambert said, "What do you think, Jimbo? Join me for a joint? High test Wowie."

Quint shook the sleep out of his head. He smelled pot.

"I got a loaded pistol here. Ever play with a weapon when you're stoned?"

Quint swung out of bed. "Don't believe I have."

Lambert said, "See here's the pistol. An automatic. Nine millimeter. Silenced." He held it up.

"I see it." Quint squatted cross-legged in front of Lambert.

Lambert pointed the pistol at the floor and snapped off a round.

Quint jerked.

Lambert laughed. "Make you nervous?"

"Oh, hell no."

"I couldn't decide whether to beat the fuck out of you or shoot you so I decided to compromise and talk."

"Good thinking."

"You can throw a tatami mat over the hole. Nobody will know the difference. I could put a hole in your head if I wanted and take you out to sea and feed you to the fish. No body. No foul. Nobody would ever know what happened to you. You got Vivienne to open up a little about her sister. Good for you."

Quint looked puzzled.

Lambert handed Quint the joint. "We used a parabolic microphone at the North Shore yesterday. Something you might see Sean Connery use in one of his James Bond movies. It's like a dish that scoops up sound at a distance. She says she doesn't know for sure if Genevieve is a Charlie. That's bullshit!"

Quint took a hit off the joint and passed it back to Lambert. Holding the smoke in his lungs, he said, "You're a helluva guy, Colonel."

"You want to hear what I have to say, or you want to be a wise guy?"

"I'm listening," Quint said.

The joint glowed, suffusing Lambert's face with soft light. "Sometimes I'm home. Sometimes I'm out and about. Hard for me to give Vivienne the protection she deserves. If the Democratic primaries aren't going well by our standards, Vivienne can look forward to having somebody drop by some night and use her for target practice or something else creative. Great sport to let her lie wondering if she's going to have a visitor. Who knows, insomnia might follow?"

Quint leaned forward. "What on earth are you talking about?"

"It's a basic brain game, Jimbo. Fear and isolation are an emotionally volatile combination."

"Why don't you just put her on the rack? Pop a few bones."

"Oh, come on. It's not as bad as all that. The deal is she's still my wife. She stays on Tantalus until you're willing to deal. You poach on my turf and I'll break your face. Ever wondered what it'd be like to walk around with your jaw wired? Having to buy fizzy crap to clean your false teeth like old folks?"

"A real sport."

"War, Jimbo. I told you this is the Vivienne War. For now she's determined to resist with every fiber of her being. While she's up there alone on Tantalus, you get to think about what might be happening to her and how you're impotent to do anything about it unless it's talking her into giving it up. After a while, slowly, inevitably, Vivienne will begin doubting herself and start identifying with us. We're not guessing here, Jimbo. This is a well-documented psychological phenomenon. Vivienne thinks she's Superwoman, but she's not. She'll come around. She won't be able to help it."

Quint said, "How long is this drill suppose to last? A week? A month?"

"How much we need the film depends on how well our side is doing. If Nixon is nominated in Miami and Humphrey wins in Chicago that will take some of the pressure off getting the film. As it stands now my mission is to deliver the Lon Be film to CBS before the conventions. But we won't know whether we'll need it for sure until the first Tuesday in November. In the meantime, if we get some political bad news and our side needs a quick boost, I'll have to have the film immediately if not sooner."

Quint was numb. "All this to give the hawks a boost."

"All this because we're fighting a war. Can you imagine the political repercussions of Americans watching journalists and innocent villagers being gunned down by the Vietcong? Talk to Vivienne, Jimbo. I don't like being all pissy and hard ass, but I've been after the Lon Be film for three years. Fun thinking of a peacenik down on his hands and knees praying someone will be nominated who's got balls enough to win this war."

"What if we just say screw you and make a run for it?"

Lambert ran the palm of his hand down his jaw. "I don't think you fully appreciate what you've gotten yourself into, pal. You're being watched twenty-four hours a day. You'll never make it off the island. You want to be responsible for an anonymous mugger breaking every bone in Vivienne's pretty body?"

Quint shifted on the bed.

"Well, do you? I'm a Lambert, remember. Who on this island will believe I would have anything to do with having my wife hammered?" Lambert passed the joint to Quint. "I don't understand Vivienne. I really don't. The chickenshit Vietcong murdered her family for Christ's sake." He looked thoughtful.

"By the way, I read your Stokely Carmichael article. Ol' Stokely's sure as hell got your number. Those do-gooders who brought him here paid good money to be kneed in the figurative crotch and few reporters, including the heroic Jim Quint were going to ask him any real questions. I thought it was supposed to be your professional duty to challenge morons on obvious horseshit, but no. You didn't have the balls to ask a real, possibly embarrassing question in front of the people who were there to be scolded for their sins. Word might have gotten back to your editors, and we all know—my oh my Jimbo—one does not challenge Stokely Carmichael with the sainted Martin Luther King recently assassinated and with posturing darkies burning down the cities. Oh, oh, I take that back. *Doctor* Martin Luther King, Jr. The flames have to be snuffed! If that means letting Carmichael get away with spouting hyperbolic nonsense, so what? What does it hurt? Reading that horseshit damn near made me puke. Jesus!"

Lambert rose, stretching his arms.

"You know, the other thing for you to think about, Jimbo, is if I don't get my way in this, I just might be moved to kill the both of you out of sheer frustration. If you have been sending and receiving mail for Vivienne, you can end all this by simply giving me the address I know damn well you've got."

Saying no more Lambert turned and left Quint's bedroom.

THE NEXT AFTERNOON, Quint and Vivienne risked Lambert's wrath by playing chess at a bench on Kuhio Beach in an unsuccessful attempt to keep their minds off what lay ahead for Vivienne when she returned to the house on Mt. Tantalus. Vivienne was a skilled chess player. Quint hadn't thought about it, but chess was played more in the Third World than in Europe and North America because it was cheap and people had time on their hands. In the Soviet Union it was big for that and because it was apolitical. It was for the same reason that Soviets were skilled at theoretical mathematics—anything to avoid the political and controversial, therefore dangerous.

It occurred to Quint that all the assertions that chess was analogous to war were bullpucky. Chess mimicked war only in the grossest sense. Yes, it took more power to capture a square than to defend it. Yes, one had to develop one's pieces. Pawns were safest when they worked together and advanced in formations. But all that was war in the abstract. The board was neat. The pieces clearly recognizable. Real war was sloppy and confusing and painful.

At sundown, Quint drove Vivienne home.

"I hate this," he said as he negotiated the curves of Tantalus Drive.

Vivienne sighed. "If we tried to drive to the airport somebody would stop us. I bet we're being followed right now."

Quint glanced in his rear view mirror. "He's there." He turned into the driveway of her house. He parked his Datsun and turned off the engine.

"For now, we're trapped, but we resist. Swear to it."

"I swear," Quint said.

She moved into his arms and they kissed. Then she pushed him away and stepped out of the car. "Go now. Sleep well. Remember, no matter what Del does to me, I won't give him what he wants. We Vietnamese have survived the Japanese, the French, and now . . ." She stopped.

"You can say it. Americans," Quint said.

"I'm ready for him. Up here." She tapped herself on the head. She turned and ran.

Watching Vivienne disappear into the house, Quint felt alone and afraid. He took a deep breath and turned around for the lonely drive back to Waikiki. As he turned onto Tantalus Drive, he passed the car that had followed him up the hill. Lambert would leave her alone the first night. He would let her have some time alone to reconsider her stubbornness before he resorted to pain games. He would save the pain for later.

34

ROGER LOBRY BECOME more straightforward in his chore of shadowing Jim Quint and Vivienne. Lobry or somebody working with him were omnipresent. Behind Quint in a car. Outside his apartment, lurking in the shadows of Waikiki. Listening in to his telephone conversations. Although Lobry might have been potentially lethal, he didn't seem threatening. He was just there like a cat eyeing a bird.

After his late-night visit to Quint's apartment, Lambert began disappearing from his house on Mt. Tantalus for odd stretches. He first left for six days and returned for two. Then he was gone for five and returned for one. As July wore on, he kept this up with unpredictable cycles. He did not tell Vivienne where he was going or when he would return, although the reason for his nights on Tantalus seemed unambiguous. Colonel Lambert wanted to give Vivienne some unnerving time alone, and he wanted Quint to know who was in charge. Vivienne was Lambert's property; if Vivienne saw Quint, he wanted it clear that it was because he was allowing it as part of his mission to recover the Lon Be film.

Lambert's deal remained in place: If Quint wanted Vivienne he would have to earn her.

Simultaneous with his mysterious absences from Tantalus, Lambert began watching Quint and Vivienne himself, but apparently not as part of Lobry's disciplined surveillance detail. He was just out there, a mysterious, malevolent lone wolf. His status with the army was unclear. Was he on some kind of leave? Was the army allowing him to torment Quint and Vivienne as part of its plan to retrieve the Lon Be film? Had his Lon Be mission been altered in some fundamental way?

When Lambert did show up at Tantalus, his routine, by Vivienne's account, was always the same. He took her out to dinner. They ate in silence. They returned home. She painted while he drank Myer's dark rum and smoked cigars on his lanai overlooking the city lights. Brooding, silent, Lambert got so drunk he could hardly walk, sometimes passing out on the couch before he made it to the bedroom.

When he was away from Tantalus, Lambert began making late night, drunken calls to Quint. The initial calls were short and enigmatic, but with the passing of terrible political days of summer, they became more disjointed and incoherent. It seemed obvious to Quint that Lambert was bearing some kind of terrible burden. Lambert was a disciplined, professional soldier, not a drinker who allowed himself to lose control.

The first call came two days after Lambert's appearance in Quint's apartment.

"Hello?"

"Jimbo!"

"Colonel Lambert. How are you doing?"

Lambert laughed. "I am the ghost." His voice was slurred.

"The ghost?"

"Of soldiers past. I speak for them. I was at Balls Bluff and Belleau Wood and Omaha Beach and Guadalcanal and Iwo Jima."

"I see."

"I bear tales of betrayal."

"Betrayal? By whom?"

"By Lyndon Motherfucking Johnson. By Robert M. McNamara and Clark Clifford and all the other chickenshit politicians."

"Betrayed you how? Because they won't let you nuke Hanoi? I don't understand."

"*Betrayal. And guys like you. Sons of bitches. Fuck you and the horse you rode in on.*" Lambert's voice was sour with bitterness. He hung up.

As the days passed, Quint and Vivienne became more emboldened, spending more late afternoons and weekends together. They were unconcerned with Lobry's detail, but they could never be sure Lambert wasn't watching—whether they were sitting in the shadows of a palm tree at Kuhio Beach or watching the belly surfers at Makapuu. When they did spot Lambert, his body language and the rage and hatred in his intense blue eyes were clear: the fury within him was building. For them, the political summer and Lambert were parallel lit fuses, burning steadily, dangerously toward the political conventions.

The ringing. Quint knew intuitively who it was. He turned in bed and snatched the receiver.

"*I'm calling you for a reason, Jimbo. I want you to know why.*"

"*Why what?*"

"*Easy to judge. A nation of chickenshits.*"

"*Are you drunk, Colonel?*"

"*Of course, I'm drunk. What does it sound like? You need to know why.*"

"*Don't be so damned mysterious. Tell me what's on your mind. Don't just mumble into the receiver. Tell me.*"

"*There's a reason for everything, Jimbo. Some of it ain't pretty, but you already know that by now.*"

The click. The buzz.

Vivienne began teaching Quint about how to stir fry, grill over charcoal, and steam in a wok, ovens being too hot and consuming too much energy in the Third World. After an early supper of Vietnamese or Chinese food they played chess or went for walks in Waikiki, before he took her home.

Their worst nightmare, unspoken but always present, was that

Eugene McCarthy would make a sudden surge in the polls, accompanied by weakening support of Humphrey delegates. They were political doves, but their survival depended on the success of the hawks.

Quint followed the debacle of the McCarthy campaign with approval. McCarthy had acted with bold resolution following Kennedy's assassination, saying nothing, after which he hid out. When he did finally emerge a week later, he remained obtuse and removed, making no direct appeals to anyone, much less undecided delegates or those who had supported Bobby. He simply asked delegates at the Democratic convention in Chicago to be responsible and make the judgment that had to be made.

When given the opportunity to please Bobby's followers by supporting gun control legislation, McCarthy said, "It's been my experience in twenty years in the Congress that you really ought not put through legislation under panic conditions." While he may have been right, the Kennedy camp, in no mood for mere logic, regarded his statement as an in-your-face smear to the memory of Bobby.

While McCarthy was apparently incapable of speaking out or showing emotion other than as a result of having a Clydesdale step on his foot, Quint and Vivienne's new hero, Hubert Humphrey, wasn't getting much in the way of public enthusiasm either. Hardly anybody showed up at his rallies. Those who did were either lethargic and uninspired Democratic hard-liners or kids screaming "Dump the Hump!" Humphrey was in an obvious dilemma. He didn't want to offend his patron in the White House, and yet he had to figure out a way to deal with sorehead kids.

"You like my wife, Jimbo. You want Vivienne, do you?"

Quint didn't answer.

"I know you do. Say it for Christ's sake. I want to hear you say it. Speak up."

"You know I do."

"Then pay the price. You covet Vivienne, but you're not

*willing to pay the price. I've by God paid the price. Where do
you think you get off? Do you think there's such a thing as a
free lunch, Jimbo?"*

Quint said nothing.

"Well, do you?" Lambert waited.

"You're drunk, Colonel."

"*Motherfucking, self-righteous little pissant.*" Lambert
slammed the receiver down.

In the middle of July, Hubert Humphrey said he favored "a shift
from the policies of confrontation and containment to policies of
reconciliation and peaceful engagement." He couldn't bring himself to say the W-word, withdraw, because that was too close to
the hideous S-word, surrender. In an effort to get adolescents off
his back, Humphrey hinted that he would nominate Teddy Kennedy as his vice president and would lower the voting age from
twenty-one to eighteen. Kids weren't so stupid as to buy such
obvious old pol payola. What they wanted was a simple sentence
of twelve words: *If I am elected president, I will withdraw our troops
from Vietnam.*

Quint found this shift in the Humphrey position unsettling.
Was Humphrey about to do a hawk to dove flop? What did the
Pentagon and Del Lambert make of this news?

Jim Quint was working on deadline the next day when he answered the phone to Vivienne crying. "What happened?"

"I . . ." Vivienne couldn't continue. She wept.

"Are you hurt?"

"I . . . I . . ." She couldn't speak.

"Do you need a doctor?"

"I'm okay," she said. "I'll be all right. Can you come up?"

"I'm on my way. Hang tough." Quint hung up the phone and
started out of the city room. He obviously wasn't going to the
toilet.

Fred Fielding looked up from the city desk. "Hey, where are
you going? We're on deadline."

"I've got a medical emergency on my hands. You'll have to trust me on this, Fred."

Fielding could see by the look on Quint's face that something awful had happened. "I'll get Sanger to finish your stuff. Steve!"

Quint raced out into the parking lot and leaped into his Datsun. He drove up Tantalus Drive and to the Lambert residence as fast as he could, cursing the waffling Hubert Humphrey for his indecision. If Humphrey was going to support the war, dammit, let him support it. Where in the hell was his spine?

He found Vivienne in a tub of cold water, her body covered with ugly welts. Quint squatted by the tub and took her hand.

"I'll be okay now," she said. "I thought the cold water might help take down the swelling. I thought I had it made. The sun was up. I'd made my morning coffee. Then I heard a key in the lock and I knew it was time."

"Del?"

She nodded. "With his air pistol. He went berserk. He said he was sick and tired of waiting and now Humphrey was going soft. He said dammit how could I force him to do this? He didn't want to do it. All I had to do was give him what he wanted."

"And what did you say?"

"I told him no. He told me to take off my clothes and run for it. If I was clever maybe I could find a place to hide. He stalked me around the house shooting at me and pumping that awful handle. It was awful. I thought he'd never stop. He was crazy. He said I was harder to deal with than a Vietcong." Vivienne smiled with more than a little pride.

"Atta girl."

"I stood my ground." Vivienne held back tears.

Quint said, "God, those things look like they hurt."

Vivienne winced as she massaged an ugly red welt on her stomach. "They'll heal. When Del left he said he'd give me another week at most before I 'knuckled under' as he put it. He doesn't understand that someone could love an improverished tropical country as much as he loves the United States. He finds that bewildering." She stood and gingerly toweled herself dry. She stepped out of the tub. "I want you to count them for me please."

"The welts?"

"Yes, please. I want you to push each one with your finger as you count. Make me feel it. Start with my backside then do my front."

Quint blinked.

She turned around. "Do it."

He tentatively pressed on a welt on her neck. "One."

She stiffened. "I will not yield. Come on, do another one. And don't be afraid. I want to remember what he did to me."

He jabbed her spine. "Two."

She sucked in her breath. "That's more like it. I will not give in."

"Please."

"There are lots more back there. I can feel them burning."

Quint ran the count to sixteen, beginning with her neck and ending with the back of her thighs.

Vivienne turned around. "You're getting timid again. Don't do that."

He clenched his jaw as he pressed on the top of her breast. "Seventeen."

"Ahhhhhh! I will not surrender."

Vivienne stoically repeated her litany of resistance as Quint finished the count on her lower thigh. Lambert had shot his wife thirty-seven times.

Vivienne took a deep breath and let it out between puffed cheeks. "After a while it doesn't hurt."

"I'm so very proud of you, Vivienne, you have no idea. Del has to learn that we won't take that shit without striking back. Maybe we'll succeed. Maybe we won't, but we will fight back. There's gotta be a way."

Vivienne swabbed her watery eyes with the back of her arm. Then she grabbed Quint's hand and pulled it onto the V.

Quint pulled his hand away and began unbuckling his pants. The loop began in pleasure.

35

THE NEXT DAY Jim and Vivienne—who was hardly able to move because of the painful welts on her body—decided to find out for themselves where her husband was holed up. Lambert's older sister Peggy had lived in a beach house in Kahala before she had died of breast cancer the previous year. Peggy had preferred the company of women to men. Her anomalous sexual taste was known to all her friends, but was an embarrassment to the Lambert family. When she died, the Lamberts had buried her quietly, relieved that the lesbian in the family was a thing of the past.

Quint remembered the snickering and jokes in the city room. But Peggy Lambert did have the house, and she had no heirs. Rather than sell it, the Lambert family used it for a retreat and lodging for visiting friends from the mainland.

Quint and Vivienne turned first to the Kahala house.

Hawaii was one of those civilized states that prohibited private ownership of beaches. Unlike places on the East Coast where a person could drive for hundreds of miles blocked from the ocean except for overcrowded parks and expensive resort property, the beaches in Hawaii were by law available to everybody. This included the exclusive Kahala district, located in the shadows of Diamond Head.

The law requiring public access was a continuing sore point to the rich and famous who lived in Kahala. They wanted the beach to themselves, thank you. While it was pleasant watching brown-bodied young men ride the curls and their admiring girlfriends didn't wear a whole lot in the way of swimsuits, the Kahala res-

idents didn't like how they got there. Outsiders got from the
highway to the water by walking down a series of public access
lanes that cut between expensive estates. Unfortunately the surfers included among their numbers an occasional thief who scaled
the security fences flanking the lanes. This required the hiring of
guards and expensive alarm systems.

Late one afternoon, Quint and Vivienne, bearing bags of beach
gear and a pair of binoculars and trailed by one of Lobry's subordinates, strolled down one of the access lanes to the beach.
Vivienne had been in Peggy's house several times, and they had
no trouble finding it. The sun was setting over the Pacific as they
found the vine-covered chain-link security fence separating the
Lambert property from land and from the beach.

The backyard of the Lambert house was landscaped with bon-
sai and contained a swimming pool and a bar on a covered deck.
A wide gate at the rear could be closed for privacy or opened to
face the white sand and the water, in which case the public beach,
marred only by trespassing proletarians, was essentially a private
beach.

Quint and Vivienne squatted in the shadows of the lane and
peered through the vines covering the fence. Lambert and a
young woman, both nude, were sunning themselves on woven
nylon deck chairs beside the pool. Quint studied the figures with
his binoculars. "She's pretty, but not in your class." He gave the
glasses to Vivienne.

Adjusting the lenses, Vivienne took a peek. "She's well en-
dowed up top. You have to admit that."

"They say anything more than a mouthful is wasted. I wonder
if they do this all the time?"

"What's that?"

"Sunbathe in the nude," Quint said. "What do you say we
check it out again tomorrow?"

THE DAY WAS warm and sunny, the kind of weather much touted
to mainland tourists by the Hawaii Visitors Bureau. Winter was
the heavy tourist season but generally reduced airfares in the sum-

mer kept the visitors coming. Jim Quint took Vivienne with him
to a sports store in Ala Moana Center where he went straight to
a glass case displaying air rifles.

Vivienne looked horrified. "What are you going to do?"

"Buy an air rifle."

"And do what with it?"

Studying the rifles, Quint said, "The son of a bitch shot you
thirty-seven times. Thirty-seven! I counted the welts."

Vivienne caught his eyes with hers. She understood. "The sun-
bathers! Now you're getting into it." She gave his arm a squeeze.

Quint bought the most expensive air rifle in stock, a German
Beeman with a rifled barrel that fired pellets. As he paid for it,
Vivienne asked him if it was a good one. Quint grinned. "It's the
same brand as the pistol he used on you. As my mother used to
say, 'What's good enough for the goose is good enough for the
gander.' "

"Do you know how to shoot?"

"Remember that first night he asked me if I had ever used an
air rifle?"

"I remember. You said you had grown up in Montana."

Quint pocketed the receipt. "I'm not proud of the birds and
squirrels I knocked off tree limbs when I was a teenager, but yes,
I know how to shoot."

QUINT AND VIVIENNE eased quietly down the lane leading from
the highway to Kahala Beach, and when they reached the vine-
covered wire fence surrounding Peggy Lambert's backyard, they
saw they were in luck. Lambert and his girlfriend, both nude,
were enjoying tall rum drinks and lying on reclining deck chairs
at the edge of the swimming pool.

Quint and Vivienne squatted in the shadows of the fence. Out
of the ocean breeze, the air was hot and sultry. Quint began
pumping the Beeman.

Watching him, Vivienne looked alarmed. "Not too much," she
breathed.

Quint whispered, "The more pressure I give it the more accurate it is. I'll only get one shot, so I have to give it some pop."

"Don't hit the girl. She hasn't done anything to us."

Quint eased the muzzle through the fence. "I don't shoot non-combatants. This is a war zone. He knows better than to let his guard down."

"And don't hit him in the face. You could put an eye out."

"Or even kill him," Quint said. "Not to worry. That's not what I have in mind." He gave the Beeman one more tough pump and put his sights on Lambert, who was lying on his back with his thigh up.

Quint waited.

Lambert, mopping himself with a towel, got up to fix a drink at the bar on the lanai.

"Shoot him. Do it," Vivienne whispered.

"Shooting him in the ass is no kind of payback. Patience."

"What are you waiting for?"

Quint concentrated on his target. "I used to be able to hit a sparrow's head at twenty yards. That's just about the size of what I'm looking at here." So small the V of Del Lambert's universal nexus, so large the consequences. From eels to elephants. The source of necessary urge. Marauding baboons. Punks rumbling in the streets. Soldiers toughing it out at Khesanh.

Lambert bent over to give a drink to the girl. He straightened.

"Turn around. Turn around," Quint whispered.

Lambert turned.

The V. Quint pulled the trigger.

Lambert screamed and fell to his knees, both hands at his crotch.

"Run, run, run!" Quint said, as he grabbed Vivienne and they sprinted back up the lane.

Out of breath, they reached the highway and jumped into the Datsun. Quint fired up the engine. He was pumped. His hands were trembling as he drove too fast toward Koko Head.

36

*A*FTER FLIRTING MOMENTARILY with a soft position on Vietnam—a moment of indecision that had moved Del Lambert to use Vivienne for target practice—Hubert Humphrey stiffened his resolve to prosecute the war to an honorable conclusion. Whether Humphrey's retreat from his hard-line position was occasioned by a careful studying of poll data or by Lyndon Johnson's wrath was unclear. Whether he was personally a committed hawk or a closet dove was equally ambiguous.

August. The rage continued. The cities burned.

The political conventions drew ever closer.

"Hello, Jimbo. Is that you, boy?"

"Me," Quint said.

"Well, your little lady is made of pretty tough stuff. Vivienne. Miss Saigon herself."

"Yes, she is."

"You fought back. See what you'll do when you're pushed?"

"It's the Vivienne War. You said so yourself.

"I take it you were trying for a nut."

"The base of the V, that's right."

"You were high, got me on the base of my dick."

Quint laughed. "That'll do. You richly deserved it."

"A surgeon at Tripler dug the pellet out. Then I had to sit around with my crotch packed in ice with nurses snickering behind my back. No fucking air rifle is gonna take me under, but I guess you know that already. I'll get my licks in. Fun making you wait and wonder how and when."

    "I'll be ready."

    "You'll never be ready for me, pal. Not in your wildest fucking dreams. Forget it."

On the eve of the Republican Convention in Miami, Quint sat perched on his stool at the Round Table obsessively working and reworking in his mind the political permutations of hawk and dove. The regulars discussed the latest round of ghetto burning and the upcoming convention; if they lacked enthusiasm for the candidates, it was because the larger country, weary of war and rebellion, was cool to the candidates who proposed to lead them out of the morass.

Abner Barnhouse thought the problem of blacks burning their neighborhoods was best explained by cultural anthropologists. "We had a round of burning three years ago, then last year. For millennia, archaic people in the tropical world have whacked down and burned a portion of the forests that's good for a year or two of tuber crops before the underbrush crowds its way back. Then they move on and slash another area. What we're looking at here is an urban form of slash and burn agriculture."

"You want to tell me the crop," Jerry Fortier said. "Not squash and yams."

"Television sets and dubious publicity." *Har, har, har!*

"Right," Fortier said.

Mayer was disgusted. "The country is coming apart, Abner. Use your brains, don't play with them."

While Republican pretenders to the White House throne could barely conceal their joy over the prospect of facing either Eugene McCarthy or Hubert Humphrey, the regulars, likely all Democrats, seemed simply resigned.

Abner Barnhouse said, "Wonderful choice, a poetry-reading moron and a suckbutt nincompoop."

"Enough already," Miki said.

Richard Nixon had begun his political career by lying about his opponent, Helen Gahagan Douglas. Nixon had helped prove that the elegant state department official Alger Hiss, a liberal, had spied for the Soviets, an act for which he was never forgiven. He had avoided getting pushed off the ticket with Ike in 1952 by making a famously maudlin speech on television, denying that he had any kind of illegal slush fund in his Senate office. Nixon said he would not give back gifts that included his dog Checkers and his wife's "good Republican coat." After his 1962 defeat in California, he promised to quit politics for good, saying reporters wouldn't have "Dick Nixon to kick around any more."

There were those regulars who claimed to have been grateful for that declaration. Others claimed to have missed his maddening presence in recent years. Throughout his career Nixon had been portrayed as, variously, a sniveling coward, an insecure jerk, a congenital liar, a conniving twerp, a posturing fake, a whining little horse's ass, and even as a man who didn't know how to properly shave himself. None of the regulars liked him.

"Let's face it, no caricature or obloquy is beyond the pale for Nixon," Mayer said.

Sanger grinned. "No shot is too cheap, clichéd, or unimaginative."

"An open season," Barnhouse said. "Great sport."

Mayer said, "Remember the time he tried to convince people he could be as cool as Kennedy? He had a photographer take a picture of him allegedly out for a thoughtful walk on the beach. There the Dick was, gazing out to sea looking contemplative. Was he about to pass gas? His cuffs were rolled up to his knees. The only problem was that he was wearing slacks and a white shirt!" Mayer rolled his eyes.

Mikki added, "The only thing lacking was a cartoonist's balloon over his head with him saying to the photographer, 'Come on, hurry it up. Let's get this over with.' "

"It was like he was trying to upstage Jerry Lewis," Fortier said.

Mayer continued, "You have to admire Nixon in a sick kind of way. He didn't quit. His heart pumped ambition. He stayed on the road for six years eating fried chicken and boiled peas at testimonial dinners. He didn't care if he was talking before dogcatchers or governors or whether he was in Blue Balls or Boston.

And never mind the ridicule. All he wanted was political obligations, and he got them."

Now Nixon had chosen Gov. Spiro Agnew of Maryland, a former Republican moderate, to be his vice presidential running mate—this on the grounds that Maryland was considered a Southern state, although that was pushing the definition. From the standpoint of the regulars, Agnew was a fine choice.

Fortier said, "The cartoonists are gonna love Agnew. He's got that huge beak and those tiny little eyes that sink back in his head."

Mayer said, "The guy made the best-groomed list of *Men's Hair-stylist* and *Barber's Journal*. He'll be a model vice president for people who were fed up with hippie longhairs like Quint here and with riots and drugs."

Sanger liked the image of a statesman going for a walk with his dog. "Nixon plays the statesman and foreign affairs expert, see, above the vulgar name-calling. Agnew is his pit bull. He growls and chomps onto people's throats."

After Nelson Rockefeller dropped out of the race on March 21, Nixon's only competition had been the man who had inherited Barry Goldwater's faithful, Ronald Reagan of Twenty Mule Team Borax and Win One for the Gipper fame, and considering Goldwater's debacle, Reagan's chances didn't look good. It was clear from the taunting by fun-loving yippies and other plans for demonstrations in Chicago that the Republican convention was just a warm-up for the featured act. Chicago would offer maximum spectacle.

Every afternoon the regulars, dispirited over what was happening to their country, followed the tension leading to the Democratic convention. By all accounts this was to be a convention as might be imagined by P. T. Barnum—including the threat, or promise, depending on one's point of view—of yippie girls humping hallucinating delegates in Chicago.

"Lace the water!" Abner Barnhouse cried. "Send in the girls!" *Har, har, har!*

"Oh shut, up, Abner," Mayer said.

Miki Hasegawa made a face. "I agree," she said.

————

"What I wanted to talk to you about tonight is air-headed liberalism. You a liberal, Jimbo?"

"I'm not anything that can be defined by one word."

"Do you even know what a liberal is?"

"You're not listening, Colonel. You accuse your critics of ignorance and cowardice, but you don't know how to listen. I say again, I'm not anything that can be described by a label, tag, or bumper sticker."

"Bullshit!"

"I don't like the war, but that doesn't mean I agree with everything in the great society."

"Let me tell you what the great society is all about, Jimbo. It's about a misguided notion of the perfectibility of man. We've got all those bleeding hearts convinced that if they just pass enough high-minded laws, why then everything will be hunky dory. If we put those blackies in fancy new public housing, see, why then they'll take pride in their surroundings and behave just like folks in the suburbs. If we put 'em in school with white kids, they'll forget all about torching the streets and hit the books and spend more time in the chem lab. See how that works? It's like whitewashing a rotten barn. Looks fancy on the outside, but the inside is still loaded with termites. You listening, Jimbo?"

"I hear a drunk who can do a lot of push-ups."

"I've had a couple, I'll admit. Myer's rum. Good shit. Old Joe Stalin thought he could produce a perfect Socialist man in a single generation. He went so far as to sack the biologists who said it couldn't be done. Dumb son of a bitch. You can't change the nature of V overnight, pal. And shooting it with an air rifle doesn't do one fucking bit of good. You have to deal with the nature of the beast. We're all of us the same. LBJ. You. Me. Your pal Stokely Carmichael. General Giap. You can't legislate our brain stems."

Lambert hung up.

On his way to work the next day, Quint glanced in his rearview mirror and saw Roger Lobry waving him to the curb with his hand. Quint parked his Datsun at the curb. Lobry pulled in behind him.

Quint got out and strolled casually back to Lobry's car where Lobry waited. "Want to sit for a minute? We need to talk," Lobry said.

"Sure," Quint replied. He slipped onto the passenger's seat.

Lobry reached over the seat and snagged a large thermos. "Coffee? I made it just before I came on watch. I grind my own beans. Good stuff."

"Sure, I'd like some coffee," Quint said.

Lobry retrieved two cups out of the glove compartment. As he poured the coffee he said, "You hit Lambert on the side of his dick."

Quint accepted his coffee and took a sip. "Say, this is good."

"Dumb stunt on your part."

"He had it coming. You should see what he did to Vivienne. He is always giving us lectures about the Vietnam War. That was retaliation VC style. Tit for tat."

"If it hadn't been for us guarding your place, you'd be dead by now."

Quint smoothed his mustache with the side of his forefinger. "You had people following us. You have the house on Tantalus wired so you know what he had done to Vivienne. Your people saw me buy the air rifle and take it to Kahala. What did they think I was going to do with it?"

Lobry pursed his lips. "We're doing our best to keep everybody calm and cool. Colonel Lambert is under orders to keep his distance. He's a professional soldier, so however sore his cock is, he'll do as he's told. But we don't want any more air rifle episodes. If you pull a stunt like that again, we can't guarantee your safety."

"Lambert's been drinking," Quint said.

"We know."

"Calling me up at night, drunk. Getting sloshed every night he spends on Tantalus. What's that all about?"

Lobry grimaced. "He was ordered to retrieve the Lon Be film.

He's been at it for close to three years. The film is still out there. Maybe it's getting to him."

"You listen to the tape of the betrayal call?"

"I did."

"What's that all about?"

Lobry hesitated. "We're not sure. There are few career soldiers who have served in Nam who don't feel betrayed in one way or another. Did Vivienne ever tell you where her sister is?"

Quint shook his head.

"She ever tell you anything about Lon Be other than what we recorded on the North Shore?"

"No."

"Have you been sending mail for her on the side? Mr. Postman?"

"I have not."

Lobry sucked air between his teeth. He clearly didn't believe Quint. "You have to remember, Jim, war is an extension of politics. The politicians think war is too important to be left to the military. The Pentagon feels just the opposite."

"So what do Vivienne and I do besides hang out and wait for the convention?"

"My advice?"

"Please."

"If Vivienne is using you to communicate with her sister, we'll eventually find out one way or another. The best advice I can give is to tell us what we want or show us where to find it. Failing that, until the convention is over, you'll just have to go with the flow. Or maybe even until the general election, who knows?"

"Right. Tell me, is this game ultimately benign or lethal?"

Lobry frowned. "What do you say we take this one step at a time."

"Lethal then."

"We're all of us on a short ration, Jim. So few years, so much to get done. Doesn't do us any good to worry about it all the time." Lobry checked his watch. "Say, you better get going, hadn't you? You've got a deadline coming up." He paused, then added. "You know Jim, if you had any brains, you'd figure this out for yourself. Look at motive. Put two and two together."

"And in this case two plus two equals?"

Lobry grimaced. "It equals horseshit cubed, guaranteed. But we can't ignore it. We have to deal with it. By the way, do you know the legal definition of somebody knowingly aiding and abetting the enemy in time of war?"

"Congress has to declare war for there to be a war," Quint said. "All LBJ has is the Tonkin Gulf Resolution, and there are serious questions about how he got that."

Lobry clenched his jaw. "You're not thinking, Jim. You're not being smart at all."

As RICHARD NIXON savored his victory in Miami, riots broke out across Biscayne Bay in a black ghetto called Liberty City. Seventy police bearing shotguns were called out to quell the violence in which four people died.

On the radio, the jocks were playing the Rolling Stones's "Sympathy for the Devil," with Mick Jagger shouting out, . . . "who killed the Kennedys—when after all it was you and me!"

Laura Nyro sang her emotional anthem, "Save the Country." The chorus nailed the mood of young people across the country:

"Save the people. Save the children. Save the country. Now!"

37

On August 10, Eugene McCarthy decided on the dubious strategy of guaranteeing that convention delegates wouldn't support him by ruling them out as candidates for cabinet slots. He announced that Martin Luther King, Jr.'s widow, Coretta Scott King, would be his ambassador to the United Nations. Henry Ford's brother, William Clay Ford—a former supporter of Barry Goldwater—would be his secretary of commerce. In all, he announced six millionaires and a half dozen Republicans, none of whom were politicians.

Ten days later—a week before the Democratic convention in Chicago—Soviet tanks rolled into Czechoslovakia, putting an end to the incipient democratic revolution. President Johnson called an emergency meeting of the National Security Council, which decided nothing could be done except to cancel the upcoming summit with Soviet Premier Aleksey Kosygin.

McCarthy's response the next day was yet another political round to the temple. "I do not see this as a major world crisis. It is likely to have more serious consequences for the Communist party in Russia than in Czechoslovakia. I saw no need for a midnight meeting of the United States National Security Council."

Later, McCarthy attempted to pacify the emotional voters who by his standards were bawling and drooling like confused cattle. He either understood that it was dumb not to show any public sympathy for the poor Czechs or his writers deliberately handed him a practical joke that he failed to recognize. In attempting to clarify his silence, he said, "Of course, I condemn this cruel and violent action. It should not really be necessary to say this."

ON THE NIGHT of Sunday, August 26, with Lambert in his Kahala house, Quint and Vivienne watched the videotapes of the
pre-convention action in Chicago that had arrived from the
mainland. Nothing seemed to have gone right for poor Chicago.
The people who installed telephones had gone on strike. Not to
be outdone, the electrical workers went on strike too. Bus drivers
and cab drivers then struck, effectively paralyzing the city before
the convention had begun.

Mayor Richard Daley had posted billboards in the city saying
MAYOR DALEY, A FAMILY MAN, WELCOMES YOU TO A FAMILY
TOWN. As they had been promising for months, the fun-loving
yippies, not caring a whole lot about matters of family, gathered
in the Windy City to torment the delegates.

Daley would have none of it. He put the city's twelve-
thousand-member police force on twelve-hour shifts. He called in
the Illinois National Guardsmen too, six thousand of them as well
as six thousand regular army troops. The guardsmen and soldiers
were equipped with rifles, bazookas, and flame-throwers. There
would be no throwing of food at Mayor Daley's table, thank you.

Quint and Vivienne watched in stunned disbelief as helmeted
police with riot shields, yelling "Kill the Commies!" waded into
Lincoln Park bent on clearing yippies responding with "Oink,
oink, shitheads!"

Watching this with Quint, stoned, Vivienne said, "My God,
what is happening to your country?"

Quint said, "Your husband sees it as a civil war."

"Is he wrong?" Vivienne asked.

"No," Quint said.

LINCOLN PARK WAS only a skirmish. The radicals kept up the
pressure throughout Monday and Tuesday, but the action was
restrained because no self-respecting yippie wanted to be in jail
and miss the action of nominating day, Wednesday, August 27.
The skirmishes were a form of parties for the radicals. Nomination time was to be a kind of yippie prom.

Early Wednesday afternoon, Lyndon Johnson's surrogates defeated the peace plank by a vote of 1,567 to 1,041. The embittered peace delegates from California and New York responded by slipping on black armbands. The losers stood on their chairs yelling, "Stop the war! Stop the war now!" as the folk singer Theodore Bikel, a delegate from New York, rose to lead them in a dramatic singing of "We Shall Overcome." A priest in the New York delegation then led a prayer, which was followed by murmurs of "Amen" and "Shalom."

As news of the defeated peace plank spread throughout the city on radio and television, enraged supporters of Eugene McCarthy joined the yippies and other radicals in Grant Park, across the street from the Conrad Hilton Hotel where Eugene McCarthy and Hubert Humphrey both had their headquarters. By the time the nominating speeches began, their angry crowd had swelled to ten thousand.

Helmeted police too gathered, bearing riot shields and armed with billy clubs, Mace, and tear gas.

Finally, a young man wearing an army helmet shimmied up the flagpole to remove the American flag.

The police moved in and dragged him off.

More demonstrators gathered around the flag and replaced it with a red T-shirt.

The police responded again, and, with network television cameras carrying the action live to a stunned republic, the battle was joined. The radicals, who had come prepared with balloons filled with paint and urine, threw them at the cops in addition to rocks, bricks, boards, and everything else they could lay their hands on. In a near surreal scene of violence, police beat and pounded on every live body they could find, including innocent passersby, and soon an eerie white fog of tear gas spread out into the melee of shouting, screaming protesters.

As the pitched battle raged outside, in the amphitheater of the convention center, Senator Abraham Ribicoff of Connecticut rose to nominate South Dakota Senator George McGovern for president. "With George McGovern as president," Ribicoff said, "We would not have such Gestapo tactics in the streets of Chicago."

The television cameras zoomed in on Chicago's scowling Mayor Daley, standing twenty feet behind Ribicoff. "Fuck you!" he said.

Ribicoff scowled back. "How hard it is to accept the truth. How hard."

With the convention twisted by anger and bitterness, the speeches continued and eventually the balloting began. At 11:47 P.M., Pennsylvania gave the vice president 103 votes, putting Hubert Humphrey over the top as the Democratic nominee for president. In the end, Humphrey received 1,761 votes, McCarthy 601, McGovern 146, with other candidates collecting 100.

Before the night was over, New York delegate Alex Rosenberg was arrested on the floor for refusing to show his credentials to a security guard, and in the confusion that followed, another security guard slugged CBS correspondent Mike Wallace in the jaw.

Was that it then, was the Lon Be tape rendered moot with the nomination of Hubert Humphrey? Was Del Lambert's obsession rendered moot by the nomination of Lyndon Johnson's vice president to succeed him? Quint didn't think so.

38

WITH LAMBERT GONE, Quint and Vivienne watched the televised rage and confusion in Chicago every night at his apartment after which he took her home. By the end of Thursday, after five days of violence, hundreds of demonstrators had been beaten, clubbed, and gassed, and sixty-five newsmen had been arrested, beaten, or both. The wrath of the police ranged from the ridiculous to the sublime, going so far as to arrest Abbie Hoffman for having the word "Fuck" printed on his forehead.

On Thursday night Hubert Humphrey selected Sen. Edmund Muskie of Maine to be his vice president. In his acceptance speech, the same Humphrey who had hidden from the violence all week—yielding nothing to the peace movement—now pounded the lectern with his hand and thundered, "Where there is hatred, let me sow love. Where there is injury, pardon. Where there is doubt, faith. Where there is despair, hope. Where there is darkness, light."

A regular Gandhi was Happy Hubie.

Four years earlier, at the Democratic convention in Atlantic City, Bobby Kennedy had introduced a film honoring his assassinated brother Jack. The delegates, many of them openly weeping, had responded with a twenty-two-minute standing ovation. As the convention closed in Chicago, Teddy Kennedy, speaking by telephone from Hyannis Port, did the same thing for Bobby. The delegates, united in their emotion, rose to give Bobby an ovation similar to the one they had given to John in 1964.

The ovation continued, for five, ten, then fifteen minutes with hand-scrawled signs appearing on the floor saying, *BOBBY, WE*

MISS YOU and BOBBY BE WITH US. After this, delegates gripped by the emotion of the moment began a robust singing of "The Battle Hymn of the Republic." After five minutes of this, the New York and Illinois delegates finally sat down as a signal that the demonstration had gone on long enough, but the singers would not stop—certainly not those defeated, distraught, but still defiant supporters of the peace plank.

"Glory, glory hallelujah!"

Mayor Daley—very likely no great believer in Humphrey's professed ideals of love, pardon, faith, hope, or light—finally had had enough. He supported the boys in Vietnam. His man had been nominated for president. Chicago was his town. Daley took the tribute to Bobby as a personal affront, and inasmuch as his henchmen occupied fully one-fourth of the gallery, he sent word that they should begin singing, "We love Daley," which they did—to the tune of "The Battle Hymn of the Republic."

"We love Da-ley. His truth goes marching on."

The delegates were not about to be drowned out. Louder, they sang, "Glory, glory hallelujah!"

Unlike Humphrey, Daley was apparently capable of being embarrassed, or at least of switching tactics. He sent Ralph Metcalf to the podium to ask for a moment of silence for Martin Luther King, Jr. If the bleeding heart peaceniks wanted to spit on Negroes with the nation watching on television, let them sing through prayer for the civil rights martyr. After all, two leaders, not just one, had been slain that year. That did the trick.

THOSE PEOPLE WHO had never tried marijuana did not understand what a pot flash was all about. They lived their lives in fear of the unknown and the demon weed was one of those tempting mysteries that had become associated with the rebellious generation of baby boomers. Quint had always been convinced that the famous munchies, a side effect of being high, were because cannabis heightened the senses. Food somehow tasted better. When Quint was high, beer tasted especially wonderful, even Primo. Art was enriched. Ideas became fun. Thinking became a form of play.

This was partly because weed had the effect of putting the observer at a slight remove from reality. This quality of the absurd led the imagination down paths that were ordinarily blocked. The commonplace and ordinary suddenly became outrageous or ridiculous. Likewise, the outrageous and unthinkable became commonplace. None of these heightened qualities were observable to the outsider; they were entirely internal. As Quint was the first to admit, one person's high was another's plain dumb.

Quint was sitting stoned with his arm around Vivienne watching the interminable rehashing of election poll numbers on the tube when he began thinking about the night Del Lambert had ordered Vivienne to strip. He remembered their embrace and the whispered words.

You should know I am doomed.

His mind drifted.

Lambert had introduced Quint to his wife and encouraged them to fall in love, yet continued to regard Vivienne as his property. She was turf, the core of the Vivienne War. In Lambert's opinion all struggle began with sex. Lambert was defending his testicles. To defend the birthright of one's country, one's nurturing homeland, was to fight for men, women, and children. That was at the heart of the war in Vietnam. The Vietcong were Communists, yes. But they were nationalists first. They too had their pride.

You should know I'm doomed.

Lambert had tried to make Quint understand the war from his point of view—both intellectually and emotionally. He wanted Vivienne to know also. He wanted, as he himself had said, to cut to the chase, to the clichéd nitty gritty, fuck the pretense.

Why?

Because he knew that something was going to happen or had happened with regard to the war that required an explanation of motive.

Whose motive? Johnson's? Westmoreland's? Lambert's? Having to do with what?

Lon Be.

Betrayal.

Quint gave Vivienne a squeeze. "Vivienne, I think it's time for you to tell me the whole story about Lon Be. This story is missing a critical link. It's there I know, but I can't put my finger on it. It's not good to put it off any longer."

Vivienne sighed. "You'll have to be patient and let me tell it my way."

"Go for it." Quint handed Vivienne the bong.

Vivienne took a hit and leaned back with a lazy, glazed look in her eyes. "Vince Carelli and his photographer arrived in Lon Be about ten o'clock in the morning the day before their scheduled filming and interview with my grandfather and the other people in the village. As mayor, my grandfather invited them into our house for sweet rice cakes and tea. My grandfather hated the war, but he didn't hate the Americans. He was a kind man. He had a responsibility to the village. He wanted to be a good host. My sister and I helped serve the tea."

Quint looked puzzled. "Say again? You helped serve tea? You were there?"

"Yes, I was."

"You saw it happen?" Quint sounded incredulous. "You were a witness?"

"Along with Genevieve and several others who escaped, yes."

"Does Del know about this?"

Vivienne said, "He knew about Genevieve all along, but not about me until recently."

"I don't understand. Why didn't you tell me that earlier?"

Vivienne said, "Because it's dangerous knowledge. Bad enough that I was a witness. I was hoping you wouldn't be harmed for what you clearly don't know."

"Why is being witness to a Vietcong atrocity dangerous knowledge to somebody in Honolulu? That doesn't sense."

She hesitated. "You'll have to bear with me."

"Tell me the rest. Do it."

Vivienne, looking drifty, remembering, said, "Vince Carelli and the Australian photographer Henson were flirting with Genevieve and me. They weren't crass or obvious, but it was clear they thought we were good looking. My grandfather wasn't dumb. He could see what was going on. But we were properly modest, and he was proud that the American and Australian thought his granddaughters were attractive. Suddenly, we heard the sound of automatic rifles outside. We had no idea what it was, but we knew it wasn't good. Henson grabbed his camera, and he and Carelli went outside to see what was happening. My grandfather went with them. Genevieve and I could see what was happening through the window. There were eight of them. Six of them were shooting everything that moved with their automatic rifles. Two more had gas cans that they used to set fire to the houses and huts along the main street of the village."

Quint found himself asking. "VC firing AK-47s. How many?"

Vivienne shook her head. "Not VC."

"No?" Looking puzzled, he took another hit on the bong.

"Green Berets with M-16s."

Quint held the smoke his lungs. His mouth fell open. "What?"

"American Green Berets slaughtered the villagers at Lon Be, Jim. They murdered my family in cold blood. They killed the CBS correspondent and his photographer. It was never the VC. It was Americans."

"Americans? No."

"I'm afraid so, Jim."

"No."

"I saw it," she said.

Quint was disbelieving. "You mean to say you've been bearing that secret with you all these months without telling me? Lambert wants to destroy the film, not give it to CBS?" Quint repacked the bowl of the bong. Watching Vivienne's eyes, he took another hit. They were not lying eyes. She was telling the truth.

Vivienne said, "They were like wild men, Jim. I'd never seen anything like it and believe me by that time I'd seen plenty."

"An American unit? You're sure?"

"Green Berets. They killed and burned and killed and burned and killed and burned some more. Outside, I heard Carelli yell,

'Jesus!' I saw that Henson was filming what was happening. I saw that the leader of the Green Berets had seen them. He was holding his M-16 at his hip. He shouted, 'What are you doing here, you dumb bastards? You're not supposed to be here until tomorrow!' "

"The officer in charge. What did he do then?"

Vivienne had a distant look in her eyes. "He shot them down. I saw my grandfather, Carelli, and Henson all straighten, and there was blood everywhere. Henson was filming his own murder when he was knocked backward from the bullets hitting him. Genevieve stepped through the door and grabbed his camera. We both retreated through a rear entrance and escaped. The Green Berets didn't kill everybody in the village, close to a dozen of us escaped, but in the confusion, I got separated from Genevieve and never saw her again."

"Oh, Jesus!" Quint put his hands over his face. "Why did you marry a Green Beret?"

"I thought I might be able to learn something useful for General Giap."

"Did you?"

Looking chagrined, Vivienne shook her head. "After I got to Honolulu I received several letters from my sister, each from a different address. None of them said anything. She asked how was I doing and so on, but they each had been opened. Del needed a way to keep me from catching the next plane back to Vietnam. What happened, I think, is that he did the logical, soldierly, dutiful thing at the Pacific Club."

"He gave you to me."

"As long as I'm here, there's a chance that I'll lead him to Genevieve and eventually the Long Be film. He hates you with a passion that goes beyond sexual competition. I just wanted to have one genuine love in my life. Beyond that, I didn't want to talk about it. I still don't."

Quint said, "I'm hungry. Do you suppose you could make another batch of that sweet rice candy?"

Vivienne gave him a kiss. "Thank you. By the way, that's the same kind my grandmother served to her guests that day. You'll help?"

"Sure," Quint said.

"After that I want to work on my painting. It's almost finished, and I'm in the mood."

"Whatever," Quint said. He flopped back on his sofa, stunned by the awful truth.

39

$\mathcal{B}$Y THE TIME Jim Quint got home from the Round Table the next day, the pretty and handsome faces on the tube were predicting a Richard Nixon victory in the upcoming election. Quint found Vivienne working hard on her painting. The little girl in the painting was coloring with crayons. She had a glass of juice. There was a bottle of Biere "33" in front of Quint. The woman who was to be Vivienne—her face was sketched in—had a clear glass cup of Vietnamese coffee. In addition, there was a bowl of tropical fruit, and blue and white soup bowls, large ones for mom and dad, a smaller one for the little girl. The street in the background was crowded with carts, motorcycles, bicycles, and people going about their business. This was Saigon, Quint knew.

Seeing him, Vivienne put down her brush. Her hand strayed to her denim shirt. She unfastened a button and casually parted the top. "What do you think?" she asked.

"About your painting or what's in there?"

She shrugged. "Either."

"I like the painting. I like what's in there too."

"Really?" She undid the rest of the buttons and parted the shirt.

"Are you trying to seduce me, Vivienne?"

She grinned.

Quint took her in his arms. "Well, aren't you the horny little lover." He led her into his bedroom.

QUINT THOUGHT VIVIENNE was unusually quiet and reflective as they had a supper of chicken with lemongrass and fish cakes with Chinese cabbage. When they had finished and sat drinking Vietnamese coffee, Vivienne said, "I want you to go for a walk, Jim. I need some time alone to finish the painting."

"Complete your face."

"Yes. Faces are hard. I have one more to go, and I want to be able to concentrate. You should take a walk down Kalakaua and have yourself a drink, maybe a Mai Tai or Fog Cutter. Smoke a little before you go. Mellow out. By the time you get back, I'll have finished the painting. I've been working hard on it, and I want to see how it looks. This is important to me, it really is."

Quint could tell that this was a serious request, from Vivienne's heart, and it would be wrong to argue with her. He also found it unsettling for reasons that were unclear. Even more unnerving was the passion of her kiss and her embrace as he stood at the door. Her eyes welled up with tears. "Go," she said.

He hesitated.

"Go. I'll be all right. I'm just feeling emotional is all. My period is coming up. No big thing."

Was her period coming up? Quint couldn't remember.

She said, "The painting is for you, by the way. A special gift. I want it to be right."

"A gift for her, don't you mean?" Quint glanced at the unfinished painting.

Vivienne looked momentarily confused, then she smiled. "The little girl. Yes, for her too. Also, I want you to take this." She handed Quint a six-by-eight-inch manila envelope. "Don't open it until you get back or you know the time is right."

Looking puzzled, Quint took the envelope. "What do you mean when the time is right?"

"You'll know, believe me. You must promise."

Quint felt a rush of anxiety in his stomach. He was frightened. He sat. "I'm not going anywhere."

Vivienne pushed him toward the door. "Oh, yes you are. I want to finish my painting in peace. You've been real good about giving me space when I need it. Don't ruin things now. Come on, get out of here." She tapped the envelope in his hand. "Not until you get back or until you know it's time. Repeat it to me."

"Not until I get back or until I know it's time. Something's wrong here."

"Everything's just fine. We made it past the convention, didn't we? Humphrey was nominated. He's not going to change his mind about the war. We'll make it past the election. Everything will be just fine. Guaranteed. Out now. Give me a little privacy. Thank you, Jim. I love you."

"Thank me for what?"

"Never mind. I love you."

"I love you too." Quint gave her another kiss.

"Don't make this any harder than it already is. Go, Jim. Out of here."

Quint stepped outside into the balmy Honolulu night and closed the door. He didn't believe for a second that everything would be okay, but if Vivienne wanted to finish her painting in private he felt he should respect her wish. He loaded his little pipe with Wowie and took a leisurely hit.

Inside, Vivienne turned on one of her Beatles records. She liked to listen to the Beatles while she painted.

"Yesterday, all my troubles seemed so far away."

40

JIM QUINT WENT for a stoned walk along Diamond Head down Ala Wai Boulevard with the canal of the same name on his left and the Ala Wai golf course on the other side and the Waikiki tourist district on his right. After a walk of about a mile, he turned right on Kapahulu Avenue. He took another hit on his pipe as he walked past the Honolulu Zoo on his left. After a couple of hundred yards he came to the ocean and sat for a while at the base of a palm tree in Prince Kuhio Beach Park.

Sitting there looking out over the water at the setting sun, Quint once again traced the sequence of events as he understood them. He took another hit and then walked Ewa on the makai side of Kalakaua Avenue, the gut of Waikiki. Suddenly, on the sidewalk in front of him was Del Lambert, who had a distant, resigned look about him.

Considering what Quint had done to him with an air rifle, Lambert seemed surprisingly amiable. "Well, by God, if it isn't our resident Charlie!"

"You know, Colonel Lambert, all these months you've regarded me as a hack who doesn't know what he's doing. I watch and I listen, but don't say much, it's true. It's my nature. Well, maybe I was an ignorant hack in the beginning. I allowed myself to be sucked into your game knowing it wasn't smart. In addition to the attraction of Vivienne, I was curious about where it would take me. It turned out to be quite a trip."

"And where did it to take you?"

"To a terrible secret, for one thing."

They came upon a green bench on the seaward side of the sidewalk.

"Shall we sit?" Lambert asked.

They sat.

They said nothing for a full minute, then Quint said, "You know why it is you people won't be winning the war in Vietnam? And by you people, I mean you, the military establishment, not the United States of America."

Lambert shrugged, "I don't know? Vietcong sympathizers in the United States carrying air rifles? Tell me."

"Vivienne."

"Oh?"

Quint said, "She once told me that the difference between the two of you is that she's fighting for her country and you're not. She's right. I watched her. The more you pushed, the more determined she became. Remember the night you used her breasts for target practice? She saw the punishment coming but she didn't care. She pushed her chest right out at you. 'Here, do what you will. I can take all you can offer and more, but you'll never defeat me.' You shot her twice, and she didn't flinch or make a sound. You burst in on her in the middle of the night and pelted her thirty-seven times with your screwed pistol. You know what she did the next morning? She had me push each one of those welts with my finger so she could remember the pain. With each count, she vowed, 'I will not yield.' "

"Tough lady," Lambert said.

"Your problem is you don't understand how anybody could love a country so poor and wretched as Vietnam. You're always talking about discipline and commitment and heroism. You know why those boys shed their blood on Omaha Beach? Because they believed that unless they stopped the Third Reich, Adolf Hitler wouldn't rest until he sent Panzers down the main street of their hometown. People are smart enough to know that Ho Chi Minh isn't thinking any such thing. He just wants you out of his country. Vivienne *is* Vietnam, and she's on the beach ready to lay everything on the line if necessary. That's why you won't be winning."

Lambert had a faraway look in his eyes. "And what about the kids in the streets? You got that figured too."

"The only constant in American political or cultural life is change, Colonel. You see change as a challenge and it is, but nobody can stop the clock by brute force. Things turned ugly and got out of hand because of the war. They'll likely stay ugly until there's some kind of resolution."

"What about Lon Be? What do you think you know about Lon Be?"

"I know a Green Beret killed Vince Carelli and his photographer and the villagers of Lon Be, not the Vietcong. You've been pursuing that film all this time because you wanted to suppress it, not release it."

"You're getting close. What do you say we find a bar and have a drink while we talk?"

"Let's do it," Quint said.

THEY WALKED ALONG Diamond Head on the makai side of Kalakaua Avenue, turning at length into the lanai bar at the Ala Moana Hotel. They found an empty table and sat. Quint ordered a Heineken beer. Lambert went for a double shot of Jack Daniels black label bourbon. After their drinks had arrived and the waiter was gone, Lambert said, "Everything that happened since that day at the Pacific Club had a reason. None of it just happened."

"I didn't think it did."

Lambert sighed. "We had an incident this year at a village called My Lai. A platoon commanded by a moronic Lieutenant William Calley wiped out a bunch of civilian Vietnamese. A journalist named Seymour Hersh has been talking to people who were there. If we're able to keep a lid on it, it'll be a miracle. Shit happens in war, but people don't understand that."

"And Lon Be? What happened there?"

Lambert sucked air between two of his teeth. "Hard to know where to begin a story like this. Do I begin with the truth, or do I start with the operative lie and go back to the truth? Your druthers."

"I know at least part of the truth, but that doesn't make any difference. Start with the lie. That's what I've been having to deal with for the better part of a year." Quint sampled his Heineken. "Boy this beer tastes good. Everything tastes better when you're stoned."

Lambert thought a moment, then said, "I was the intelligence officer in charge of that area of the Mekong. My people had the contacts among the Vietnamese in the area, so after the Lon Be massacre the Saigon command put me in charge of retrieving the film."

"Westmoreland's people were operating under the impression that Vietcong had committed the atrocity, but you knew better."

"Correct. When we learned that one of the surviving witnesses, Genevieve Thanh, had a sister living in Saigon, we ran her down. She turned out to be a beauty."

"Vivienne."

He nodded. "At first CBS made weekly inquiries, then monthly, then, slowly, their producers began to get the picture. Of course, we wanted to be on the good side of the networks, but the odds were never good that we would ever recover the film. We had reason to suspect that Genevieve had gone to work for the Vietcong. Why she would want to work for the Vietcong after they had slaughtered her family was a mystery, so we didn't know whether it was true or not. As our sole link to Genevieve, Vivienne was our only chance at recovering the film. Then some sport hit upon the wonderful idea that I should put a move on Vivienne as a way of getting to Genevieve."

"Duty, honor, and country."

"Westmoreland's staff was convinced that the film was of incalculable propaganda value. The Vietcong casually wasting an American journalist in the middle of a slaughter of innocent villagers? What a propaganda score that would be!" Lambert sighed.

"Vivienne told me she married you in hopes of learning something useful to Ho Chi Minh," Quint said.

"She might have hoped for that, but that wasn't her main mission."

"No?"

Lambert shook his head. "At first we didn't know whether there were any surviving witnesses or not. Maybe Vivienne knew the details of what the VC had done to her family. Maybe not. Since my house on Tantalus was wired to record Vivienne's telephone conversations and any visitors she might have, the army knew the marriage was in trouble. Hard to expect anything else, I suppose. Last January, in the middle of Tet, a colonel flew in from the Pentagon. This was an election year, and command was worried that the film might surface." Lambert fell silent. The distracted look returned, seeing but not seeing.

"So what did he suggest?"

Lambert smiled bitterly. "He said only reason I had married Vivienne was because I had been ordered to. If she was unhappy that plan obviously wasn't working out, and there was nothing to prevent her from returning to Vietnam. Since she was our only connection to Genevieve Thanh and the incriminating tapes, we had to do whatever it took to keep her in Hawaii—short of keeping her prisoner." He watched Quint, saying nothing.

"And?"

"He said we had to take the logical next step to keep her in place. Set her up with a new lover! He was quite specific. He wanted a dove on the war, preferably somebody Nguyen and Genevieve Thanh might logically use and trust as a conduit to CBS."

"Nguyen Thanh?"

"Vivienne's brother. I'll tell you about him in a minute." Lambert turned, glancing at Lobry, then returned his attention to Quint. "The colonel didn't care how I kindled the spark, only that I gave Vivienne grand passion with a peacenik and saw to it that she got to spend plenty of time alone up there in the big house."

"To encourage her to contact her sister."

"Or Nguyen. Correct. He flew back to Washington, leaving the details to me. When I talked to Vivienne on my way into the Pacific Club that day, I could tell she was interested in you. When I found myself sitting beside you, a longhaired reporter and hippie asshole, I knew I had my mark. Everything went okay until the end of May or the first week in June when our people in Saigon began hearing that it wasn't the Vietcong who killed those people at Lon Be." He locked onto Quint's eyes. "It was *my* unit."

"Your unit? Were you there?"

"Yes, I was."

Quint blinked.

Lambert said, "The army had never questioned my official report that my unit was in a different part of the delta on the day of the atrocity. But there had been witnesses who escaped. The rumor surfaced, as I knew it one day would. Now let me tell you about Nguyen. Nguyen Thanh, a captain in the North Vietnamese army and Vivienne's oldest brother, is one of the most cold-blooded, meanest cocksuckers you can imagine in your wildest nightmare. An ambush artist who loves to mine trails. A dead shot in the moonlight. He murdered three of my closest friends and tortured a fourth until he lost his mind. Finally, I'd had enough of his horseshit. We all had. We thought to ourselves fuck you and the horse you rode in on, pal, and *that*'s why we did our number at Lon Be."

Lambert paused, remembering, then continued as though he was telling Quint about a bar fight the previous Saturday. "Oh, I'm here to tell you, Jimbo, it was so, so very sweet. The motherfucking civilians back in Washington had imposed restrictions on us that made it impossible to win. Everything was a political calculation. When you go into combat it is to win. Only to win. Second place doesn't cut it. You should never, ever commit troops to combat unless it is to win or if you have an honorable way to get the fuck out if you have to. And to have that chickenshit Thanh hanging out there in the darkness picking us off one at a time was just too fucking much." Lambert clenched his jaw at the memory. "Thanh's family lived in Lon Be. We knew he was using the village as his headquarters, hiding behind civilians. Our plan was to show CBS the aftermath of a VC atrocity. So the day before Carelli and his photographer were supposed to show up, we filed a report of our day's activities putting us in another part of the delta, then we just strolled into that fucking village and mowed down everything that moved and torched the place. Only Vince Carelli and his photographer had showed up a day early. A day early! Why? The stupid sons of bitches! Morons." Lambert shook his head bitterly.

Quint said, "Vivienne was there that day with her sister. She witnessed the whole thing."

Lambert sighed. "People were racing out of the back of that little house like rabbits. I always suspected Vivienne might have been one of them." Lambert grimaced.

"Are they going to try you for murder?"

Lambert smirked. "And admit what had happened? No, no, no. A CBS film of Green Berets slaughtering villagers is ammunition for the peaceniks."

Quint held up his hand for another Heineken. Was Lobry behind him, watching this conversation? Quint turned and yes, there was Lobry. Their eyes met, and Lobry nodded in recognition.

Lambert leaned forward, looking at Quint straight on, his face earnest. "Vivienne is both tough and loyal, you're right. Formidable. It wasn't until this morning that I learned the complete truth."

"Which is?"

"All this time her brother and her sister have been building a case against me. They managed to trace my unit step by step on the day of the massacre. Vivienne married me in order to take me down one day. She came on to you so strongly because she needed a way of communicating with her brother and sister." He held up his hand. "Yes, yes, she fell in love with you, I grant that. I take it you have been sending and receiving mail for her."

Quint nodded.

"From the beginning all she wanted was justice for her family. Can you imagine the discipline and the determination?"

"I can now that I've gotten to know her," Quint said.

Lambert finished his whiskey and caught the waiter's eye, signaling for another round. "People back here don't have any idea what it's like to fight a war like this. The motherfucking Charlies

are everywhere, setting booby traps and shooting at us from the
darkness and the cover of jungle. It's an infuriating, impossible
mission." Lambert suddenly looked old and sad.

Quint found it impossible to hate Lambert. Disagree with him?
Yes. Hate him? No.

Lambert said, "You say change is constant. Why is that? I say
Charlie Darwin had it right dead-on, life is a neverending quarrel
about balls and pride and turf. But if you view turf in the limited,
literal sense, like dogs marking their territory with piss, you don't
understand the nature of struggle. In the end, all the fancy articles
in the *Journal of Foreign Affairs* and all the learned pieces on the
op ed pages of the *New York Times* are so much rhetoric. In the
beginning, I thought you were an ignorant little bastard with too
much influence for your education and years. Turned out I was
wrong." Lambert managed a self-deprecating grin.

Quint laughed. "And I thought you were a sadistic fucking
robot. A militarist moron. I was wrong about that too."

"Thank you, Jim."

"No Jimbo?"

"No, it's time I called you Jim. You've earned it. You and
Vivienne were real soldiers; I have to hand it to you. You never
yielded an inch. Regular Charlies both of you." Lambert stood
and they shook hands. It was hard for Quint not to feel sorry for
Lambert. Also difficult not to admire him in a strange way. To
the very end, Colonel Del Lambert had honored his convictions.

Lambert started for the street, then stopped, standing beside
Roger Lobry but ignoring his presence. To Quint and for Lobry
too, he said, "There's one more thing, Jim. It's difficult for me
to admit, but I think I owe it to you to be completely honest.
The Vietnam War is so fucking stupid it makes me want to puke.
The fact is we're afraid to do what it takes to win for fear of
dragging the Russians and Chinese into it, so we're wasting all
those young men's lives to no good purpose."

"You might be right," Lobry said, mildly.

Lambert said, "The horseshit! All the blind, self-deceiving,
totally unnecessary horseshit. The kids are right. They ought to

lasso the balls, and where necessary, the tits, of the president, his cabinet, and the entire United States Congress and string 'em from the highest tree. Hell, I even hope they find the Lon Be film and turn it over to Mike Wallace."

"You say Vivienne's brother and sister documented the case against you?"

"They nailed it. Took them more than two years, but they traced our unit almost minute by minute. They had everything except the film. They could have simply assassinated me, but they wanted more than that, the treacherous bastards."

"You said you didn't know until this morning. What happened this morning?"

"A telephone call to the Judge Advocate General."

Quint said, "From Vivienne?"

Lambert sighed. "She did what she had to do."

Quint saw that the tip of Lambert's left shoe was covered with blood. "You've got blood on your shoe. Where did that blood come from?"

Lambert looked down at his shoes. "I don't know. There's so much blood, it's hard to know where any of it comes from. From a razor knick. From a bar fight. From a mortal enemy. From an innocent who got in your way. The stains build up. After a while everything is a blur." The fit and loyal soldier, embittered, defeated, destroyed, strolled casually out of the bar.

41

JIM QUINT JOINED Roger Lobry. Together they watched Del Lambert walk up the sidewalk crowded with tourists.

"What do we do now?" Quint said.

"We trail him," Lobry said.

They followed Lambert as he crossed the street. He stopped in front of the International Market Place where vendors peddled aloha shirts, souvenirs, and necklaces made of koala nuts and seashells imported from Indonesia and the Philippines. With tourists looking on in amazement, Lambert took a small automatic pistol out of his pocket.

Calmly, he put the muzzle to his temple. The pistol made a loud pop! Colonel Ball Bearing Buns, scion of Hawaii's Lambert family, a man with seemingly everything he had wanted, pitched forward onto his knees, his brains splashed onto the sidewalk.

With people yelling and screaming behind them, Quint and Lobry walked up the sidewalk on the mauka side of Kalakaua Avenue, headed to Pearl City toward his apartment. In a few minutes the wailing of sirens joined the confusion behind them. They picked their way through the curious tourists rushing toward the International Market Place. They were apparently the only ones on the street who didn't want to see more.

Finally, Quint said, "Lambert had blood on his shoe."

"Yes, he did," Lobry said.

"Not his blood."

"I don't think so."

Quint stomach twisted. He thought his heart was going to pop out of his chest. When they got to Aikini Street, they turned right, and Quint saw the blue lights of the white squad cars of the Honolulu Police Department outside of the small apartment building where he lived. He didn't have to be told why they were there.

Quint dropped to his knees and abruptly vomited on the sidewalk.

Lobry squatted beside him.

Quint retched until he thought he was going to turn himself inside out. Then he stood and wiped his mouth with the back of his hand and wept. He thought of all the husbands and wives and brothers and sisters and sweethearts who had lost their loved ones in Vietnam. He could barely get the words out, "Who did this? You or him?"

"He did."

"Whose idea?"

"His. He started this business. He wanted to finish it. If it had to be done, he wanted it to be him. If he had lived, their next step would be to leak their case to the press. We would have eventually been forced to prosecute him, even without the film. Now maybe we can put it behind us."

They stood in the shadows of a palm tree. Lobry waited patiently while Quint wept. Finally, Quint got his emotions under control. He felt weak. He got out his little pipe and loaded it with Maui Wowie. If there ever was a time to get stoned and stay stoned this was it. "You smoke?"

Lobry shook his head no. "Colonel Lambert got carried away. Slaughtering an entire village served no useful purpose. What he did, he did in the heat of the moment. We understand that. But we can't condone it. We certainly can't let the American people know about it. He paid the necessary price. A patriot."

Quint thought about that. "Let's trace that logic, what do you say? You say Lambert got carried away. Slaughtering an entire village served no useful purpose. What he did, he did in the heat of the moment. You say you understand. No you don't. You don't understand shit."

Lobry sighed.

"The United States is not threatened in this particular fight. If it were, the chickenshit radicals you despise would be lined up around the block to get in to the army recruiters. They did it when the Japanese bombed Pearl Harbor. They'd do it again."

Lobry said, "Let's not rehash all that. We both know it goes nowhere."

Quint knew he was right. The war would go on. In such passion as attended the Vietnam War logic was irrelevant. The brain stem prevailed, not the cortex. The future was sealed. The bloody drama, nurtured by ignorance and misconception, sustained by hubris, would play itself out.

They walked on in silence.

Finally, Lobry said, "For the last year, we suspected an American unit might have been involved in the massacre at Lon Be, but we didn't know which one. Lambert knew we were closing in on him which is why he started drinking. Vivienne called us from a pay phone this morning to tell us the complete story—pieced together by her brother and sister and Vietnamese nationals with access to our records. She gave us the details that only an eyewitness to Lon Be would know. She said they had been hoping to find the film but that it apparently had been lost. If they'd found the film, she said, it would have been shown on American television by now."

At last Quint understood. "Vivienne waited Lambert out for two years. When you didn't find the truth yourselves and the Democratic convention was finished, she made her call and did what she had to do."

"She was a Vietcong bent on bringing down a war criminal."

"A beautiful, educated, talented Charlie," Quint said.

"Who fell in love with the postman. Correct. There's no doubting how she felt about you. It was clear from her body language and the way she looked at you. All of us on the surveillance detail were envious of you. She was truly extraordinary. In the jungles they pull the trigger of an AK-47. Vivienne simply slid a dime into a pay phone. As the dime rattled its way home, her fate was sealed."

Lobry was right, Quint knew. In thanking him so earnestly, Vivienne had wanted him to know she was grateful for the six months of passion they'd shared. He stepped under a streetlight and opened the envelope Vivienne had given him. It was a photograph of a beautiful young Asian woman. Quint didn't have to be told who it was. Except for her eyes, Genevieve Thanh could have been Vivienne's identical twin. Her eyes, huge brown orbs with an expanse of white so admired by Asians, were stunning. He turned the photograph over and on the reverse side, in Vivienne's handwriting, was a short note:

Hey, Jim, don't make it bad. Love always. Vivienne.

Quint gave the photograph to Lobry.

Lobry said, "Genevieve Thanh. Even better looking than Vivienne, if that's possible. Smart as hell too. Or so they tell me."

It was hard for Quint to believe anybody could be more beautiful than Vivienne. He studied the photograph. Lobry had a point, Quint had to admit. Genevieve had real presence. Those eyes! He hoped Vivienne had gotten to finish her sister's face in her painting. He turned the picture over a second time, momentarily puzzled by the "Hey, Jim, don't make it bad!" Why had Vivienne chosen that phrase?

Quint heard a song playing on a transistor radio being borne along the sidewalk across the street by a happy group of hippies heading for the heart of Waikiki. The song on the radio, a current Beatles hit, had been one of Vivienne's favorites. That the hippies should have been listening to that specific song at that time and at that place was of those mysterious coincidences that Carl Jung called a synchronicity. Coincidence. Synchronicity. By whatever term, Quint knew Paul McCartney was singing "Hey Jude," for him:

"Hey, Jude, don't make it bad, take a sad song . . ."

Quint quickly put his hands over his ears. He didn't want to hear the end of the line. Was it really possible to make such a sad song better?

Then Mick Jagger sang the lament that had recently popped to the tops of the charts:

"I can't get no sat-is-faction."

" 'Hey Jude' for me. Del Lambert got 'Sympathy for the Devil.' " Quint wondered, as he listened to Mick Jagger growing dimmer in the soft tropical night, if those two songs—a rock and roll yin and the yang—might not reflect the tortured soul of 1968.

42

THE COLUMBIAN INN was a hub-bub of activity as Jim Quint stepped inside, passing the poster of O. J. Simpson, the most recent of the enlarged photographs of sports heroes Tosh Kaneshiro had on the walls. Simpson was breaking every NCAA rushing record imaginable in propelling USC toward the Rose Bowl and was a lock to win the Heisman trophy. In a year when Negroes seemed bent on burning the cities to the ground, the likeable Simpson seemed downright white. He was a black jock people could support with enthusiasm.

The Round Table regulars were all there that night, Barnhouse, Jerry Fortier, Steve Sanger, Phil Mayer, Babs Parsegian, and Miki Hasegawa.

"Hey, Big Jim, plop your Montana butt down," Abner Barnhouse called.

Quint did, ordering a Primo. And he took a sample of the chicken and long rice—rice noodles—which Kaneshiro was offering as election night *puu puus*.

The talk that night was not of the Humphrey-Nixon race that had become a tiresome subject, but about two cultural fronts in 1968. Election cycles came and went but changes in the culture were enduring. On the first front, women, having been freed sexually by the Pill, were now eyeing male perks; this promised to be a protracted struggle of uncertain consequences. On the second, blacks determined to seek their fortunes in a white world had escalated the violence that marked every summer since 1965.

In January the Associated Press had opened 1968 by reporting an incipient movement of "women's liberation" in which the author used the word "sexist" to describe "male dominated institutions."

The regulars debated whether "sexist" would match the likely half-life of such recently coined words and phrases as "groovy," "uptight," and "right on," or would it endure. The males at the table were playfully skeptical. Babs Parsegian and Miki Hasegawa thought otherwise. It was their sense of humor that enabled them to endure this most barbarous of years. Should they laugh or weep? They chose to laugh.

On most issues Phil Mayer automatically took the liberal position. But the opportunity of razzing Babs and Miki was too good to pass up. "You women own the damned country. You've got us jumping through every kind of imaginable hoop. You control the only commodity that really matters in the end." He leered at Babs. "No pun intended."

"Yeah, sure," Babs said.

Sanger leaned to one side, scoping Babs's behind. "You got a nice end, it looks to me." He grinned.

Mayer said, "If we want it, you make us pay the maximum. What's wrong with the free market? Isn't that what this country is all about?"

"Guys like you are why this thing is just getting started, Phil," Miki said mildly.

Barnhouse murmured, "Next, it'll be the queers. Fag liberation. You wait." Barnhouse rolled his eyes, pleading to the heavens, "Today Yamani's tea party. Tomorrow an equal number of male and female editors. After that we get female combat soldiers and prize fighters." *Har*, har, har. "What's the matter with you, Quint? You sucking up to the women by not speaking up?"

Quint managed a tepid grin.

"Coward," Mayer said.

"Got his mind on the Colonel's wife," Sanger said.

Seeing that Quint had his mind somewhere other than the table, the regulars turned to the complicated question of the future of blacks in the U.S.

Before 1965, federal law had prohibited discrimination based on race, religion, or national origin. None of this information could by law be included on an application for employment. The idea was that the law should be colorblind; applicants should be judged solely by their qualifications. Now, under the aegis of the great society—and spurred by Lyndon Johnson's 1965 call for "affirmative action" on behalf of Negroes—the government was actively collecting data on race, sex, and age.

As Fortier understood it, the country needed to do something to accommodate the blacks. "We've got to find some way of dealing them into a better life. This craziness can't continue."

Abner Barnhouse, as usual, took the crass line. "The notion that all men are created equal means that by natural right all citizens should be treated equally under the law. If all men were literally equal, we wouldn't have track meets and spelling bees."

Sanger who usually sat and listened to the talk, argued that political payoffs in democracies had traditionally taken the form of preferential dips into the national treasury. "Incumbents use pork to buy reelection. The Nazis argued that there were more Jewish bankers and intellectuals than was justified by their number in the population. What if politicians in Washington started adjusting opportunities to please X or Y kind of voters?"

"A spooky possibility," Fortier admitted.

"Jim Crow in reverse," Barnhouse said. "Lyndon Johnson's 'Something Less than the Great Society.'" Barnhouse had gone so far as to look up the meaning of the words in the phrase "affirmative action." "The word 'affirm,' a verb, means 'to declare firmly. To maintain to be true. To uphold. Confirm.' The word 'affirmative,' an adjective, means 'giving assent, confirming. Positive. Optimistic.'"

Mayer said, "You want to tell me we should sit around with our thumbs up our butt and do nothing? Jerry's right, we can't continue with this kind of hatred."

"I agree with Phil and Jerry," Miki said.

Quint didn't think fairness was to be feared. Who could argue that blacks should be shut out of opportunity because of the color of their skin? It went without saying that the emerging push for sexual equality would change the way males did business. What was disconcerting about most arguments was the logical extreme.

Barnhouse was so loaded he could barely stay on the bar stool. "You know something, we're all of us whores. We wear 'objectivity' like dime store perfume. We give our readers intellectual quickies. *Har, har, har!* We pander. We titillate. We thrill. We give succor. We whisper shocking things in the ears of our readers. We never write anything truly wholesome or uplifting that's not staged for somebody's benefit. We know who the major is humping on the side. We know which pols hang out with crooks, but we say nothing. Whores we are. *Har, har, har!*"

Mayer rolled his eyes. "Yeah, right, Abner."

Quint grinned. Barnhouse had a crazed point in a way. It was true that the regulars had been numbed by their experience, and they did sometimes talk about their readers as hookers did their johns. Listening to their talk, Jim Quint sat silently, still stunned by the events at Waikiki earlier that night. He held the photograph of Genevieve Thanh below the edge of the table and took a quick peek.

Sanger caught him looking at something but didn't see what it was. "Hey, what've you got there?"

"Nothing," Quint said.

"Bullshit, let's see," Barnhouse said.

Quint showed them.

Mayer said, "Hey, a real beauty. Who's she?"

"She's Vietnamese. Her name is Genevieve Thanh," Quint said.

"She's beautiful," Miki said. "Go for it, Jim."

"I'd do it to her, that's fact," Barnhouse said. "She'd bend like a willow."

Quint gave Barnhouse a look and slipped the photograph into his shirt pocket. The regulars knew they should say no more, and they didn't. Sitting there, thinking of the painting and the photograph, he broke down and wept.

Miki, not knowing what had gone wrong with Quint's life but knowing it was traumatic, put her arm around him and gave him a squeeze. The rest of the regulars, pretending that he wasn't weeping, began a self-conscious attempt to talk about the election, but that wasn't going far and they knew it. The Round Table lapsed into one of its rare silences. Something awful had happened to one of their number. They all knew it must have something to do with the photograph, but they had no idea what.

That's when an officer of the Honolulu Police Department strolled into the Columbia Inn, asking if anybody knew where he could find a *Star-Bulletin* reporter named Jim Quint.

43

SHORTLY AFTER DEL and Vivienne Lambert were in their graves, Jim Quint sent a letter to Genevieve Thanh using the Hong Kong address Vivienne had given him. Over the next four months Quint exchanged letters with Genevieve in which he introduced himself and gave an incomplete account of what had happened to her sister. In January, he cashed in his accumulated vacation time with the *Star-Bulletin*, rolled up Vivienne's passionately rendered painting, slipped it into an aluminum tube, and flew to Hong Kong to meet Genevieve in person.

As the Northwest Airlines flight neared Hong Kong, Quint remembered the definition of a year by the sardonic San Francisco newspaperman Ambrose Bierce—a period of 365 disappointments. Quint believed it would be difficult for the fortunes of history to possibly deliver another such wretched stretch of misery as 1968. He was convinced history would see that year as a turning point of the American twentieth century—the high point of a cultural revolution that would leave the United States forever changed. From then on, the sentimental paintings of Norman Rockwell that graced the covers of the *Saturday Evening Post* would be quaint, nostalgic reminders of a time that was forever in the past.

Quint suspected there would never be another cycle like it in his lifetime and that the value of his memories would appreciate, a form of writer's saving account. Smart to remember this, he told himself. But it was Col. Del Lambert who had taught him the remarkable parallels between private and public passion. Lambert's biological imperative of which Mr. Darwin wrote those many years ago—denied, misunderstood, dressed in curious drag—was lying always beneath the surface of the text. Males marking their territory with piss and pistols. Love of a woman. Love of country. The hate of principles betrayed! The rage!

Lambert had called 1968 a bitch, a witch, a harridan, a harpy. Quint understood what he had meant. The character of a year was determined by a combination of storms, disasters, history, politics, sports, fashion, movies, lives, and deaths—all those events and high points packed into summaries printed and broadcast between Christmas day and New Year's Eve. That and the events of one's private life. Ordinarily a year was most vividly defined by the personal territory of friends and adversaries, loves, joy, tears, triumph, and loss.

The songs lingered in the imagination. Love too. And sometimes hate. In the end, a year was more than an abstract measurement of sidereal time based on how many times the earth circled the sun. Quint understood that he carried the past with him, a kind of existential flotsam and jetsam that altered his life in small ways and large. It was in this way that 1968 had transformed him, often in subliminal ways of which he was unaware. There is a quality of a year that remains personal and individual. The year of the boomer uprising meant one thing to a soldier in the jungles of Vietnam and quite another to a young man or woman in the streets of heady protest.

Quint saw 1968 one way. Vivienne saw it a second. And Col. Del Lambert very much a third way. History in the manner of Kurosawa. For Quint, the year was a time when the public events that were history in the making had become one with the texture of his personal life in a way that he would have thought unimaginable.

Vivienne. Vietnam. The resonant, evocative sounds of her name and that country—where hormones and history became one in the mysterious nexus of the V—were forever folded into the recesses of his memory. It was Vivienne and Lambert who taught him the meaning of V. Each made a contribution. One thing was certain, Lambert was far more complex and unpredictable than

Quint's youthful stereotype of a career military officer. When Quint had first seen him at the Pacific Club, he had thought Lambert was predictable.

The strange thing was, and maybe a little hard for Quint to admit, but Lambert wasn't all wrong about soldiers and soldiering. The country needed soldiers like it needed yard dogs, to keep marauders from stealing its chickens. What it didn't need is for those dogs, eager as they are, to prowl around in other people's yards pretending their chickens were American property.

It had ultimately been the consequences of Tet, the Chinese New Year of 1968, that had brought Quint and Vivienne together. The indomitable, implacable, courageous Vivienne had taught him why the United States would not be winning the war in Vietnam.

Jim Quint landed at the Hong Kong airport at ten o'clock in the morning of the eve of the Chinese New Year of 1969.

JIM QUINT'S EARLY afternoon lunch with Genevieve at a dim sum restaurant on the Kowloon side of the Hong Kong colony began awkwardly, but Quint soon worked up the nerve to get to the heart of his mission, that of explaining in more detail Vivienne's fate, which he thought Genevieve deserved. He had the painting rolled up in a tube.

Quint told Genevieve everything that had happened to her sister and him and Del Lambert. He started with his meeting Vivienne as she sat in a Mercedes Benz in the parking lot outside the Pacific Club. He told her about the strip. He told about the night Lambert shot Vivienne's breasts with his air pistol while she sat unflinching. He told of the night of the thirty-seven welts. He told her about Vivienne's painting and about her murder. "Your sister taught me what love of country was all about."

"You're the mailman," Genevieve said.

"Yes, I am."

"In her last letter she said you'd be bringing me something."

"She did?" Quint was momentarily taken aback, but then he understood. "That would be this." He unrolled the canvas. On seeing it, Genevieve was startled. She glanced up at him, deeply moved, then returned her attention to the painting. Knowing she was surely to die soon, Vivienne had not only embraced life, but through the romantic vision of her painting, she had sought her own curious resurrection.

"Me," Genevieve said.

"And me," Quint said. "She worked on that painting for months. She put her heart into it. It is impossible for me to tell you how much it meant to her."

"It's beautiful," Genevieve said, catching Quint's eyes. Then her face bunched up and she wept.

"A sister's love. A kind of masterpiece," Quint said.

Genevieve stared at the painting, her eyes wet with tears.

Quint said, "Vivienne saved your face for last. Until that final night, I assumed that the figure was her and the child was ours."

"She knew what was going to happen to her."

"From the beginning. The artist as guerilla. What Vivienne had with me was temporary, and she knew it. The painting is her prayer and blessing."

Quint reached over and took Genevieve's hand, holding it tightly as her small body shook with grief. Genevieve wept for her family, for her sister, for herself, and for Quint—all caught up in the awful, avoidable tragedy that had destroyed her country and was tearing his apart.

Later, on a stroll through the shopping district of Kowloon, Genevieve told Quint that the CBS film of Lon Be had been lost by the thief who stole the camera; he was only interested in fencing the camera on the black market in Saigon. Of course there was no telling that to the Americans, especially after they learned of Del Lambert's involvement.

Quint remembered Vivienne saying that "Marxist economy" was an oxymoron and that Communism was doomed. She had hated the brutality of Ho Chi Minh's soldiers, but she also felt Vietnam's fate was rightly that for the Vietnamese to decide, not Americans. Eventually, they would find freedom, but in their own time and in their own way. Cooperative predators, Lambert had said. It occurred to Quint that such soul and heart and beauty as was to be found in life was between individuals. The ugliness and the grief of cant, dogma, and blind loyalty—all the hateful, debilitating *isms*—lay in groups.

Vivienne had called Genevieve a bohemian. By Asian standards she was too. She and Quint had a common interest in books and writing, and they quickly became comfortable with one another. At dusk, the Hong Kong police cleared the traffic from Nathan Road and the crowds began gathering to usher in the Chinese New Year. The British didn't like the business of fireworks. Cleaning up the red paper the next day was an expensive chore—totally unnecessary by the tidy British standards. But this was not really a British city. It was Chinese. Their turf. The British were only there until their lease ran out in 1997. It was the Chinese custom to scare bad spirits away with fireworks and paper dragons on New Year's Eve.

As darkness descended, the firecrackers began to pop. The racket rose and grew in a mad crescendo that Quint knew would continue for hours.

Asians did not approve of public displays of affection. There was no holding of hands or casual embraces by couples such as one saw in North America and Europe. As the fireworks grew from loud to a crazed din, popping and cracking, the crowd consumed Quint and Genevieve, and soon they could see the colorful dragons making their way up Nathan Road. As they waited in the crowd for the dragons, jostled this way and that, their hands inadvertently touched, then gripped tightly. The communication was clear. The link was joined. Vivienne's fervent wish had come to pass. Their fate was sealed.

"Hey, Jim, don't make it bad, take a sad song . . ."

JIM QUINT GOT a job with the Associated Press covering Vietnam. The little girl that was the issue of his marriage to Genevieve looked remarkably like her aunt. When she reached the age of the child in the painting, the United States, having declared victory in Vietnam, airlifted the last of its citizens from Saigon, and Quint moved his family to Hong Kong, where he found work with the *Asian Wall Street Journal*.

In her little crayon-loving namesake, Vivienne was reborn in more than memory, and the cycle of love and affirmation continued in the face of such execrable misadventures as the Vietnam War. From the nexus of the sublime V sprang the complementary yin and yang of strife *and* life. Such a lovely bounty. Vivre!